PRAISE FOR THE NOVELS
OF EMMA WILDES

"A luxurious and sensual read. Both deliciously wicked and tenderly romantic. . . . I didn't want it to end!"
—*New York Times* bestselling author Celeste Bradley

"A stylish blend of dangerous intrigue and scorching desire that is bound to captivate fans of Amanda Quick and Nicole Jordan." —*Booklist*

"This wickedly exciting romance will draw you in and take hold of your heart."
—*USA Today* bestselling author Elizabeth Boyle

"Regency fans will thrill to this superbly sensual tale . . . deliciously erotic . . . a spectacular and skillfully handled story that stands head and shoulders above the average historical romance."
—*Publishers Weekly* (starred review)

"Wickedly delicious and daring . . . a page-turner that captures the era, the mores, and the scandalous behavior that lurks beneath the surface."
—*Romantic Times* (4½ stars, top pick)

"[A] gem of an author . . . keep[s] readers riveted to each scandalous scene—and everything in between."
—Romance Junkies

continued . . .

Also by Emma Wildes

Ladies in Waiting

Twice Fallen
One Whisper Away

The Notorious Bachelors

Our Wicked Mistake
His Sinful Secret
My Lord Scandal

Seducing the Highlander
Lessons from a Scarlet Lady
An Indecent Proposition

RUINED BY MOONLIGHT

A WHISPERS OF SCANDAL NOVEL

Emma Wildes

A SIGNET ECLIPSE BOOK

SIGNET ECLIPSE
Published by New American Library, a division of
Penguin Group (USA) Inc., 375 Hudson Street,
New York, New York 10014, USA
Penguin Group (Canada), 90 Eglinton Avenue East, Suite 700, Toronto,
Ontario M4P 2Y3, Canada (a division of Pearson Penguin Canada Inc.)
Penguin Books Ltd., 80 Strand, London WC2R 0RL, England
Penguin Ireland, 25 St. Stephen's Green, Dublin 2,
Ireland (a division of Penguin Books Ltd.)
Penguin Group (Australia), 250 Camberwell Road, Camberwell, Victoria 3124,
Australia (a division of Pearson Australia Group Pty. Ltd.)
Penguin Books India Pvt. Ltd., 11 Community Centre, Panchsheel Park,
New Delhi - 110 017, India
Penguin Group (NZ), 67 Apollo Drive, Rosedale, Auckland 0632,
New Zealand (a division of Pearson New Zealand Ltd.)
Penguin Books (South Africa) (Pty.) Ltd., 24 Sturdee Avenue,
Rosebank, Johannesburg 2196, South Africa

Penguin Books Ltd., Registered Offices:
80 Strand, London WC2R 0RL, England

First published by Signet Eclipse, an imprint of New American Library,
a division of Penguin Group (USA) Inc.

First Printing, September 2012
10 9 8 7 6 5 4 3 2 1

PUBLISHER'S NOTE
This is a work of fiction. Names, characters, places, and incidents either are the product of the author's imagination or are used fictitiously, and any resemblance to actual persons, living or dead, business establishments, events, or locales is entirely coincidental.
    The publisher does not have any control over and does not assume any responsibility for author or third-party Web sites or their content.

ALWAYS LEARNING   PEARSON

For Dr. Jeffrey Dikis and his lovely wife.

ACKNOWLEDGMENTS

The process of publishing a novel involves many people on different levels, and while it might start with the author, it certainly is not my creation alone. I would like to thank my agent, Barbara Poelle; my editor, Kerry Donovan; and all the other people behind the scenes including the copy editor, the art department for such a fabulous cover, and all those involved in making this book the best it could be.

Chapter 1

The Awakening

The first impression was of jeweled colors: sapphire, brilliant ruby, golden topaz . . .

Lady Elena Morrow's eyes fluttered open and she suppressed a small moan. Her head ached, her mouth was dry, and she came to the startling conclusion she had absolutely no idea where she was.

Stone walls rose all around her and the faint colored illumination came from several stained-glass windows set in arched niches high above where she lay on what appeared to be a bed, though she was on top of the coverlet, not under it, and she shivered slightly, as she was clad only in her lacy chemise.

In a surge of panic she sat up, which proved to be a mistake, as the room spun and nausea caused her eyes to close again as she struggled to remember just how she might have gotten into this strange room. Bracing herself on the softness of the mattress with one hand, she pushed the fall of loose hair away from her face and took a deep breath.

Think . . .

Her last memory was of the theater. The performance, the music, the glittering crowd . . . she'd worn a new gown of aquamarine silk . . . Slowly she opened her eyes again to survey her unfamiliar surroundings.

It was at that moment she realized she wasn't alone.

How she hadn't noticed before was bewildering, but she was hardly clearheaded, and as she glanced over she wondered for a moment if she was hallucinating.

The man sprawled carelessly on the bed next to her was half-nude, wearing a pair of doeskin breeches and nothing else. It was so shocking she blinked, her gaze traveling over the muscled contours of his bare shoulders and the flat plane of his stomach, finally shifting back up to his face. He had glossy dark hair, disheveled against the white linen of the pillow, and in profile his features were clean and masculine: straight nose, high cheekbones, downy ebony brows, a mouth that was parted just slightly in sleep, his tall body relaxed and taking up a good deal of the bed.

The one they shared.

The situation registered and she scrambled to her knees in scandalized horror, more confused than ever.

A strange place, and, worse, an unfamiliar man. What in the name of heaven could be going on?

Or *was* he unfamiliar?

Doing her best to stay calm, Elena tried to think, incredulously recognizing the infamously handsome features of Randolph Raine, Lord Andrews. It wasn't as if they actually knew each other—he hadn't even asked to be introduced to her this season, and if he had done so her mother would have probably fainted dead away—but it was impossible to be part of the beau monde and not know of him.

He was the reigning rake of the *ton*, his reputation more wicked than sin itself, his name a byword for seduction and forbidden pleasure.

What is he doing half-naked in the same bed with me?

The infamous viscount stirred then, as if her horrified gaze touched his psyche in some way even through his sleep, and he took in a long sighing breath before moving one arm above his head in a careless arch. Even in repose he looked dangerous, with an almost beautiful cast to his features and all that tousled raven hair. . . .

Yes, that was his nickname, wasn't it? Not that her mother or aunts would even mention him in front of her, but still tidbits had sifted through to her awareness. *The Raven.* She'd seen it in the society papers. A titillating and amusing nickname, but at the moment all she could think about was his notoriety.

There was no doubt in her mind he was about to open his eyes. She hadn't the slightest notion of what might have prompted her current fantastical circumstances, but Elena was suddenly reminded that she wore only a thin, semitransparent shift, and upon the first swift perusal of the room, there was nothing to use to cover herself. The bed linens might have been an option had he not been on top of them, but given his height and solidly muscled body she doubted she could shift him even one inch.

What is this place, she had to wonder with frantic assessment, as her eyes scanned the room and she found not even a stray blanket or other furniture besides the ornate bed; a screen in the corner that hopefully concealed the necessary; and a small table that held a carafe, two glasses, and a lamp.

With a true sense of urgency she wondered what had happened to her clothes, because the viscount was waking up and . . .

Sure enough his eyes opened, the thick fringe of his lashes lifting. He stared at the stained-glass window for a moment and then with a sweeping glance surveyed the entire room, arrested when he saw her kneeling there next to him. He muttered, "What the devil?"

She'd had exactly the same reaction and a part of her was relieved he seemed as startled as she was, but another part was more puzzled than ever.

In a swift, athletic motion he levered up on one elbow and shook the hair out of his eyes, his tone husky. "What is this? Who are you?"

Considering she was the one clad only in a slip of flimsy silk, the warmth of embarrassment flushing her skin, she responded tartly, "I have not the slightest idea as to what *this* is. How did I get here?"

"How did *you* get here? As I've never seen you before and *here* is a mystery to me, how would I know?" He sat up fully and ran his long fingers through his thick hair. His eyes were dark, his skin a light bronzed tone that reflected the dappled multicolored light from the unusual window high above them. Then his eyes narrowed. "Just a moment. I retract that. I do know who you are . . . Whitbridge's daughter?"

The evident consternation in his direct stare confused her even more. It was genuine, she would swear to it, and, besides, why did she remember nothing of arriving at this place? And, as bizarre as it was, apparently neither did he.

Elena nodded, her lips trembling. Whatever was happening there was no doubt her father was undoubtedly frantic. How long had she been here? "Yes, Lord Whitbridge is my father."

Her companion swore. It was under his breath but telling in intonation, and she caught the sentiment if not the exact words. After looking around the room again he finally said evenly, "I don't remember anything. I can count on one hand the times in my life I've been so foxed an entire evening got away from me and those were a decade ago, not to mention I doubt I'd ever forget bedding *you*. I wasn't drunk, so how in Hades did I get here?"

The young woman in beguiling dishabille, who at the moment had turned a very becoming shade of pink, looked at him as if he were the devil incarnate, complete with cloven hooves and a forked tongue.

Perhaps he was, come to think of it.

Irrefutably, Ran would never have said anything so blunt in front of a young, unmarried—even if very beautiful—woman under normal circumstances, but virginal misses were not his provenance. Were he concerned with fine manners and social graciousness at the moment, he would apologize for being so indelicate, but, the truth was, they *were* in bed together in a room he didn't recognize and he had no idea how either one of them had gotten into this predicament.

Finesse be damned at this point in time.

The earl's golden-haired daughter looked at him with enormous blue eyes, the pale upper curves of her full breasts gleaming above the lace of her demure chemise, the soft rose of her lips provocative. He'd seen her only in passing before, but up close, her beauty was as dazzling as all the rumors held it. "You . . . you didn't," she stammered, her blush deepening. "We didn't . . . we couldn't have—"

Fucked? Luckily, he didn't say that out loud. Courtesy was not his first priority right now but at least he didn't vocalize the crudity.

"Exactly my point," he grimly interrupted, partly because he was still unnaturally groggy and had an appalling headache, and partly to spare her, since it was obvious to him she didn't know exactly what she was referring to in the first place. "But you have to admit certain conclusions could be drawn over our location and state of mutual undress."

What he would like to have said was that while he might be known for his largesse in the bedroom, at least it could be said of him that he remembered his paramours—but he made it a point to never discuss his private affairs with anyone.

Still, that raised the question: Why was he here, in bed with the delectable daughter of an earl, who happened to be a young woman he'd never even met?

As far as he knew, there were no rumors about Whitbridge's finances being suspect. However, Ran was a very rich man and his initial reaction to this unusually compromising situation was suspicion. There was a reason he stayed away from the eligible young ladies angling for wealthy, titled husbands. At not quite thirty, he wasn't interested in the restrictions of marriage yet. But if he had to do his duty and acquire a wife in order to sire an heir, at least he wanted it to be his choice.

"If this is a ploy you will wish you hadn't tried it," he said through his teeth with less civility than he might otherwise have used due to his aching head. "I can't be coerced."

In answer she just looked at him in evident confusion. She appeared to think he might have suddenly lost his mind, which, in light of his current circumstances, he wasn't sure he hadn't. "What?"

"I won't marry you."

In any other situation her horrified expression might

be amusing, but he wasn't in a particularly jocular mood. She stammered, "You surely do not think that I . . . I . . . that this . . . Are you insinuating . . . ?"

He lifted a brow.

This time it was anger that tinted her cheeks as she gathered her composure. Scathingly, she informed him, "My lord, your legendary charm seems to be in abeyance. I hope it does not offend your sense of self-worth, but rest assured, you are certainly *not* what I am looking for in a husband."

If she was acting she was quite good at it.

He took a moment, unclenched his jaw as he registered her sincerity, and reminded himself she was lovely enough it was unlikely she would need to resort to such drastic lengths to capture a rich husband. "It's been done before," he said with less steel in his tone. "A man manipulated into a compromising position and honor-bound to marry the young lady."

"My understanding is that *honor* is a rather loose term to you."

She was wrong. He played the game only with ladies who were as willing and as detached as he was, but Ran was well aware of his reputation. "You don't know me," he said curtly.

"I am starting to wish that was still the case," she shot back, her cheeks flushed.

If she were innocent he deserved the set-down, and it sounded like she meant it.

The infidelities of his class left him somewhat jaded. He'd been first seduced by one of his aunt's friends, a countess whose much older husband was not that attentive, and after that enlightening experience he'd seen enough of the value most of his privileged acquaintances put on their wedding vows to have a jaundiced view of the institution of marriage itself. It was his conclusion that while some species of animals and birds mated for life, human beings were not sophisticated enough for that sort of loyalty. It was usually a mercenary arrangement and if he was honest with himself, he'd always thought there should be much more to it.

He swung his legs over the side of the bed and stood abruptly, wondering where in hell the rest of his clothes might be, not to mention his boots. In his experience, and he had to admit he had quite a bit, the usual scene of any seduction had clothing strewn on the floor or any other convenient surface as the participants disrobed in the heat of passion. Not interested in defending his morals, he asked, "Now that we've established neither one of us want to be here, why *are* we? What do you remember?"

"Attending the theater." She lifted a trembling hand to smooth back her shining hair, the long pale strands gilded by the colored light, her expression disconcerted, but to her credit she wasn't in hysterics like most spoiled young ladies might be. "I was waiting for my father's carriage. It is unclear to me what happened after that."

His last recollection before waking? Ran wasn't sure. He contemplated it for a moment, rubbing his jaw. "I was leaving my club. I'd met friends there for dinner and a whiskey or two, but as I said, I was hardly inebriated enough for this. My last impression was of stepping out onto the street."

The floor was cool stone like the walls and from the circular shape of the room it appeared to be in a tower. When he strode purposefully to the door he already knew what he would find.

As he suspected the door was barred on the outside.

He tried it and then set his shoulder to it, but it was solid and didn't move even a fraction. When he turned back around his delectable companion had gathered the blanket from the bed and covered her partial nudity, her eyes pools of inquiry.

Had their circumstances been different, he might have experienced a twinge of regret, but as it stood, it was just as well.

"Locked," he said unnecessarily.

"Why?"

"My very question." He saw the glasses on the table and was grateful—at the moment, for later he might wish for something stronger—that the pitcher was full of water. First he poured a glass for his companion, guessing if she'd been given the same vile drug that he'd obviously been dosed with, she might also be thirsty. She accepted with a chilly thank-you, and when he'd taken a long cool drink for himself, he asked neutrally, "Can you think of any reason someone would wish to kidnap you?"

"My father is wealthy."

As was he, so it was a possibility. But in Ran's case his funds were not available without his presence to sign the proper documents, so that was an oversight on the part of their abductor. However, now that his throbbing headache was easing a little, the whole thing seemed like perhaps there was more behind it than money. To start with, why take their clothes?

"I suppose it could be we are going to be ransomed," he conceded slowly, wondering what drug they'd been given, because he'd drained his glass of water and was still thirsty and his headache pronounced enough that he was glad the room was shadowed.

"You don't sound very convinced, my lord. Why else

are we here? If they had wished to harm us they certainly had every opportunity."

He *wasn't* convinced. A young debutante locked in a room with a man who had a reputation for seduction?

When he looked at it that way, the angle reflected an interesting light on the situation.

"There is harm, my lady, and *harm*. And the difference can be subtle."

She was sitting on the edge of the bed now, her slender, shapely form wrapped in the concealing folds of the coverlet, and she regarded him with discomforting directness. "If you will excuse me for saying so, Lord Andrews, you are much more likely to have enemies than I am."

"Perhaps," he agreed with a hint of cynical practicality. "But would they exact vengeance by locking me in a room with a beautiful young lady?"

Chapter 2

The Ultimatum

There was something very civilized about pouring a cup of tea, even in the middle of a *very* unconventional conversation, and though it had taken some effort, she'd actually gotten her husband to abandon the paper.

"May I offer you more, my lord?" Alicia Wallace, Lady Heathton, offered the delicate cup, her hand remarkably steady in her estimation, the saucer wobbling only for a moment.

The man sitting across from her just stared at her as if she'd gone mad.

And perhaps she had.

But *something* had to be done.

"You can't be serious." The words were said through his teeth, his fine-boned face drawn into a mask of disbelief.

"Of course I am," she said with what could hopefully be called admirable composure. "You are out of tea and I poured you another cup. Would you like sugar?"

His gaze flickered to the porcelain cup and he took it almost savagely, some of the liquid slopping over the side to drip on the extremely expensive Oriental rug. "No, thank you," he bit out.

She strove for the same poise she'd promised herself she would maintain when she'd begun this conversation. "Now, then, would you care to hear my terms?"

"Alicia, there are no terms. You are my *wife*."

"I am so glad you recognize that fact." She smiled, but in truth she was shaking inside. It was difficult to challenge her husband in this way, but maybe it was necessary.

No, it *was* necessary.

Benjamin's mouth tightened. "Of course I do. Are you attempting to make some sort of point?"

"What is my favorite color?"

Sweeping back an errant lock of hair from his brow, he said with obvious exasperation, "What?"

"Just answer the question."

His handsome face was a study in confusion, and, truthfully, that alone was progress, for he rarely showed any emotion beyond composed, distant, and preoccupied. Though she had to admit when he chose he could be charming, those instances were few and far between. Not because he was cold by nature—she knew firsthand he was not just intelligent, but also a passionate man—but because he evidently did not feel the need to share with her anything about his feelings.

About his life.

That needed to change.

She was tired of living with a stranger.

After trying several different methods of getting his attention, she'd unfortunately come to the dismal conclusion they were going to have *to talk* about it. Six months into their marriage, she knew him little better than she had before they'd said their vows.

Perhaps *he* liked it that way, but *she* did not.

"I have to confess I haven't the slightest idea what your favorite color might be." Ben sat back with an ironic smile. "I don't think men dwell on such things. For that matter, I doubt you know what mine is either. For—"

"Dark green," she interrupted serenely. "You favor it in your waistcoats, the racing colors you chose for your stable, even the hangings on your bed."

Vivid hazel eyes narrowed. "I've never really considered it. What if I told you that your conclusion is incorrect?"

"Then you would be lying, and while I acknowledge you are not perfect, you do not usually tell falsehoods."

That silenced him and he even smiled, albeit a bit reluctantly. "No, I don't, but I admit to not being sure exactly what is going on here, madam. I believe you just told me you would not share my bed any longer."

"No," she corrected softly, hoping he saw the poignancy of her expression. "I said I do not think we should be together as husband and wife in that way until we know each other better. That isn't a refusal but a suggestion."

"Lord, Alicia, we've been married for nearly half a year."

"Exactly my point."

He muttered something under his breath she didn't quite catch, and perhaps it was just as well, for it involved a word she'd never heard before. He reclined, tall and lean, his long legs extended, attired casually this afternoon in a dark coat, buff breeches, and polished boots, his white shirt open at the throat. The informal attire suited him, and since she'd pried him out of his study with some difficulty to make him join her for this conversation, the lack of a cravat was not his fault. She found she liked him like this, his dark blond hair a bit tousled because he habitually ran his fingers through it when he was concentrating—an endearing mannerism to her mind—so he didn't look quite so ... unapproachable.

Sometimes he was so guarded she had no idea how to break in.

Covertly, she studied him. His features were familiar: high cheekbones, chin a bit square, straight nose, eyes striking with their gold-green color under arched brows just the slightest shade darker than his hair ... There was no question he was a very attractive man. Alicia knew when the very eligible Lord Heathton had noticed her she'd been the envy of most of the eligible ladies of the beau monde.

However, the marriage was not quite working out as she expected. Her handsome husband was the farthest thing from romantic and it rankled. Until now she'd said nothing, waiting for the intimacy to grow between them. But it hadn't, and if she didn't do something, she had come to the conclusion, it never would.

Therefore the ultimatum. This was up to her. If left to him, they would live out their lives this way. It was a leap of faith, but, then again, they needed to leap together. If she fell she'd been on the precipice since the day they'd said their vows anyway.

He bit out, "Though I think this is all ridiculous, please go ahead and be more specific. What exactly is it you want from me?"

The question alone was a coup, and Alicia did her best to not look triumphant in any way. She carefully set aside her cup. "It is very simple. I think if we are going to share a night together, before that we should share something significant that does not involve ..."

When she trailed off, not sure how to finish the sentence, Benjamin did it for her in a sardonic tone. "Sexual relations?"

Yes, that was precisely what she meant, but his voice held a dangerous edge and so she simply nodded rather than responding directly.

"Forget the tea. I need a brandy." He rose and stalked—that was the only way she could describe it— across the informal parlor and picked up a crystal decanter to pour some of the amber liquid into a snifter. Then with his back still to her, he took a hearty swallow before he turned around. His gaze was direct and challenging. "You do know you can't do this without my permission. I have conjugal rights and if I wish to exercise them you are not supposed to refuse me."

That, of course, was her real weapon in this small battle she'd chosen to engage. He would never force her.

Never.

Ever.

That conviction gave her confidence.

And at least some measure of power in a world where women had very little. His autocratic statement was no doubt due to the blow to his male pride, so she didn't take offense. She might not know him as well as she'd like to even after months of marriage, but that he was caught by surprise was obvious, and she wasn't above pressing that advantage given the nature of the cause.

"I think, my lord," she said with a quiet smile, "we can come to terms without drastic measures being taken on either side. I am not asking for much. For instance, would you like to go on a stroll through the gardens?"

* * *

For years he'd played a secret role in helping the Crown untangle untidy messes here and there, but damned if he knew what had just happened.

Benjamin Wallace fought the urge to just storm out of the room, but that seemed ill advised considering his lovely wife was currently holding him hostage by threatening to banish him from her bedroom.

He'd been—in a word—ambushed. *Unthinkable.*

A part of him was furious because he'd done his best, ever since the day he'd sat down and coolly arranged the marriage with her father, to have exactly the kind of relationship with his wife that he'd always envisioned once he sacrificed his bachelorhood to duty.

He wished to live his life, and she was free, within limits, of course, to live hers. She appeared on his arm at certain functions, oversaw the menus and other aspects of the household, and though it hadn't happened yet, she would bear his children. All very civilized, all very much in his control, and nicely ordered.

He'd never expected to be blackmailed.

It was unsettling to realize a small part of him, a completely foreign facet he didn't recognize, was intrigued at this sudden show of independence. Alicia had always been biddable enough, acquiescing to his decisions without argument, always the gracious hostess and dutiful wife. In bed it was much the same. She allowed him to touch her as he wished and never refused him unless it was an inconvenient time of the month. And when he left her for his own chamber she never failed to sweetly bid him good night.

However, if he was painfully honest with himself, her submissiveness gave him an uncertainty about whether she even enjoyed his attentions. He hadn't realized it bothered him until now, when he found himself gazing at her from across the room, his mind only remotely registering the question she'd just asked him.

She was very attractive. That went without saying, for he had selected carefully once he'd decided it was time to marry, and, truthfully, Alicia had caught his eye right away. Graceful, with a delicate femininity that drew him, she had glossy hair so dark it was almost black. At the moment she had her hair caught up in a sleek, simple chignon that complemented her pearly complexion and compelling, huge, dark blue eyes, their color reminiscent of deep water at midnight, cobalt and mysterious. This afternoon she wore a light blue gown that emphasized her dramatic coloring and accentuated the curves he'd explored on those shrouded nights when he'd visited her bed.

The nights when, he could now admit to himself, he felt vaguely like an interloper. As if he were not there by invitation but by permission, granted but not necessarily because his presence was wanted. And yet he hadn't been aware of it before this moment.

Perhaps she wasn't the only one dissatisfied with their current arrangement.

Damn all.

"A walk in the garden?" He cleared his throat and then finished his brandy in a swift, irreverent toss that almost made him cough. "I fail to see what that will accomplish, but fine."

A vision in pale azure silk, she stood and murmured, "Thank you."

It rankled to be thanked for such a small thing as taking her for a simple walk. Was he really that . . . indifferent? It was true he tended to approach most matters in a very analytical way but he hadn't done so with his marriage. In his selection of a wife, yes, but the reality of their relationship, no. Or had he? Again he had a flicker of discomfort even as he offered his arm and she laid her hand on it, her head dipping downward in demure composure.

Or perhaps she was just not meeting his eyes on purpose.

And tantalizing him with the glimpse of her nape, which was both beguiling and deliciously feminine. He led her toward the French doors down the hallway off the breakfast room that opened to the terrace, a sense of the ridiculous lingering as they stepped into the afternoon sunshine. "Do you have a particular path in mind?" he asked with as much neutrality as possible, the hint of her perfume mingling with the scent of the blooming flowers.

"To the right. I know it isn't original but I love the roses. They are classically romantic, I suppose."

I'll have to remember that, Ben thought wryly. *Favorite flower: rose.* Duly filed away so if questioned again about her particular preferences, he would have at least one answer. If he knew her favorite color he could find a rose that hue and perhaps ingratiate himself twice over.

The sun was warm, the breeze a gentle caress, and to his surprise he found he wondered why he never bothered with the gardens except to occasionally admire them from the window of his study. *I'm a busy man,* he excused his abstraction, his boots crunching the gravel as they walked, her long skirts brushing his legs.

"Such a beautiful day," Alicia commented.

He slowed his stride to match her shorter one. "I agree."

"It always seems a shame to me how people hurry

through life, throwing away lovely afternoons like this." She lifted her face toward the sky and smiled.

Benjamin let his gaze slide over her, lingering where the swell of her breasts filled the bodice of her demure gown, at the arch of her slender throat, the glistening pink of her lips. He worked long hours, but, his estates needed managing, his fortune was maintained by careful supervision of his business affairs, and he did have a seat in the House of Lords, which took up a considerable amount of his time. He shrugged. "Obligations are what they are. Not all of us give up lovely afternoons voluntarily."

"I suppose there could be a certain validity to that argument, my lord."

"Why is it I have the impression I have just been disagreed with again, but in the most subtle way possible?"

There was a slight mischievous twitch to her mouth. "Perhaps you have been. I think a person must *make* time in life for what is important. And most do, only their vision of importance is often different from that of others. We are all unique, so that isn't an astonishing conclusion."

He was fascinated—a bit unwillingly—by that utterly feminine teasing smile. He asked, "And what do *you* think is important?"

She seemed to contemplate the answer, her profile defined in the slanting sunlight, her long lashes slightly lowered. Then she murmured, "I find much of my attention focused on you, my lord."

Benjamin was silent, not at all certain how to respond to that. Of course, he was her husband, so it made sense she would consider him a central figure in her life, but, truthfully, he'd not made that adjustment. She was his wife but they didn't spend all that much time together. He traveled to London frequently and as it was the season, she was in town also, arriving just a few nights before, but not because he had requested her presence. He'd always been under the impression she liked the country and so he'd left her there.

They would spend even less time together if she carried out her threat.

Truly, a man should not have to make concessions to bed his own wife, but he had to admit that a pleasant stroll through a garden was not really asking much.

Leaves fluttered as the breeze brushed past. There was a small pond in the walled garden, lilies on the surface, fish moving in flashes of gold beneath the water. Some enterprising member of the gardening staff had artfully made a small waterfall over some mossy stones, so the cascade made a pleasant sound as it splashed downward.

Alicia stopped, bent, and picked a small white flower he didn't recognize—but he was hardly a botanist—and, smiling, tucked it into the buttonhole of his jacket. "A gift, my lord, so you can remember the first time we took a walk in a garden together."

Amused, he caught her slim wrist, circling it gently with his fingers. "Alicia, I believe men are supposed to give women flowers, not the other way around."

"One of your problems is you have some archaic preconceived notions of how men and women should act toward each other."

His brows shot up, but she looked so lovely standing there in the warm late-afternoon sunshine, her rich hair shining, a hint of gold on her flawless skin, those long-lashed eyes holding a shimmer of laughter, that he found it impossible to be insulted. "Do I? How so?"

She took him by surprise yet again. "You've never kissed me."

Benjamin gazed down at his wife in bemused consternation. "At the risk of arguing with a lady, I beg to differ. I most certainly have, Alicia, and you know it."

A blush touched her delicate cheekbones but she held his gaze. "A perfunctory offering at best."

"You have an interesting approach, madam. Tell me, how do you know if a kiss is perfunctory or not? I was unaware you had any experience before me."

Damn all if he didn't feel a twinge of something that might even have been jealousy, which was an irrational emotion he didn't believe in at all.

His wife said softly, "Do you think a woman, experienced or not, cannot tell if a man puts true emotion into a kiss?"

At that moment, to his chagrin, he knew what she meant. He'd kissed her but usually it was a formality before he took his pleasure, the merest brush of his mouth on hers in the dark as a prelude to their joining. Unprecedented in his adult life, his own face flushed at that all too astute observation.

Had he really been so self-serving?

She went on with charming, hesitant sincerity. "I am not particularly worldly but have no illusions over whether or not there have been other women, before me or maybe even after our marriage. I am your wife so there was no need to seduce me, but surely you have done it before. The flower is for you to remember this afternoon. Perhaps you could gift me a real kiss so I can treasure it always?"

A kiss? His beautiful wife was asking for a real kiss.

She is young, a voice inside him chided. Idealistic, ro-

mantic in the way women were, and it appeared he'd
bungled things badly by assuming she was as satisfied as
he was with their arrangement. He had had no idea before this afternoon that she was anything but content
with their marriage.

How on earth could he refuse that challenge? His
gaze dropped to her mouth. Her lips were soft and inviting and . . .

At that inopportune moment someone cleared his
throat.

He glanced up to see Yeats hovering partway down
the path, the elderly butler's apologetic expression clearly
stating that he might have just overheard part of their
exchange. "Yes?"

"Sorry to intrude, milord."

Poor timing indeed.

Drily, Ben said, "What is it?"

With two gloved fingers the elderly butler extended a
card. "Lord Whitbridge is here. He insists on seeing you
at once."

"My uncle is here?" Alicia looked pleased, though
Benjamin wasn't sure why. Her mother's brother could
be a bit pompous, in his opinion, and he wasn't particularly delighted to hear of his arrival, especially right now.

Yeats cleared his throat again. "Yes, my lady, but while
he sends his regards, he wishes to see his lordship alone."

Chapter 3

The earl sat very upright and Benjamin noticed the efficient Yeats had ushered him into a comfortable chair by the fireplace and given the man a generous snifter of brandy.

Always one step ahead was Yeats. Ben was grateful that his visitor had not been seated behind his desk, for, truthfully, Lord Whitbridge held quite a commanding presence. Instead Ben took that chair and nodded in greeting. "Good afternoon."

His lordship sat back and stared at his glass with an intense scrutiny, as if he were judging the quality of the beverage. But after a few moments he glanced up, his features tight. And without even the courtesy of a greeting, said, "My daughter is missing."

Ben was hardly a contemporary so it wasn't as if they were close acquaintances, but still, the blunt disclosure was a bit startling. Slowly he responded, "Elena?"

"She is my only daughter, is she not?"

It was rather difficult not to take exception at the man's waspish tone, but maybe the circumstances warranted a certain edge. Ben said calmly, "Alicia said nothing to me about it."

"That is because she doesn't know. And before she hears of it—before all of London proper hears of it—I would like you very discreetly to find Elena."

As he was hardly the keeper or seeker, for that matter, of flighty young women, Ben's brows lifted a fraction. "I am sure I have no idea why you think I can help you."

The earl was still fairly fit in his middle age, his thinning blond hair brushed back from a high forehead, his blue eyes steady. He was immaculately dressed, composed, almost lofty as he surveyed the confines of the comfortable study with its somewhat faded draperies and a fine layer of dust on the shelves. Ben preferred to have it cleaned only upon his orders, and habitually he forgot about it. Perhaps tomorrow he would order a good airing.

Lord Whitbridge spoke in a crisp cool tone. "I am told you can and I trust my source."

"What source?"

"The Iron Duke himself. He's an old friend of mine and apparently an admirer of yours. He swears if anyone can accomplish the task it is you. He said to tell you he was calling in a favor, but I would think our family connection to be quite enough. Imagine my surprise when I went to him and asked who could help me and your name was the first that came up."

The condescending tone was hardly flattering, but, again, Ben had always done his best to seem unremarkable. It was a cultivated talent and it had served him well.

But Wellington knew the truth.

Well, hell and blast. This wasn't what he needed after that confounding scene in the garden with Alicia. Where had his very orderly day gone? Ben blew out a short breath. Once—only once—he'd asked for special consideration from the duke and been granted it, and it was true he owed the man. "I'm flattered in his confidence but also retired from his service."

"You won't even hear me out?"

Ben wouldn't have or so he told himself, but Elena Morrow was his wife's cousin and he knew Alicia was fond of her.

At his hesitation, Whitbridge said in a voice that cracked slightly, "When you have a child, you will perhaps understand the depth of my desperation."

The evidence of emotion when his guest sat so negligently in his chair and sipped from his glass caught his attention. In fact, if he was to wager on it, he would place money on the probability that his austere lordship was moved almost to tears and the man was usually so dignified his bearing could almost be called haughty. Ben had never particularly even *liked* his wife's uncle before this moment, but damn all if the man wasn't more human than he let on.

Devil take it.

Thoughtfully, as if he were tuned to the nuances of the meeting even before it happened, Yeats had also poured Ben a snifter of brandy. He picked it up and took a sip. This appeared to be an afternoon that needed extra fortification. "I will listen," he said evenly, "if you keep the recital short, to the point, and without emotional inferences. Just the facts, if you will, in as concise a manner as possible. What happened?"

Whitbridge seemed grateful for the excuse to blink several times and compose himself. "We were at the theater and she never came out to the carriage once the performance was over. As you know it was drizzling last eve, and I went out to stand with the footman to wait, and my wife joined me but Elena never emerged from the crowd. At first we thought she must have met a friend and been detained for a few moments, but after a while we became irritated at the delay and then alarmed, so we sent someone looking for her. There was no trace."

That *was* curious, and despite his vow to relax easily into the role of a cultured gentleman and his conviction he didn't miss the hunt, Ben found himself intrigued. "No one saw her leave?"

"No one saw anything." Whitbridge was emphatic. "When I realized what had happened I questioned the footmen and attendants myself. She retrieved her cloak, but after that, nothing." He stopped, seemed to recall the admonishment to not show his feelings, and then added hollowly, "It is as if Elena has just . . . vanished."

Not certain how diplomatic he had to be when the man was seeking his assistance, Ben took another sip from his glass before he said neutrally, "Elena is quite lovely and Alicia has mentioned her popularity more than once since her debut this season. Is it possible she has eloped with one of her many suitors?"

"No." The earl decisively shook his head.

"You sound very certain." Considering the young lady's age and the ridiculous romantic notions women entertain upon occasion—his own wife a case in point that had a pertinent immediacy—Ben wasn't nearly as certain. It seemed to him the most likely explanation for the whereabouts of the errant Lady Elena. She was the reigning belle of the *ton*, her blond beauty both fashionable and striking. "I am sure the idea doesn't please you, but what if she had a penchant for a man you would not approve of? It has happened before."

"She would never worry her mother and me in such a

fashion, trust me. If she *had* run off—which I don't think is what occurred for a moment—she would at least leave us a note of some sort. She's always been a very level-headed girl. It would be very out of character to be so inconsiderate. Besides, she is newly engaged to Lord Colbert."

That jibed with how Alicia had always described her. Not prone to vanity even with her current level of popularity and inclined toward physical pursuits like riding and archery rather than embroidery and practicing the pianoforte, which did not please her mother.

"I take it you have already made certain he isn't also missing. They would not be the first couple to decide that a long engagement is inconvenient."

"Of course." The words were crisp and the look Ben received was disparaging. "I did not wish to alarm him unduly, but naturally I sent someone to find out if Colbert was aware of the situation. He was very much in residence and had no idea."

So the word was out, which made discretion somewhat of a dicey proposition. It also did not mean Lady Elena had not hared off with another suitor, but it was hardly politic to point it out.

"You can think of no one who might be a part of this?" Ben leveled a direct look at his guest. Truly, he had no time to dabble in an investigation. But if he had to—and it appeared he must, though his new life was supposed to be calm and free of intrigue of any kind—he needed to get started at once. He had taken over the role of earl . . . it wasn't all that challenging, but it was his duty, and his schedule was already quite full.

Besides, with every passing moment, he knew from experience, locating a missing object, be it an important document, a valuable piece of information, or, in this case, a person, became more of a challenge.

"No one," the earl said and drained his glass in one convulsive swallow.

"Women confide in each other. I can ask Alicia if—"

"No!" Whitbridge thrust himself to his feet but at least he had the grace to calm his voice. "I want as few people to know of this as possible. Colbert knows but I was obligated by honor to tell him. I am fond of my niece, but Alicia is young and female and perhaps might not understand the ramifications if she divulged our family's current dilemma. I prefer you say nothing, Heathton. Understand?"

Just when he was supposed to be dedicated to pleasing his wife he was supposed to keep an important secret from her?

Perfect.

He muttered, "I understand, but this is deuced bad timing."

A full day.

By the illumination, albeit difficult to discern through the colored glass of the windows, it was at least late afternoon, so they'd been locked in this room at least a *whole* day.

Ran fought the urge to pace.

He was restless by nature anyway and usually he rode every morning without fail for exercise. Not to mention that they'd been so far given nothing besides the water, and the delectable Lady Elena was probably also hungry and God knew he was famished.

"When do you think they will at least extend us the courtesy of more water?"

It was a good question and followed his own thoughts directly, and, actually, he had to admire Elena Morrow for asking it so calmly. He was close to wanting to pound on the door in frustrated fury yet again. So far that tactic had proven useless. The walls were too smoothly constructed to scale and the window too high to reach even if the bed were dragged under it. To escape it would have to be through the door, which was as solid as if it had been constructed to withstand a battering ram from an invading army.

"It seems like the least of common decency to do so," he agreed, trying to ignore that even though she was wrapped in a sheet, he well remembered what she looked like in just her shift. "But as you have witnessed, pounding on the door and letting whoever is behind this know that we are not only awake but full of questions has done absolutely no good."

Maybe that is the idea, he wondered wryly. To starve them to death was a bit crude, though he was still mystified as to why anyone would wish either of them harm. There was no doubt he had a few people out there who disliked him, but to *this* extent? No, he could think of no one.

His most recent mistress, Beth, perhaps, but they had parted ways in a friendly fashion. And besides, while she was undeniably luscious in an overblown fashion most gentlemen found appealing, she did not have the deviousness to somehow drug him and maneuver him into his current predicament. To her credit, he also doubted she had the malice in her either. They had freely enjoyed each other and that was the extent of it. The affair had been pleasant but brief.

Lady Elena held the sheet modestly closed at her

throat, a faint frown on her lovely face. "I must admit the idea that someone touched me while I was unaware of it is . . . disturbing."

"I like it as little as you do," Ran admitted, leaning a shoulder against the cool wall. His coat, cravat, shirt, boots—all were missing and he had no recollection of removing them. "It gives me a feeling of helplessness I acknowledge affronts me as a male."

"Females experience helplessness quite often," she said with a hint of asperity. "Perhaps it is retribution for your sins."

"Perhaps." For the first time since he awakened, disoriented and locked in a place he had never seen before, he smiled. She had been perfectly right earlier; he had made no attempt to be anything but marginally civil so far, and she was not only younger, but no doubt did feel quite vulnerable. Quietly, he went on. "But while I have my faults, a disparaging attitude toward women is not one of them."

His reassurance might have been a good idea, for she visibly swallowed. "I've no doubt you have great admiration for my sex, Lord Andrews, but that is nice to hear."

What he might have said next was interrupted by the sound of the bar lifting on the door, the scrape making him straighten out of his negligent pose, every muscle going tense. He was not feeling very charitable toward whoever had orchestrated their imprisonment.

However, the young boy who entered was certainly not the villain. No more than ten years of age or so, he carried a tray full of covered dishes. Behind him came an elderly man with a carefully balanced salver with two different decanters and crystal glasses.

Immediately Ran demanded, "Why are we here?"

He didn't get so much as a glance in response, and the boy hurriedly set down the tray on the small table. Ran waited a moment while neither of them said anything and then moved purposefully toward the open door.

"Not so fast. I'd stop if I were you, milord."

The pistol leveled in a very businesslike way at his chest did give him pause in the doorway. A swift glance revealed more stone walls and a circular staircase, the ceiling low, going downward outside the room. Ran prudently took measure of the man standing there blocking his exit. The guard had graying whiskers a bit unruly around a pugnacious jaw and his jacket showed some wear at the hem, but the gun was polished to a high sheen. The thickness of the guard's shoulders and his implacable expression weren't all that promising, and as efficiently as the kidnapping had gone so far, Ran should have known it was foolish to expect an easy escape.

"What is it you want?" he asked evenly, still eyeing the gun.

"Just for you to stay put without a fight, guv. There's food, drink, and a lovely lady. Sounds like a fine evenin' to me."

"Who hired you? I can pay more."

The man just chuckled. "I never tire of you rich toffs trying to best each other . . . but no, thank you. I'm decent satisfied as it is and not inclined to take me chances."

That was some information but certainly not enough. So their abductor was wealthy . . . though Ran had already come to that conclusion just from the quality of the bedding and the beauty of the stained-glass windows in their intimate little prison.

"I am Viscount Andrews and the young lady is the daughter of an earl," he said through his teeth, taking a step forward, gauging the distance. "What the purpose of this abduction is escapes me, but—"

"Don't try it," the man said with emphasis, brandishing the pistol. "You're expendable, milord. I've orders to shoot ye if there's trouble. Stand back and don't move."

He was expendable? That was interesting. Up until this moment he'd thought he was the target of the abduction, but perhaps not. "Whose orders?"

"Never you mind. Just stay where ye are." The barrel pointed directly at his chest.

Still, he tried one more time. "Why are we here?"

"Enough with yer questions."

As incredible as it seemed, there was enough evident sincerity in that terse statement that he believed it. Ran stood there woodenly while the older man and the boy scurried past him. And then the door shut, the bar scraped back into place, and once again they were imprisoned.

Wonderful.

It had all happened so fast, he wasn't sure whether to swear blasphemously or sit down and put his head in his hands. "Damnation," he muttered, as much under his breath as possible, unclenching his fists, not even aware he'd made them.

"He actually pointed a gun at you." Lady Elena's voice quivered, and when he glanced over, her face was ghostly pale.

"I noticed." He consciously loosened his jaw. He wasn't just a privileged aristocrat—he'd served in the Peninsular War. That gave a man a sense of when the enemy was serious, and their jailor with the firearm had been very committed to his purpose, if he was to judge. "Our captor is quite lethally determined to hold us here, as far as I can tell."

"I am having difficulty making sense of all this," Elena murmured, her eyes glimmering in the multicolored illumination. "Why would he possibly do that?"

"I'm no more enlightened than you are." His smile was crooked and he tried to make light of what happened. She was obviously shaken and he was a bit off balance too. "But he did have a point. At least there's food and drink. Perhaps I am not happy over being dragooned, threatened, and made an unwilling captive, but we both need to eat, and I, for one, could use some wine. Can I pour you a glass?"

Even as he refilled her crystal glass in a gentlemanly display of civility, Elena could sense the frustration in the man who then seated himself across from her at the small table.

Not that she blamed him, since someone had leveled a gun at him. Though she'd been shocked, he merely seemed angry, settling into his chair in an impressive ripple of muscle, his dark eyes shadowed.

"That was delicious."

"I agree." His tone was sardonic. "I suppose we should send out our praise to the chef. It seems incredible to say it under these conditions, but the meal was superb."

It had been. Roast duck, cherries in a tart sauce, creamed potatoes, tiny peas in butter, and they'd found under one of the covers a pudding studded with dried fruit with a sweet vanilla glaze over the top. Between them they'd devoured almost every bite of each course.

Elena contemplated her empty plate and then nodded, fingering the slender stem of her glass. "You are perfectly correct, my lord. It was a lovely meal."

Even to her ears it sounded ridiculously stilted. The sudden curve of his smile confirmed it in the first surfacing of that infamous charm. "I see we are in character," Lord Andrews said, still clad only in his breeches, his dark hair boyishly tousled, faint dark stubble on his lean jaw giving him a rakish look. "Trying to be painfully polite despite our unusual circumstances. How very British of us."

"I suppose it is." A small laugh escaped. It had been impossible to eat and at the same time keep the sheet clutched around her, so she'd settled for letting it slip down to cover her bare legs, trying to tell herself that ball gowns had low necklines so her shift was not so very different. And, as notorious for his lascivious pursuits as he might be, Lord Andrews had kept his gaze scrupulously on her face as they ate, the bared upper curves of her breasts apparently not of interest. She had to admit after a few moments it put her at ease, and she'd been hungry enough that it was a relief to just enjoy her food without worrying so much about her modesty.

So far he was *not* living up to his wicked reputation.

For which she was grateful, she assured herself, gazing at him over the rim of her glass as she took another sip of wine. And it was true: while the whispers about his affairs were frequent and it was common knowledge that he'd bedded numerous of the *ton*'s most dazzling beauties, his aversion to marriage was also common knowledge. Certainly that had been his first reaction to being locked in a room with *her*.

It made Elena a bit curious as to why someone like Lord Andrews, who was reputed to be very wealthy and had a title, was so opposed to taking a wife. True, he was still young—she doubted he'd seen his thirtieth birthday yet—but most men in his position understood about duty.

Not that it mattered. She most definitely did not want a promiscuous rakehell for a husband, no matter how good-looking or smooth-mannered, so his fears were entirely unfounded.

"I must admit I am out of my element." He sat back, his eyes heavy-lidded. "I don't have a lot of options."

Having absolutely no idea as to what specifically he was referencing, Elena just looked at him.

He gestured at the window above with his half-full glass. "The sun is going down. The light is fading."

She wasn't enlightened.

"The floor or the bed?" he elaborated with a slight ironic lift of a brow. "Soon it will be pitch-dark in here, I imagine. Where will I sleep? It is up to you."

"Oh." It was disconcerting to realize exactly what he was saying and even more so to face the reality that he was absolutely right. A cold stone surface was not particularly fair to him when the bed was large, but the alternative . . .

"I will take the floor," he told her, effectively reading her mind. "Or you can take my word that I won't touch you."

The pragmatic tone of his voice moved her. That, as well as the fact that so far he'd been remarkably restrained and not overcome with lustful urges. Just the opposite. She couldn't decide if she should be piqued or not that the normally scandalous Lord Andrews was more interested in a decent night's sleep than in her.

But if he was as tired as she was perhaps that was

understandable. It could be the wine and the rich food
or the aftermath of the kidnapping, but she was already
drowsy, relaxed in her chair, though she had to acknowledge that even as sleepy as she was growing—and he was
right; the illumination was fading—she couldn't imagine
huddling on the hard floor.

Or making someone else do so either.

It seemed fair enough, even in the company of London's most notorious libertine, when she offered, "We'll
share the bed."

Chapter 4

He'd never thought of a doorknob as an ominous thing. It was just a household fixture, one that operated a simple mechanism, but at the moment it represented much more.

How much more? Ben had to wonder as he eyed the closed door between his wife's bedroom and the earl's suite he currently occupied. He handed his cravat to his valet. "Has Lady Heathton returned yet this evening?" he asked as casually as possible.

Morton nodded, taking the snowy white cloth and folding it neatly. "An hour ago, my lord."

Ben made a noncommittal sound and sat down to take off his boots. Alicia had attended a rout with her sister but he'd declined, preferring instead to stop over at his club, with a calculated side trip to the theater where Lady Elena had last been seen the night before. There was no performance that evening but a rehearsal was in progress, and he'd persuaded the caretaker to let him in. He'd examined the lobby, finding that indeed there were side doors behind the thick crimson curtains that led to service corridors that had access to the back of the building. Amid the chaos of the sets and props and dressing areas for the actors, there was certainly ample opportunity to hide if one wished, and he had strolled through unnoticed, no one giving him a second glance. The alley behind the building was dark but wide enough for a carriage, and there were several doors to allow the cast to arrive and leave without having to use the main lobby meant for the patrons.

An orchestrated escape would be easy enough.

Slip through one of those doors, go through the backstage bustle and out to a waiting vehicle . . . he still wasn't at all sure the beauteous Elena did not run off with a lover. The difficulty was how to gain information about her personal life without spreading her disappearance all over London society like wildfire. Lord Whitbridge wanted discretion and Ben could not blame him. His daughter's reputation was at stake. Her maid had been questioned and sworn to secrecy and paid well to keep that promise, but apparently the girl had known nothing.

And somehow Ben was supposed to keep the news from his wife. That didn't bode at all well for a mutually satisfying reconciliation of their current rift.

"Is there anything else, sir?"

Startled, Ben glanced up, realizing that Morton was looking at him inquiringly and his dressing gown was laid neatly on the turned-down bed. "No, thank you," he murmured with a slight nod.

"Good night, then, my lord."

The young Irishman left and Ben began to unbutton his shirt, but his gaze went again to the door into the adjoining suite and his fingers stilled. "Damnation," he muttered, indecision not something he usually struggled with, but this afternoon and his wife's ultimatum were very much on his mind.

Perhaps Alicia was asleep, in which case it was only polite to leave her alone. His pride actually urged him to simply ignore her presence in the very next room and let this whim of hers pass.

On the other hand, he *was* her husband. In their world, that meant he controlled everything in her life: her pin money, the events she chose to attend, where she resided.

But, truth be told, he had never considered exerting that level of autocratic control over her. However, it chafed to admit he hadn't really considered their marriage in terms of friendship either, and that seemed to be what Alicia had been saying earlier.

Were husbands and wives meant to be friends?

It wasn't at all what he intended when he married her. He didn't wish for a companion; he wanted a wife, a mother for his children, and a hostess for his guests. It was a simple equation.

But he'd be damned if he was not reluctant to try that connecting door, in case she rejected him.

The decision was taken away from him as the door opened and Alicia came into his bedroom without so much as a knock, her dark glossy hair hanging loose and brushing her hips, a light pink silk dressing gown tied at her slim waist, just a hint of lace at her bosom telling him—disappointingly—that she wore her night rail under her robe.

"Did you have a nice evening, my lord?" She stopped a few feet away, the single lamp throwing shadows on her cheekbones. "I'd retired, but was up reading and heard you come in."

Did he have a nice evening? He wasn't sure if probing into the disappearance of a missing young woman who

happened to be one of his wife's relations—all the while
forbidden to say a word about it—and a drink in the
stuffy confines of one of London's most exclusive men's
clubs qualified. He said neutrally, "On the whole, it was
uneventful."

"I suppose I should not be all that surprised at your
answer." She glanced around with interest, though for
the life of him he couldn't imagine what there was to be
interested *in*. A framed map on the wall, two upholstered
chairs in dark green velvet—he hadn't even realized that
was his favorite color until she'd pointed it out, but she
must be right, for he'd selected the fabric himself—an
armoire in the corner, the bed, of course, and a small
display of elegant snuffboxes in an antique cabinet.

To his chagrin, she focused on that singularly uncharacteristic ornamental collection and wandered over, the
hem of her dressing gown fanning out and the sway of her
hips provocative. "I have not been in this room more than
once or twice. Yet I have always wondered about this.
They are quite decorative, I must admit. Where did they
come from?"

What was decorative was her compelling beauty, all
raven hair and silken skin, and when she turned to look
at him, Ben almost forgot she'd even asked him a question. Her eyes shimmered in the flickering light, and her
lips looked soft and tempting.

Very tempting.

She still needs that romantic kiss I've supposedly ne-
glected. . . .

"My lord?"

His attention riveted on her feminine allure, it took a
moment before he answered. "The snuffboxes? They belonged to my father."

"Now, you see how much we do not know about each other? I had no idea you were that sentimental. What was he like?"

A certain masculine affront rose at being called sentimental and he evaded the question about his father. "I kept them because they are valuable," he said coolly, admiring the graceful line of her neck. "I assume he acquired them for the same reason."

She reached out and picked up an agate piece, cradling it in her palm and running a fingertip over the polished stone cover. "I would think he collected them because they are both lovely and interesting. Did he have other hobbies?"

"I have no idea."

There was a hint of reproof in her dark blue eyes when she glanced over, and he relented. After all, the walk in the garden might have been a mystifying turn of events, but it had not been unpleasant, and, he reminded himself, she'd come to *him* this evening. He would do what he could to encourage her affection toward him. "His horses," he told her. "A love of racing his stable. Something, I do admit, I inherited."

"Why?"

"I suppose because it is rather exhilarating as a sport and challenging as an owner, and—"

"No. I was asking why you had to admit it. Is there some reason you wouldn't enjoy the excitement of the races or the triumph of having one of your own horses compete against champion bloodstock and win?"

He had absolutely no idea how to respond to the direct challenge in her gaze . . . except, perhaps, honestly. Discussing his feelings was not his normal behavior, so he weighed his response for a moment with due measure. "No. Obviously not. I simply meant that it isn't precisely a cerebral exercise, but more one of primal emotion . . . the race, the wind, the final victory, and that is not how I usually see life."

"I agree. It isn't." His wife gifted him then with a compelling smile. "Now," she said in a low whisper, "we are finally getting somewhere."

It was rather difficult to imagine someone as detached and sophisticated as her husband to give up his inner thoughts easily, and Alicia had already come to that conclusion, hence her extreme strategy.

Even now while he still just stood there, his eyes were watchful and his tall body noticeably tense.

Good. She wasn't particularly skilled at it but she'd exacted some sort of response, and the disclosure he'd just made was one of the first truly personal revelations he'd given her in six months of marriage.

It was a start.

"Somewhere? I am not sure the journey is one I wish to take." His voice was wry. "Alicia, I am getting undressed and ready to go to sleep, and you've made it clear I must bring you a posy or write a bit of doggerel for you to wish my attentions. I don't have either at hand. Perhaps you should return to your bed and your book."

At no point had she ever said she didn't want his attentions. She simply wanted them to be a bit different. Or maybe a great deal more different. The problem was she had no idea what that ideal was exactly, but definitely something more romantic than his previous obligatory visits to her bed.

"I never asked for flowers or poetry," she informed him, her voice quiet.

"No? You see how much at a loss I am as to what you *do* want?"

More personal confidences would be welcome, but this evening had already showed some promise. At the same time he was resistant to the change in their relationship, which was no surprise. Before he'd had it entirely his way.

She was going to have to seduce him on an emotional level and she had absolutely no notion how to go about it.

Though it *was* helpful he was even more remarkably attractive with a glimpse of his bare chest showing through the gap in his shirt. She was much more used to seeing him formally dressed, and those nights when he did come to her, Benjamin usually shed his dressing gown after the lights were out. She knew him in a carnal way but it was only in tactile sensation, and the scent of his skin, and the exhale of his breath in the dark.

He touched her but he didn't *touch* her.

How to explain the difference was beyond her at the moment. She knew her husband was keenly intelligent but she wasn't at all positive he would understand how *she* saw it.

Particularly since she was distracted anyway by that tantalizing V of bared skin. It was rather startling to realize just how little she really knew about his body. "By all means, do not let my presence stop you from your evening routine."

And she boldly selected a chair, settling into it, seemingly nonchalant, though her pulse was racing and the bravado entirely false.

"You wish to watch me disrobe?" There was no mistaking the dangerous edge to his voice.

"I am . . . curious."

Not for the first time he looked at her as if she'd gone mad, so in explanation she said, "It has always been dark."

"I thought women preferred it that way." His eyes held a slight glitter. "And that I was expected to protect your delicate sensibilities."

"What you are really saying is that you thought a proper wife would prefer it that way," she corrected, doing her best to relax her arms on the sides of the chair as if she lounged in her dressing gown in his bedroom often and was comfortable with it. Alicia casually crossed her ankles. "Maybe I am not all that proper. Please proceed. Take off your clothes."

"If you wish, but I warn you," he said with an almost lethal softness, his fingers going to the buttons on his shirt, "if we are playing a game here, I don't know the rules and therefore might not follow them to your liking."

"It isn't a game," she responded, her gaze fastened on his bared torso as he tugged the hem of his shirt free from his breeches. "I am quite serious."

"Yes, you appear to be."

She chose to ignore the dryness in his tone, fascinated by the masculine contours of skin and bone, the ripple of muscle impressive as he tossed his shirt aside. The term *beautiful* was not usually applied to men but she thought it appropriate for *this* man. A flush touched her skin as he began to unfasten his breeches, and the way his mouth quirked upward in one corner she rather thought he somehow knew it.

It made her wonder once again about the women in his past, but that unsettling thought was banished as he stripped out of his breeches and, splendidly nude, stood there looking at her with inscrutable directness. "Be sure to let me know when your curiosity is satisfied, madam."

Never, she almost said, because she had the feeling that Ben might take a lifetime to truly know. At the moment she knew he was referring to that part of him that made him male. Not currently the hard length she had experienced moving inside her, but still rather large, though she was hardly a judge. Less than brilliantly, she said, "Oh."

"Surely you've seen drawings and statues. We are all basically the same. Now, then. Shall I put on my dressing gown, or would you care to join me in the bed, where it would be my pleasure to give you a firsthand demonstration of the delightful differences in our anatomy?"

The suggestion caused the telltale flush to deepen and a flutter in her stomach, but she hesitated to give in so easily and she doubted his claim all men were alike. Surely not all of them were so devastatingly attractive.

"You came into my bedchamber." Ben took a step toward her, his hazel eyes veiled. "And today I have walked a garden."

Alicia felt a flicker . . . of what? Panic or anticipation? He looked taller than usual and his nudity was a bit overwhelming, so perhaps a combination of both.

But her intention was for him to realize that just because she was his wife and therefore available to him under the traditional concept of marriage, she needed more and was willing to fight to get it. Today was just the start of a journey and she wanted him to see just how determined she was to see it through to the end. She rose and shook her head. "It was a nice beginning, my lord, but I meant what I said this afternoon. I do not wish for us to lie together again until we are husband and wife more than just in name."

His jaw hardened as he halted in the act of taking another step, and then he turned to pick up his dressing gown and shrugged into it. "Very well, madam. Have it your own way. May I ask that from now on you not enter my bedchamber and ask me to disrobe if you do not have the intention of sharing my bed."

"I've never shared your bed," she pointed out, which was true. He had always come to hers. And left it. Not once had he slept with her all night. "And I didn't come to ask you to disrobe; you just happened to be undressing. I came to say good night. We rarely do. There are days when you are so consumed with your horses and business affairs that I do not see you at all, and if we do not go out together in the evening, we don't even exchange a word. I thought it would be nice if we at least said good night to one another without fail."

"*I* am beginning to come to the conclusion perhaps it would better if you did not spend so much time thinking," he muttered, tying the sash on his robe around his lean waist with a firm jerk.

She suppressed a laugh that she was sure he would not appreciate at his disgruntled tone. "I am not asking for jewels or a new carriage or a trip to the modiste at your expense. What I am asking is quite simple and would please me very much."

It took a moment but then he inclined his head. "If it is so important I will make the effort. Good night, then."

Another victory. Small, but it was progress. Alicia walked toward the connecting door between their rooms. "Good night, my lord. I hope you sleep well," she said, and pulled it closed behind her.

Chapter 5

Day Two

The lamp had guttered out sometime during the night and it was dark when Ran came awake to the familiar feel of a woman, soft and warm, next to him. She was still asleep, her breathing quiet and even, and his arm was draped around her waist, her shapely bottom pressed against his groin, the silk of her hair under his cheek.

Then he remembered.

Kidnapped.

Held at gunpoint.

Lady Elena slumbered on as he gave an inward groan. No doubt habit had asserted itself and he vaguely recalled rolling over, encountering a delectable female body, and instinctively pulling her close before drifting back off.

Old habits, it seemed, truly were hard to shake. The trouble was how to extract himself without waking her and making her aware of the transgression, albeit not an intentional one.

When the same two servants and the guard came back for the dinner dishes, they had brought hot water for the hip

bath behind the screen. Though a request for their clothes
to be returned had been ignored, they had been granted
another candle since his speculation that the room would
be pitch-dark soon was accurate. Lady Elena had bathed
first and he'd followed, noting wryly that he'd not been
given a razor, which was frustrating, as he hated a beard. It
was odd how they'd used the same soap, but the scent from
her skin was different, sweet and floral and feminine.

Arousing. He was hardening already, his cock stiffening in a basic response to the equation of bed, half-naked
woman, and their closeness.

Her breasts were cushioned against his encircling
arm, the firm weight of that resilient flesh enticing, which
was *not* what he needed, and as his hand was flattened
on her rib cage, all it would take was a slight movement
and he could easily cradle one mound in his palm.

As quickly as that treacherous thought came he banished it. Not only had he given his word but the beautiful —
and very marriageable — daughter of an earl was the last
woman he'd attempt to seduce.

But it appeared someone had plotted for him to make
that very mistake. A picture had begun to form in his
mind to what the purpose of all this might be. He had
lain awake long after she'd fallen asleep and contemplated their plight with as much detachment as possible
and there seemed to be several inescapable truths.

They didn't seem to be in physical danger but just
held together against their will. One bed, and no other
entertainment to pass the time but each other? Was it
intended that he persuade her to spend that time in the
way men and women had been entertaining each other
since the beginning of the human race?

Yes.

If nothing else, the combination of his reputation and her dazzling beauty had led him to that conclusion.

She stirred then, just a slight sigh and a restive shift of her body. Ran took the opportunity to move also, carefully easing his arm away and edging back enough that they were no longer touching, and propping himself on one elbow. He should probably leave the bed, but the room held a slight chill and it wasn't as if he had anywhere else in particular to go.

It must have been close to dawn, for there was enough jeweled light he could watch her wake. The slight parting of her soft lips, the flutter of her long lashes, the quiver of her fingers near her cheek; if he'd really been her lover he might have smoothed back a loose tendril of hair from the curve of her slender shoulder. . . .

But he wasn't. He was instead a practical and worldly man, and even though Whitbridge's daughter claimed innocence in how they'd come to be in their current circumstances—and he was tempted to believe her—that didn't mean the situation was if not *caused* by her, still *because* of her.

For instance, if she needed a father for a child she carried, no one would believe him if he declined to accept responsibility. The accusation alone would not be enough to force his hand, for he also had wealth and power, but if the plan was for them to be found together, his choices would be limited. Just by sharing the bed he'd essentially compromised her.

Elena's eyes opened and though it was hard to read the expression on her face, he sensed it was momentary confusion by the swift way she glanced around and sat up, her long hair trailing in a mass of silken curls down her back.

"Good morning," he said ironically. "Or I assume it is morning by the way the window is beginning to glow."

"It wasn't a dream." Her voice was still subdued with sleep and unflatteringly disappointed.

As he'd had a similar reaction, he could hardly fault her. "I am afraid not."

She unnecessarily gathered up the sheet and modestly tugged it up to her neck, apparently unaware he really could hardly see her in the dim lighting, and the evening before he'd committed it all quite nicely to memory anyway. He'd always had a penchant for voluptuous beauties, but her slenderness accented the curves of both breast and hip, and while *voluptuous* didn't apply, she was alluring and feminine—and all too close for comfort.

The lovely Elena brushed back her hair, her sigh heartfelt. "It is rather incomprehensible. I was hoping to awaken elsewhere."

"Yes." *Incomprehensible.* Both their plight and that he'd spent the night with her in his arms. "I agree."

He slid out of the bed, wincing as his bare feet hit the cold floor, and headed for the screen. He took care of relieving himself and rinsed his hands in the now-cool water, wondering just how he could keep from going mad if he had to stay locked in this room all day again. When he emerged Lady Elena was untangling her hair with her fingers, and her eyes looked huge in the lessening gloom. She said, "Surely by now my parents are beside themselves."

A day and a half, he reflected with savage vehemence. Her parents were not the only ones who would be concerned. "I have a meeting with the prime minister this morning," he said more tautly than he intended. "One does not skip that particular appointment without the courtesy of a note. My absence will also be remarked."

"Then people will be looking for us."

Then people will be talking about us. He was more realistic, more versed in how society worked.

"I suspect they already are." Though he was allowed to live his own life, whatever could be said of his personal activities, he didn't shirk his responsibilities by disappearing whenever he wished. Maybe his family would wait tolerantly a day or two but they would soon realize something was wrong.

As for looking for them . . . where the hell were they?

He had the feeling their captor was too clever for an easy rescue, unless it was a deliberate attempt to have them discovered half-dressed in bed together.

Unfortunately, even in the gloom she seemed to sense the reserve in his tone. "But you have no faith that it will do any good, do you?" Elena's mouth might have trembled. It was hard to tell.

At least she was intelligent as well as beautiful. Honestly, he stated, "As I have no idea where we are, I can't answer that question."

"So all we can do is wait?"

He rubbed the stubble on his jaw and then shook his head. "Rest assured I have been thinking about this and if a solution comes to me, you will be the first person I share it with, my lady."

Her spirited reply surprised him. "And I vow the same, Lord Andrews. If *I* arrive at a viable plan first, *I* will share it with you."

Elena leaned forward in concentration, brushing the curtain of her hair back when it obscured her view of the table. The dappled light colored the faces of the up-turned cards and she considered them, mentally counting, and then smiled triumphantly. "You should concede the game, my lord."

The man lounging across from her lifted his ebony brows. With his glossy dark hair and the shadow of a beard, he looked rather like a romantic pirate, just slightly dissolute and a touch dangerous. This time, with the hot water delivered after breakfast, they each had been given a robe, much to her relief. His dressing gown was black silk and enhanced the rakish persona that was so well-known, his masculinity flagrant and distracting.

She was very much—to her dismay—coming to realize just what it meant to be locked in a room with him for any length of time. There had also been a pack of cards on the tray next to the scones, some writing paper, and an inkwell and pen. It didn't bode well for an expeditious release. It seemed more a ploy to help them pass the time.

He told her, "You should never warn your opponent but instead raise the stakes. If he or she hasn't been paying very careful attention, that challenge will be accepted and then your winnings are increased."

"I see." Elena laid down her cards so he could see them. "But in our case we are not wagering anything, but just keeping score of how many games we each win."

"True." His answering smile was wickedly attractive. "However, there is much more to the strategy of playing card games than the hand you receive by chance. It looks like we will have the time for me to teach you all I know."

All I know.

It was an unfortunate choice of words and she had the impression that even the sophisticated Lord Andrews regretted putting it quite that way. It was made all the worse when Elena, who could feel her blush, murmured, "I am sure you are quite accomplished."

Oh, dear.

"I certainly hope so." The uncharacteristic disconcerted look on his face was replaced with amusement almost at once. "I have practiced quite often."

"I feel certain that's true." Elena glanced down self-consciously to make sure her own robe, a pale blue silk, was still decently covering all it should.

He simply laughed, his gaze touching on where she more firmly knotted the sash at her waist before it returned to her face. "Your name ... it's unusual for an English lady."

"My mother is half-Castilian. It was her mother's name."

"Elegant Elena," he murmured.

She made a face. "I have to admit the propensity of the *ton* to give silly nicknames is something I find irritating."

"I couldn't agree more. The Raven isn't precisely flattering when you think about it. Being likened to a bird who is primarily a scavenger is hardly a compliment."

"I think they are more referring to the color of your hair, my lord. It is very dark."

And deliciously thick. The wayward thought invaded her mind. At the moment a curling ebony strand fell over his brow, giving him a boyish look that was hardly in keeping with his formidable reputation. She wondered what it would feel like to touch those ebony strands, to run her fingers through it ... Would it be warm? Or like cool silk ...

"Is it?" His tone held a subtle silky texture of its own.

With each passing moment, even in her inexperience she was beginning to understand more and more how all those women ended up in his bed. His charm was no doubt deliberate but it wasn't deceptive. He had a sense of humor even in their less than perfect circumstances, and, yes, perhaps a certain innate arrogance, but at such short acquaintance she'd already discovered it was tempered by intelligence. While he was certainly aware of his good looks—by all accounts women had been throwing themselves into his arms for the past decade—Elena doubted he was vain. He might be cognizant of his attractiveness but wasn't like the other handsome fops she knew at all.

"Extremely dark," she said with a slight lift of her chin. "Surely you've glanced in a looking glass a time or two."

"Your father's estate is in Berkshire, is it not?"

She blinked at the change in subject. It wasn't surprising he'd know, for London's elite society was a limited circle. "Yes."

"Do you prefer the country to the city?"

Was his interest genuine? The better question, she decided a moment later, was, what did it matter if sincerity was the motivation? They had nothing better to do but talk and play cards, and the inquiring look in his eyes was compelling.

"It is hard to say," she answered, considering it. "They are quite different. Back at Whitbridge Manor the pace is slow and the servants more like friends than just people my father employs. On the other side of it, London is much more exciting. I have spent most of my life anticipating my debut."

What she didn't add was that the endless rounds of

balls and teas and tedious luncheons bored her more than anything else, but she simply had no choice. Her recent engagement had been more a compromise than a coup as far as she was concerned, but at least it kept her mother from dragging her to every single event.

Engagement. Odd; up until now, she hadn't thought about how Lord Colbert would react to her sudden unexplained absence. She really didn't know him well enough to guess either, which was a disconcerting revelation. He was suitable and her father had been delighted when he'd proposed, so Elena had acquiesced. In a world where so many marriages were business arrangements, at least she'd had some measure of choice and her future husband was both pleasant and nice-looking.

"Siblings?" Lord Andrews was saying. "I'm afraid your father and I are mere acquaintances so I do not know too much about your family."

Her father, if she had to guess, hardly approved of the licentious viscount. He wasn't a puritan, but even she would concede he was a bit on the lofty side and a man with a reputation as notorious as the viscount's would not meet with his approval. She hadn't lied when she'd said that Randolph Raine was not someone whom she'd choose as a husband. Her father would not be pleased in the least.

Obligingly, she told him, "Two younger brothers. Edgar, the heir, is only fifteen."

"I have a sister just a year older than your brother. I am her guardian."

For whatever reason she found that incongruous. The disreputable Andrews was the guardian of a charge he must launch into society in just a few years? As diplomatically as possible she murmured, "I didn't know, but, then again, though people do talk about you, they don't mention those sorts of details."

His mouth twisted a little. "I can only imagine what kind they do mention."

"Actually, not too much in front of me, but it is easy enough to get the gist of it."

"Wicked is as wicked does. Is that it?"

She didn't flinch from looking him in the eye. "Just about right, my lord."

"Some of it might even be true. How is," he said with idle inflection, "the season so far?"

How come she got the impression that question wasn't idle at all? And yet the switch in topic was welcome. "I'm engaged."

"I thought I saw the announcement recently. Colbert, is it? We've crossed paths but we really are not well acquainted. Tell me about him."

The jeweled light through the windows gave sapphire tints to his dark hair and slanted a ruby streak across one lean cheek, touching the corner of his mouth. Cautiously she asked, "Could you be more specific?"

"I am still trying to make sense of this."

"How could Lord—"

"Indulge me. What can it hurt? As I said, we have nothing but time."

That seemed to be unfortunate but true.

Elena regarded him thoughtfully. "You still believe this is directed somehow at me."

He shrugged, broad shoulders moving under the black silk. "As I said, I don't know, but we both must admit that someone has gone through a great deal of trouble. For instance, that whiskey"—he pointed to a decanter that had been brought with their luncheon—"is actually rather hard to obtain and a particular favorite of mine. It isn't a secret, but, also not necessarily common knowledge. Why would our captor bother when I have been deemed replaceable and threatened with bodily harm?"

"I don't know." When she remembered the man with the pistol pointed straight at Andrews's heart, she could hardly disagree. Casting back, she tried to recall anything she could that might be related to their current incomprehensible state of imprisonment. "The season has seemed rather uneventful, if you ask me. I've had suitors whom I would deem truly serious in that they seemed more determined than the others, but quite a few eligible gentlemen have sent flowers and called. It happens every day. Lord Colbert had the advantage of my father's approval. We've only just become affianced, and, in truth, I can't tell you anything remarkable about him. He's very ... pleasant."

How inadequate it sounded when put that way.

Lord Andrews didn't comment but something flickered in his eyes. "Can you think of anyone who might resent your choosing him?"

"Another suitor? As you've mentioned before, would they lock me in with you as retaliation?"

If the tart tone of her voice bothered him, he didn't show it. "A valid point, but perhaps if there was another young lady angling for Colbert's title and fortune, there might be an interest in removing you from the fray, as it were."

She hadn't thought of that, but there were flaws in the theory. "Please explain to me," Elena said with all due practicality, "how a young woman my age could possibly orchestrate something so elaborate and costly. I certainly couldn't. My allowance doesn't include funds for rare whiskey or armed guards."

"What about one of the ambitious mothers that usually make me run in the other direction when in their company?"

That hadn't occurred to her either, but neither did she subscribe to the possibility that she was the focus of this absurd abduction. Slowly she shook her head. "I can't think of anyone who is a rival in the sense you mean."

"It might not have been obvious. But jealousy is a powerful emotion."

Elena considered him with a hint of wry humor. "Are trying to tell me you've experienced it firsthand? I somehow assumed that as London's premier rake, constancy was not your preference; therefore jealousy would be pointless."

"We are not now discussing my personal preferences," he countered mildly. "I am speaking as a man who has a title and enough wealth to have been the quarry of more than a few scheming matrons eager to gain an aristocratic husband for their insipid daughters."

No doubt he was right, for while his reputation might cause some pause, he was still undeniably a coup in the marriage mart. That is, if he had the slightest inclination to choose a wife.

A certain part of her was envious, actually. She was betrothed to a man not necessarily of her choosing but who pleased her parents and could provide well for her and their children.

The patently unfair restrictions against her gender were frustrating, but not limited to the rich and aristocratic either. "How very vexing for you," she said coolly.

"Ah, the haughty tone indicates disapproval, I assume.

You play the outraged lady very well. Yes, I find it uncomfortable to be coveted for my money and position. That is why I much prefer my relationships to involve nothing but physical satisfaction for both parties."

He said it matter-of-factly and she believed the detachment to be sincere. It was somewhat startling. "Is that why you don't wish to marry? Are you afraid when a woman shows interest it might be mercenary?"

Apparently he wasn't interested in answering questions about his personal life. Instead he changed the course of the conversation again. "My sister and aunt are in the country so they won't be alarmed yet, but my valet and my secretary will both know this is not my usual behavior. I suspect also our mutual absence will start to raise eyebrows, unless your father handled your sudden disappearance with the utmost discretion."

Though he was sometimes a bit stuffy Elena knew her father would be beside himself with worry. "He would not wish a scandal and would do his best to avoid one."

"I'm sure you're correct, but, unfortunately," the man sitting across from her said with grim conviction, "I don't think that is going to be possible."

Chapter 6

The big roan thundered around the corner, still going easy, his neck wet and his breathing audible as he went by, but he wasn't winded even though Gibbons had been pushing him and that was very encouraging indeed.

What hadn't been nearly as satisfactory was the evening before, or, for that matter, this morning. The former had involved his wife doing her best to instruct him in a lesson in severe sexual frustration and the latter had yielded almost nothing in the form of information on the winsome but mysteriously missing Lady Elena.

Leaning against the rail in moody contemplation Ben had come to the conclusion that the elusive daughter of the Earl of Whitbridge had quite simply vanished in a wisp of smoke. At this point she'd been gone for almost forty-eight hours without a word.

"Nice run, my lord. I told you he's in fine mettle. Thor has the haunches of a champion."

Ben glanced over at his trainer, roused from his musings. No one had agreed when he'd decided to let someone as young as Adam Altamont take over his stable, but the decision had been duly weighed and considered, and, eventually, he'd decided that instinct was sometimes better than logic. As his horses were winning more than ever, he still felt it a good one. "He's moving well," he agreed, feeling guilty for his distraction, since usually his horses were his passion. "Loose on the inside, though, I thought."

"He moves better when he's pressed. Without another horse he's never going to give us all he has."

That was true. His most promising young racer liked competition. Ben watched as the jockey trotted his mount to the gate and the lads ran out to lead away the horse. Interesting . . . it brought to mind the years of the war, and how when he was challenged and lives hung in the balance it had never been a question whether to act if it was a decision of how much to risk and in what way. He'd have laid down his life for king and country and had taken that road more than once, but this current situation was at once more simple and yet more complex.

He leaned his arms on the railing of the paddock. "I've an obscure question. If you were intent on eloping with a young lady who has a powerful father, tell me, how would you go about it?"

Altamont blinked for a moment, his brawny forearms also against the fence, his thick dark hair ruffled by the morning wind. There was a hint of alarm in his clear blue eyes. "My lord, please let me assume this is strictly a hypothetical question. The occasional enthusiastic titled lady is trial enough without some accusation coming my way. I vow I've been doing nothing more than training your horses."

It was impossible not to laugh. Ben hardly walked around judging the appearance of other men, but it was true that his trainer was not only brilliant with his high-strung charges but good-looking and did seem to attract considerable female attention at the race meets. "No, no accusation, though I do advise you to keep to the safer venues that do not include the daughters of earls."

They weren't that disparate in age, actually, maybe a three-year difference, which was why everyone had recommended a seasoned trainer for the expensive stable. But Ben had liked Adam immediately and, more importantly, his horses had responded in the same way. He'd seen him handle them, realized at once the affinity between man and animal, and had hired him on the spot despite his lack of experience. This would be the first racing season since his father's old trainer had retired and Ben thought the horses looked fitter than ever.

"I *do* know better," Adam murmured, his smile slight. "Always. I am not so foolish as to risk my career for a casual tumble. One word against my name and suddenly I do not get to train horses like yours. It isn't worth it."

Or no woman had made it worth it yet, Ben mused, thinking it over. It was all about perspective. "But let's say in theory you wished to spirit away a young lady who was the daughter of a powerful man. How would you go about it?"

"Off to Scotland, I suppose." Adam frowned, his shirt open at the neck, his sleeves rolled up to his elbows. "That's the fastest way to marry with the least effort, though it isn't a particularly short journey. I've never fancied that idea myself. It seems to me if a lady is worth marrying, it is worth doing it properly."

A sensible attitude. Admittedly Ben had also chosen a safe, proper course, selecting Alicia for her bloodlines, her beauty, and her serene disposition. He'd dutifully courted by calling and bringing the occasional bouquet that almost always his secretary obtained for him, and, in retrospect, maybe he hadn't quite completed the task in the way he thought he had. When he'd proposed to her, he and her father had already hammered out the marriage agreement beforehand and solicitors had been consulted, and, if looked at that way, to his chagrin, it did not seem very romantic.

However, his current standoff with his wife was not part of what might have happened to Lady Elena but an entirely different problem.

"Quite," he agreed, the scent of fresh earth, dug up by the hooves of the racers, pungent. "But not always an option. What if her father didn't approve of you?"

"If she was a true lady I doubt he would," Adam said frankly. "I might be the son of a baron and decently educated, but I have no prospects except a working man's income, and I'm not a part of the beau monde by any means. That's fine. I prefer my horses anyway, but approaching an earl for his daughter's hand . . . no. Is this about Whitbridge's missing daughter?"

It had been too much to expect all along—Ben had known it from the beginning—for this to be kept entirely quiet, but he had to admit he hadn't anticipated the news of Lady Elena's disappearance to spread so quickly. Granted, two days had passed and Lord Whitbridge had questioned the staff at the theater the night Elena had gone missing, but for someone like Altamont to know of it already was a bit startling.

"What exactly have you heard?" he asked casually, watching as Gibbons, his first choice of jockey, slid off Thor and said something to the lad who took the reins.

Adam wasn't fooled, but, then again, his quick mind and intuitive reactions were why Ben had taken a chance on such an untried trainer. "I might be a fifth son, but my older brother does move in your circles. He mentioned it to me. Word has it she abruptly disappeared and her family is looking for her. No one seems to know where she's gone. Speculation is growing."

Ben had been doing some speculating of his own. "I understand Lord Andrews is also missing."

Adam cocked a brow, watching as the roan trotted past them, one of the lads taking him to cool down. "The viscount owns some of the finest horses in England."

"Some," Ben agreed mildly.

"Not as fine as yours, my lord."

"You might be a dash prejudiced." Still, he found the quick equivocation amusing. "What he does own is the reputation of bedding Britain's finest ladies. Who can I talk to?"

Altamont leaned back, holding on to the paddock railing. "I have to say, knowing his lordship's reputation, a connection would surprise me. She is not his usual choice in a female in any way. He avoids the marriageable ones."

"That's interesting." Ben spoke evenly. "But I would like to confirm that there is no connection between him and Lady Elena. What about his stable master? The lads usually talk to the maids and footmen, and it would be a much more subtle way of inquiry."

"Prescott?" Adam answered readily enough, his gaze steady. "Would you rather I speak to him? He's Welsh and a bit prickly. We know each other, and though he feels I'm too young to be in charge of such fine horses we get along well enough. I'm going to guess you'd get little to nothing from him. We usually exercise on the same track at dawn. I could talk to him for you."

That was a generous offer, and as Ben still hadn't

explained—nor was he going to—his interest in the matter, probably prudent. It took him a moment but he nodded. "Ask Prescott if he's heard intimations that Andrews is involved seriously with anyone. And leave Lady Elena's name out of it, though it doesn't appear to be a deep, dark secret."

"It's quite puzzling as to what it is," Adam declared succinctly. "With the viscount's propensity for a very different type of lady, it seems unlikely they are together."

"Does it?" Ben wasn't quite as sure.

"I would think so."

This was all becoming rather interesting. Ben watched Thor being led away toward the stables, a powerful animal, so proud and confident, but being taken in a certain direction willingly because of the promise of a reward.

"I suppose it is possible their mutual absence is not connected." The concession was insincere. He didn't believe that for a moment.

His instincts told him otherwise.

Between the whiskey, the candlelight, the beautiful girl . . . he could almost succumb to temptation.

Almost.

Once he'd begun to understand the dynamic of the predicament they were in, Ran declined the honor of this planned seduction.

Still, she was damned tempting. It hadn't helped that he'd listened to her bathe earlier, the slight splash of the water erotic, and had watched—what else was there to do in this prison?—as she performed the very intimate task of combing out her long, damp hair, unsnarling the golden strands. The act was so feminine and arousing it had sent him to his feet to pace across the room, and hopefully she didn't realize the source of his sudden restlessness.

Elena—to the devil with their titles; he was done with propriety and her first name would do—sat across from him in a light blue robe now, her shining hair loose, and while she was as manipulated as he was, the scene had certainly been set.

No.

He refused to play this game. He knew exactly what their diabolical host wanted from him.

The bastard.

"I'll sleep on the floor tonight," Ran said more tersely than he intended. "I think perhaps it would be better."

Waking with her in his arms again was not a good option, but stating that involved admitting that it had happened in the first place. If she didn't really remember it, *he* did.

She frowned, shaking her head. "I don't think that sounds very comfortable, my lord."

It didn't sound comfortable to him either, but better than the alternative, which might involve a weakened state of resolve. It wasn't that he actually doubted his willpower, but more that he had come to the conclusion this wasn't about the two of them but something else entirely.

Perhaps he should just be blunt.

"All of this," he said with as little intonation as possible, "is designed so we are coerced into not only sharing our meals, the washbasin, and the close quarters, but also that bed. Whether it is aimed at you or me, Colbert, or for an unfathomable reason someone else, the intention is hardly subtle."

"I realize that." She gazed across the room, her profile

clean and lovely. The long shimmering strands of her hair brushed her waist as she turned her head finally and met his eyes. "I might be not nearly as sophisticated as you are, but I understand clearly the purpose of this abduction."

Suddenly Ran was struck with the impulse to laugh, not out of amusement but because he admired the lift of her chin and the defiance in her eyes. "I see. So we both know the intent but not the motivation." Carelessly he picked up the decanter of whiskey and refilled his glass. "We always come back to that. Any thoughts? What about your father? I assume he has enemies, as all powerful men do."

"That has occurred to me." Elena sat composed, her voice prim but holding a thoughtful note. "I'm afraid I am not well-versed enough in his business affairs to suggest a specific culprit. I suppose it is plausible that someone might wish to get back at him through me."

"He's had more time on this earth to antagonize others than we have," Ran agreed sardonically, but further elaboration would involve his own political opposition to the conservative and loyalist views of Lord Whitbridge, and, at this point in time, that was hardly useful.

"He's certainly antagonized me once or twice," his lordship's daughter murmured with a hint of the humor he was starting to appreciate, "but never enough I felt the urge to retaliate. You would know better than I. Is his position in the House of Lords worth this?"

She was quick minded, he would give her that. The implications were interesting to him also. "I don't know," he answered honestly, "because while I don't agree entirely with his opinions, I suppose I am not rabid enough to ever consider ruining someone else's life to prove my point. Besides, while your father is influential, a scandal involving his daughter would not change the course of the way he votes for Britain's future policies or how he debates the new agricultural laws. He'd be injured personally, but this won't influence the course of history."

Propping her chin on her palm she murmured, "I agree. It seems excessive."

Women were not usually offered the option to agree or not, as it was hardly important if they did. Ran took a sip of his favorite whiskey and registered how intriguing he found the lovely Lady Elena's sense of independent self-worth. "I suspect you were a mischievous child. Weren't you?"

She laughed in a low melodic sound. "I don't know. Perhaps. I've always liked horses more than embroidery. Does that count?"

"Of course." He could picture her in a riding habit, graceful in a sidesaddle, her cheeks tinged pink from an early-morning breeze, golden hair under a plumed hat, slim gloved hands on the reins . . . She'd be skillful and swift and the most beautiful one there. . . .

Damn.

"Do you hunt?" He asked it too abruptly.

"No."

She didn't, he discovered, because she deplored the actual sport, but she liked a canter through the countryside much more than a London ball, and the *ton*'s most-favored beauty smiled at the recollection of summer pastures and bucolic fields. She stated in her concise way, "Someone of your level of sophistication might not understand this, but I am not all that interested in the whirl of society."

He understood it quite well actually, and though he

spent far too much time in London because his obligations required it, she might be surprised to learn he also
preferred quiet mornings and green pastures and the
sound of singing birds. However, defending himself was
never something he bothered to do, so he just regarded
her with amused consideration. "How unconventional,
Lady Elena."

"Rather like spending the night in the same bed as
the infamous Lord Andrews. That takes *unconventional*
to new heights."

"Perhaps, but nothing happened."

Well, not *nothing*. He'd wanted her and that was
something, and he wanted her now and that was even
more significant. It wasn't just her beauty either, which
was unusual enough to give him pause. Yes, she was desirable, but she also reminded him intellectually of the
independent ladies he favored normally, not an ingénue.

She murmured, "No, nothing has happened."

Yet. The word hung there like a presence in the room.

Maybe he would have said more but she lifted her
hand then to brush a lock of hair away from her cheek.
That simple motion emphasized the fullness of her
breasts under the material of her robe, and he allowed
his gaze—and his mind—to wander just a fraction.

Indisputably, she was already ruined if anyone discovered their mutual captivity.

Of course someone would. That was the intent of it
all.

There were quite a few ways to make love and leave
the woman a virgin.

And he'd considered all of them this afternoon.

Chapter 7

The London Times: Society Section, July 19, 1816

> *Has the raven flown away, taking a little bird with him?*

Ben set aside the newspaper and contemplated his cup of coffee. He'd forgotten to add cream, he noticed absently, reaching for the small silver pitcher and pouring in a dash, and stirring the already cooling beverage in abstraction. Whitbridge had, as predicted, been unable to keep the disappearance of his daughter a secret. Perhaps if Andrews hadn't also suddenly gone missing it would have been possible, but Ben had known if they didn't discover Lady Elena's whereabouts quickly, word would leak out no matter how discreet they were about the search.

For a second time he scanned Altamont's prompt note, his trainer's script surprisingly neat. Yes, trainers did exercise the strings early, but this was swifter than he'd expected.

> *Prescott scoffed at the idea his lordship would carry off Whitbridge's daughter. More to come soon if further information possible.*

More to come soon? What the devil did that mean? In the early-morning sunlight he leaned back in his chair and contemplated rakehells and innocent maidens. As far as he could tell the two had no connection whatsoever, or else the rakehell lost his status and was forced to marry the no-longer-so-innocent maiden.... Either way they both were removed from their familiar footing in society.

"Good morning, my lord."

Glancing up, he saw his wife gracefully enter the room, her demeanor composed as if what happened before she'd exited his bedroom the other evening never occurred. This morning she wore a lemon-colored gown of some frothy material that set off her lustrous dark hair, and when a young footman hurried forward to pull out her chair, she gifted the man with an entrancing smile.

It irritated Ben for no obvious reason. She was always gracious with the servants and he expected no less of someone who was charming and good tempered by nature— *With the exception of when she is banning me from her bed,* he thought caustically. Perhaps that was the source of his angst.

"You don't normally read the society section," Alicia observed, coming over to give him a most chaste— disappointingly so—kiss on the cheek as he'd risen at her entrance, the faint waft of her perfume instantly distracting. Had he not known better, he could have sworn the affectionate gesture was merely to peer at what he'd been reading.

"How do you know?" he asked with equanimity. "Quite often we breakfast apart."

Almost the moment he said it he regretted it, for it

gave her an opportunity to expound on how little time
they spent together, but Alicia merely went to sit down
opposite on the other side of the table, poured coffee
from a silver pot into her porcelain cup, added two lumps
of sugar, and pursed her soft, very tempting mouth. "I
often peruse the paper later, and if one is observant she
can tell the parts that have been folded and read from the
crisp lines of the other sections. I know what interests
you."

He was apparently married to a detective. Ben considered his answer, decided that neutrality was a cowardly course of action, but usually a prudent one, and
reached for his cup. "Lord Whitbridge is family. I saw his
name and it caught my eye."

The absolute truth.

"And Elena is missing." Alicia nodded, her smooth
brow furrowing. "Yes, I heard. Everyone is talking about
it. At first I thought it was just another ridiculous rumor,
but it sounds like it could actually be true. Is that why
Uncle Thomas wished to see you?"

All the gossip didn't bode well, but since word was
obviously out if it appeared in the *Times*, even if the reference didn't have Elena's name maybe they could use
that to their advantage. He was more interested in *how*
the rumor was spreading than the fact it was going about
so quickly. He avoided answering Alicia's direct question
and instead asked one himself. "Tell me, how did you
hear it?"

His lovely wife paused in taking a sip from her cup
and gazed at him. "My sister told me. We are both close
to Elena, and Harriet is naturally very worried, as am I."

"Did she also mention Lord Andrews?"

"No. Why would she?"

She was going to hear it sooner or later so he might as well tell her. It was right there in the paper. "He seems to also be mysteriously absent."

"The viscount? And Elena? Surely you can't be serious?"

Ben shrugged. "She's a very beautiful young woman and Andrews has a penchant for lovely females. It makes sense to me. Tell me, did Harriet mention the source of her information?"

His wife's spoon clattered onto her saucer. "My cousin did *not* run off with Lord Andrews."

"How do you know?"

Emphatically Alicia said, "She wouldn't. For that matter, *he* wouldn't. In case you have not been paying attention, he has a rather legendary aversion to the idea of marriage. Besides, I've not heard even one whisper of a connection between the two of them. How ridiculous."

Secrets, he wanted to point out, *have been kept before.* Instead he asked again, "Where did Harriet hear of your cousin's disappearance?"

"I . . . I don't know. She didn't say." Alicia's fine brows drew together as she looked at him in open consternation.

He could, of course, ask her to inquire, but that was more obvious than he'd prefer. He trusted Alicia to the extent that if he specifically asked her to not say anything, she wouldn't. Then again, he would have to explain why he was interested.

Perhaps even have to mention that he'd once been a spy in the war, although, to be truthful, his time had been spent mostly in London, making sure the War Office ran as it should. Spy wasn't quite right. Investigator sounded better.

Either way that revelation was hardly necessary and not something he wanted her to know. He was used to being secretive and old habits were difficult to break.

"You must admit it is an unusual situation. I have to wonder if the source of the information might know more about what has happened to Lady Elena, and since your uncle is a friend I am naturally concerned," he said smoothly. Claiming Whitbridge as a friend was actually stretching the truth, but in his experience the truth was an elastic entity when it needed to be.

"I've always thought you rather didn't care for him all that much," his wife said with unsettling insight.

"If we weren't friends why did he come to confide in me about his missing daughter?" Before she could comment he added, "While concern is only natural on our part, I am sure there is a logical explanation for the situation."

"I hope so," she said quietly, sitting across from him in her—he couldn't help but notice—very flattering summer gown. The soft material draped her breasts and the color *was* becoming.

And when the hell he had started to notice if a woman looked particularly fetching in a certain shade?

It was clear he'd lost his mind, but she'd pushed him into it.

It wasn't all that difficult to summon a smile and ask in a very husbandly fashion, "What are your plans for this day?"

If her dazzling smile was the reward for such a plebeian question, he decided a moment later, perhaps he should ask it more often. Obviously he'd done something right, but, honestly, he wasn't sure what. He'd only made polite conversation at the breakfast table.

However, it occurred to him that he rarely inquired as to her activities, assuming, perhaps erroneously, that it demonstrated he was not a controlling husband dictating her every move. She said softly, "I am glad you asked."

Perhaps he'd just made progress toward ... well, a goal he'd never considered difficult to achieve before recent events. Her bed had been open until the baffling ultimatum.

"I am supposed to go to a rather dull luncheon," his wife informed him. "I thought about sending my regrets in a last-minute cancellation, but we are supposed to attend that soiree tonight so it might seem rude to skip one and attend the other."

"Soiree?" He picked up his coffee.

"We accepted, remember? The Heatheringtons?"

He didn't, actually. It must have showed, for she gazed at him in open reproof. "Benjamin, your secretary said you approved the invitation. I was very pleased, for rarely do we attend events together."

"You and I didn't discuss it that I recall," he muttered defensively.

"Absolutely true." She took a genteel sip from her cup.

Why she was looking at him triumphantly wasn't exactly a mystery. He'd fallen into the trap much too easily. "I meant ..." he trailed off. Actually he'd meant what he'd just said: he never addressed their plans with her. The invitations she wished to accept were given to his secretary and he sorted through them when he had the time, usually refusing the majority. Ben cleared his throat. "I don't recall committing to the affair, but if you say so, I must have. What time do you wish to leave?"

"Not too early. We can dine together beforehand. That would be lovely."

The amazing thing was his beautiful wife looked as if she really thought it *would* be lovely. He wasn't nearly as confident. Not because he eschewed her company, but because he wasn't quite so sure he could live up to the ideal she had of what marriage represented.

This damned test of his ability to be a good husband was irritating, but the potential reward . . .

He was thinking a great deal about that, which he guessed was exactly what she wanted from him. "Fine," he said neutrally, rising and dropping his napkin. "I'll be back in time to change for the evening. Please excuse me."

Perhaps it isn't a garden stroll, he thought grimly as he left the room, but it was a concession, for he disliked society events for the most part. He had a full day already with his solicitors, and, on top of all that, he was supposed to find the elusive Lady Elena and return her to her family, all while keeping the gossip to a minimum.

Easier said than done, but most of life was that way. As he asked for his horse to be brought around, he wondered what else could happen to confound his existence.

The looming scandal was the talk of the *ton*.

There was no doubt about it. Despite Ben's reassurances that there was a good explanation for Elena's unexplained absence, Alicia's cousin's disappearance was causing quite a sensation.

Alicia lifted her cup of tea and tried to appear serene when inside she was quite cold and troubled. It had been a shock to hear Elena was missing yesterday, and then an even greater one to realize that the notorious Lord Andrews also appeared to have vanished at the same time. Gossip had it the viscount left town without a word to anyone and none of his staff or family had the slightest idea where he might have gone.

"... is said to be keeping her," Lady Dorchester said in a smug tone, "though I have never given credence to the rumor."

Lady Dorchester had given credence to every other rumor she'd ever heard, so Alicia gritted her teeth, though the urge to defend Elena almost overwhelmed her. Unfortunately, as puzzled as she was by her cousin's sudden absence she really couldn't think of much to say, but it was impossible to stay completely quiet. "Whom to be keeping whom?" she asked, her voice cool. "I assume we've had a turn in subject, for surely we are not still talking about Elena."

"Oh, dear." Lady Dorchester waved a careless hand. "No, of course not. We are talking about"—her voice lowered theatrically—"that foreign countess Andrews favored."

The change in status from ingénue to married lady meant she was allowed to hear such scandalous insinuations, but it was all still disconcerting to her. *Favored* carried a connotation that was wickedly suggestive, but, then again, they were talking about Randolph Raine.

Surely—*surely*—Elena would not be involved with the handsome young viscount and not mention a word.

Alicia was half inclined to ask Ben to look into it. She didn't know what it was he actually did during the war but had a vague idea he gathered information. That might be useful now. Maybe he could help with this ... this growing awkwardness.

"Well"—Evelyn Borroughs waved her fork—"it isn't like Andrews has not done this sort of thing before."

"He has?" Adele Rockfort scoffed. "When? He most certainly has never run off with a lady of good family, Evie."

Alicia would have backed up that statement but it wasn't necessary. A dainty woman with snow-white hair who was a contemporary of her grandmother observed, "No matter that Andrews is a very charming rogue—he isn't a fool. If he wished to marry the girl he would have, but this is an unnecessary scandalbroth."

That was no doubt accurate. Though Alicia didn't know his lordship well, the truth was, any eligible young woman knew his interests did not lie with the unmarried misses of the *ton*, and the mutual absence of Elena and the viscount did not make sense.

"If he has run off with my cousin," Alicia said with deliberate intent in an effort to be supportive, "he would be a genius, not a fool, for she is not only beautiful but also gracious and intelligent."

At this point all of the women in the room turned to stare at her.

"Elena is wonderful," she declared stoutly, "and, to my knowledge, she's never even met Lord Andrews." Her cup rattled into the saucer as she replaced it. "She certainly has never mentioned him to me and you all admit you have never seen them so much as share a waltz."

"Lady Heathton," one of the matrons finally commented, "I am sure if your cousin is blameless, she will be duly exonerated."

The speaker was Winifred Tomlison, who was the dowager Countess of Something-or-Another, but at the moment Alicia was too irritated to remember. The woman had the nerve to add, "*You* must admit that their mutual absence is quite the coincidence."

Guilty until able to prove otherwise. That hardly seemed fair, but Alicia had the sinking feeling that was how it was going to be from the condescending intonation. "I feel confident we will find that there is a logical explanation for all this," she responded, realizing as she said the words that they actually belonged to her husband.

Well, when analyzed that way, Benjamin wasn't always that communicative, but when he did speak it was always well thought-out and worth listening to.

When she left the luncheon on a murmured excuse a few moments later, she could swear the speculative gazes followed her out the door and left a clinging residue she wished to wash off.

If this glancing blow from the upcoming vitriol of her cousin's disappearance was any indication, how was Elena going to feel? To say Alicia was concerned was an understatement. Only a year apart in age, they had shared enough time together that she knew Elena was sensitive and, despite her recent popularity, not a person who reveled in the attention of society in any way—and especially not this one.

Where the devil was she?

Chapter 8

Day Three

It was nothing. A mere brush of his fingers against hers as they both reached for the clotted cream at the same moment, but it sparked a startled awareness and an absurd blush warmed her cheeks.

It didn't help at all that Ran politely withdrew his hand and there was a definite gleam of wicked amusement in his eyes over her discomfort at the inadvertent contact.

He had the most beautiful eyes. Elena had never really thought about that part of a male before this incarceration. Naturally a woman noticed the usual things like the breadth of a man's shoulders, his height, the whiteness of his teeth when he smiled, the line of his jaw, and how he tied his cravat . . . but she hadn't realized the impact of the way a man—especially a devilishly attractive one like the scandalous Andrews—could look at a woman.

As if those midnight blue eyes could see *everything*.

The realization of his presence so close to her—the careless tie of the sash at his lean waist, the fact he was naked beneath the smooth silk of his robe—was unsettling. . . .

"Please," he said affably. "Ladies first, of course."

It was a little irksome that he could be so blasé when she was so affected, but Elena murmured, "Thank you."

She was getting used to the multicolored muted light and the way it gave the room a surreal glow. The truth be told, it was very romantic in an aesthetic sense. She put the cream on her scone, took a dainty bite, and touched her mouth with a napkin. "What do you think this room was used for before?"

"Before *us*, you mean?" His smile was ironic. "Before someone decided it was the perfect place to hold two people against their will as their lives no doubt disintegrate with each passing minute?"

Put that way it sounded awful, but there was no denying the probable truth. How *would* they ever be able to explain this? "Before us," she agreed, setting aside her pastry, wondering at the same time as she said the words how often other women had sat across from him in this fashion, drinking tea and nibbling on their breakfast in nothing but a thin robe, after spending the night in his bed. It was currently late afternoon and they were having high tea, but still . . . surely there had been many intimate mornings.

Maybe not that *often,* she decided upon reflection. She might be young and inexperienced, but she had the impression that while Lord Andrews was a celebrated lover, he was not a man who lightly shared intimate details of his life.

In fact, he didn't share his life at all as far as she could tell. By the sheer necessity of circumstance there was little for them to do but converse, and she was starting to get more of a sense of him other than just the persona so whispered over by society, but he didn't share personal information freely. What she had discovered had come in chance remarks and small comments.

For one, he loved his family. He spoke fondly of his sister and aunt and part of his anger at his current predicament was how worried they both would be over his unexplained absence. As annoyed as he was at being detained involuntarily, they were obviously his main concern.

Interesting, that. She would never have given him credit for being so sentimental or sensitive before their enforced proximity, but there was much more to the man than met the eye, and considering their mutual incarceration that was lucky for her. If, indeed, the purpose of this was to destroy one or both of them, Lord Andrews was not cooperating.

"This was a meeting place for assignations, if I had to venture a hypothesis," he said, the words weighted, "for a lord and his mistress." He gestured at the bed. "There are some modifications that tell me this was used for illicit trysts."

"Modifications?" The word was spoken without thought, and she eyed the main piece of furniture in their prison with an assessing eye. "I see nothing unusual about it. It is beautifully carved, but otherwise it is just a place to sleep."

His smile was lazily wicked. "Do you see the rings? What do you suppose those are for?"

She had no idea.

He was correct: there were two gold rings, each mounted on either side of the elaborate headboard, but she wasn't quite following him. In truth, the attachments really didn't seem to have much purpose. "I'm not certain."

"I didn't think you would." He laughed but then ruefully shook his head. "And I most certainly should not explain. In case you have not noted it I am doing my utmost to not be a bad influence on your maidenly sensibilities."

"I have noticed."

Their gazes met. Deliberately he said, "Then I shouldn't tell you."

"My lord, you do a great deal of things you should not do. Is that not correct?" She found the slight dimple in his cheek fascinating when he smiled. It gave him a boyish air at odds with the power of his tall frame.

"Not the past few days."

"No," she agreed, not quite sure why she was playing with fire in this fashion, but she truly was curious. "Not the past few days. You have been the model of decorum. So you should be allowed a small infraction. What are the rings for?"

"Model of decorum? I am fairly sure that's the first time in my life I've been referred to that way." He stretched out his long legs and lounged back. "As for the rings, it's a game some men and women like to play . . . a fantasy giving the illusion of not having a choice."

She still didn't quite understand and her confusion must have shown, for he went on.

"Bondage is an aphrodisiac for certain lovers. Some women enjoy it. Men, too, I've heard, though I must admit it doesn't appeal to me."

"Bondage?"

"Being tied up before and during sexual intercourse. There are those who find it to enhance the experience. Obviously it makes one partner dominant."

That blunt declaration was enlightening enough that she blinked and then blushed, but she had to admit it was all very interesting. In a shocking way, of course, but still interesting. No doubt Lord Andrews was a very font of information on a subject she knew virtually nothing about.

Why not ask, she thought recklessly, for they had nothing but time to talk. No one else would ever have this sort of conversation with her. "I admit I've never heard of such a thing. Why would that appeal to anyone?"

"As I said, it's a fantasy. The helplessness is supposed to add to the pleasure."

Were Mother in the room, she would faint dead away over his frankness, Elena thought with a twinge of humor. "I would think feeling helpless would not be enjoyable at all."

"If you truly were helpless. There is trust involved but that goes without saying when making love. Usually the male is larger and stronger than the female anyway. A woman gives the gift not just of her body in the bedroom but of her trust also."

"I had never thought of it that way." He was right, of course. Yet despite the obvious strength of his tall, athletic body, she wasn't the least bit afraid of him. Quite the opposite. Elena felt protected more than vulnerable.

"Perhaps we should change the subject." His voice was dry but his gaze was speculative under slightly lowered lashes. "I am sure this topic is inappropriate for a proper young lady."

"I disagree." Elena looked back with a hint of challenge. "No one will ever know what we discussed during our time here, and, quite frankly, I'm very curious. It seems to me that young women in my position are expected to marry, often to secure a family bloodline by producing an heir, but no one really explains how one leads to the other. I've never understood why it is such a secret, but when asked my mother is so vague that I have given up."

"I hardly think she'd approve of you asking *me*."

"She wouldn't," Elena admitted. "As I said, I'm not likely to tell her about this conversation and, actually, I'm asking you because I think there is a good chance you will be honest with me."

Dark brows lifted slightly in sardonic amusement. "If I cooperate I will lose my status as a model of decorum and I have had it for so short a time."

She stifled a laugh. "I doubt you were destined to keep it for long anyway, my lord."

"That's probably true," he agreed with an unrepentant grin. "So, go ahead. Ask me whatever you wish and I will be as frank as possible, though, your mother aside, I would think Colbert might be the one to take the greatest offense."

The reminder of her fiancé was disconcerting, as she realized for a few moments she'd almost forgotten he existed. "I can't imagine asking *him*," she admitted, thinking of his lordship's almost forbidding politesse.

"Well, he isn't here," Ran said drily. "It appears I am your only option, my lady."

She seemed to be carefully weighing her first question.

If he could resist her request he would, but the beauty sitting before him with her tumbled fair hair and an inquiring look on her face made it impossible.

Or maybe he didn't *want* to resist. He should, of

course. It went without saying. He'd done his best to concentrate on any other subject besides the topic she wanted to discuss since he'd woken up in the same bed with her.

She was too bewitchingly lovely, and though of the upper class—her family's wealth significant, her launch into society lauded—so far he'd found her uniquely unspoiled. For a man who thought he knew a great deal about women the anomaly was unsettling. He was sophisticated enough he understood that beauty did not mean depth—more often quite the opposite. Lady Elena wasn't vain or petulant or a dozen other traits he disliked.

Thank God.

He was forced to admit their captor might be cleverer than he first imagined. Their shared captivity was having a predictable effect on his libido—that was intentional, he knew. But it was also producing an unexpected sense of camaraderie and friendship.

So, despite the warning voices clanging in his brain, he decided to answer whatever she asked. Why not? After all, she was right: no one would ever know what they had conversed about together and he found the curiosity in her gorgeous eyes irresistible.

"Why is it my understanding that some women do not enjoy the attentions of their husbands but others seek lovers? That seems to be such a contradiction."

At least that was easy enough to address. "Obligation is rarely as enjoyable as the forbidden. I'm afraid that is human nature. It works both ways also. Men may choose their wives with many factors in play, such as political connections and bloodlines, but when choosing a lover, a man or woman usually selects what actually attracts them in a physical sense. As it is a very physical act, obviously the latter choice is a more enjoyable experience."

"How physical?"

That delicately asked question was a bit more difficult to define without describing the mechanics. He lifted his brows. "Let me say enough so that when done properly the two parties should be breathless and pleasantly exhausted afterward."

Her smooth brow furrowed. "I see."

No, she didn't, and he would love to drag her the few feet to the bed and demonstrate, but that was ill-advised. Ran went on. "However, making love is like an intricate game on another level also, since emotions are usually in play. It involves not just the body but the mind. The balance of power is always shifting. It might be a man's world, but women tend to hold power over men because our sexual desires are more"—his smile was brief—"base, shall we say? In the bedroom, at the least, we are much simpler creatures. When aroused gratification is paramount."

The jeweled light shaded the look on her face as Elena obviously contemplated what he'd just said. "In short, you want us more than we want you? Having experienced this season with the fawning gentlemen in attendance, I would give credence to that theory, except the young ladies seem to be just as intent."

That was astute. Ran murmured, "But the goals are remarkably different. Men wish to have a willing bedmate and women often want a protector. They both take and give."

"A trade, then. How . . . mercenary. I'm trying to decide which gender is worse."

"It isn't always that way. Sometimes the pleasure is

the only consideration." He'd bedded married women, but never if they didn't have an understanding with their husbands. The tendencies toward loveless matches in the aristocracy rendered a set of rules that allowed wives to follow their own inclinations once a legitimate heir had been born.

Thoughtfully she considered him. "I suppose that must be true. For instance, you are not married, but rumored to have ... well ... many times."

His marital status being contemplated by a very eligible young debutante gave him pause. "As long as everyone understands the rules before the game begins, it is a fair trade rather than a bargain struck."

"I suppose what you are telling me is that women *do* enjoy sharing a man's bed if he is of their choice?"

And possess some finesse and the desire to please her. Ran chose not to go into the details of how a man needed to understand the complexities of female arousal. The conversation had gotten uncomfortably immediate already. If the table wasn't between them she might even notice his growing erection, and that, he would have to explain, was the graphic difference between men and women.

He could be a great deal more enlightening about *male* arousal but it just wasn't wise.

The temptation was, in fact, damned foolish, and he wasn't a fool. Or so he liked to think anyway, and his instincts with women were usually correct.

Careful.

"It always depends on the two people involved," he informed her neutrally, a part of his wayward mind speculating that she would be responsive in bed because she was so refreshingly without artifice.

He had no doubt that her dazzling beauty was why men had flocked to her, but the more perceptive ones would have sensed that underlying sensuality because she wasn't skilled enough—or jaded enough—to hide it and hadn't recognized yet the power that aura wielded.

But she would, because she was sufficiently intelligent to realize it eventually. He didn't intend to be that vulnerable, but there was a certain licentious temptation to be the man to teach her how to play the game.

A game he was very, very good at, by all accounts, and he enjoyed immensely, which was a bit of a problem.

Or *more* than a bit at the moment.

"I have just one more question." She regarded him directly, her robe delectably draping her slender figure.

He was weakening, damn all. The resolve not to touch her was born of self-preservation and outrage over their circumstances, but the cracks were widening and the temptation not helped by their current conversation.

"Yes?" His gaze involuntarily strayed to the slight part in the material of her robe where it covered her breasts.

And she noticed, for her cheeks took on a faint pink color. "How do you know?"

"Know what?"

"If it is a fair trade, as you put it."

Ran explained slowly, "Sexual pleasure is dependent on how receptive the lovers are to each other. I don't think attraction can be defined—it just happens. When you marry duty is involved, but that is entirely different."

An ambiguous answer at best but a truthful one. From her few remarks on her engagement she didn't appear to be emotionally involved with Lord Colbert, which was a pity.

But she was attracted to *him*. Ran knew the signs well enough, and though she wasn't skilled enough at flirtation to be deliberately provocative she managed it anyway.

You want her. She wants you. There is privacy and a bed. . . .

"It *sounds* less than satisfactory," Lady Elena muttered, resting a slender hand on the table. "But it still makes no sense to me. If so many women take lovers and some of them are married, they must find pleasure in it. As a husband, why not offer it to your wife instead?"

A palatable silence descended as he contemplated the answer. She didn't yet understand the nuances of choice and male privilege—and when the hell had this discussion turned from a titillating discourse on sexual practices to something else entirely? He didn't want to destroy any romantic notions she might have over her upcoming nuptials.

"I've never been a husband so I don't know."

"When you marry, I assume you will do your best to—"

He didn't normally interrupt a lady, but now the conversation had definitely taken the wrong turn. "There is more in this room that indicates that it was used for illicit trysts."

Lade Elena glanced around, diverted, thankfully, from the less than desirable topic of any marriage, much less his. "What? There is hardly anything in here at all. No armoire, just this small table and chairs, and the screen and hip bath."

"Exactly. It was never used as a bedroom in the sense someone lived in it. The sole purpose is the bed and a place to bathe afterward."

"Why would you bathe afterward?"

Her innocence should be off-putting, not intriguing. *Damn.* He'd never wanted a grass green girl in his bed. *Woman,* an errant voice whispered in his brain. *Every inch a woman.*

Damn all if he didn't want her enough to listen.

Hadn't she just asked him a question . . . ? He cleared his throat. His cock was rigid now, throbbing with the beat of his heart. "For it all to work with the greatest sensation for both male and female, our bodies ready in certain ways. It is also a bit messy after climax."

The blank look on her face was predictable. "Climax?"

It did him in, and his voice took on a telltale huskiness when he said, "Though I still vow not to cooperate with our mysterious captor, I would love to demonstrate."

Chapter 9

Was she being seduced?

Although she did not have any experience with it, Elena rather thought so. It was in the subtle change in his demeanor, in the intensity of the viscount's gaze. Their discussion, which she had certainly encouraged, hadn't helped a bit, and his last statement was definitely contradictory.

Surely either a woman was compromised or she wasn't.

"You know I have no idea what you mean." She said the words softly but an unexpected heat raced through her body and she regarded his dark beauty with as dispassionate an eye as possible. Unfortunately, an understanding of why so many women had graced his bed became clearer by the passing moment, and it wasn't just his masculine appeal.

Fair trade.

He was . . . not just polite but genuinely considerate. Other than their initial exchange in which he was suspicious—understandably so; she'd been suspicious too—of why they were locked in together, he'd always been thoughtful and solicitous, though she knew the strain of forced idleness was difficult for a man more used to action.

If he'd changed his mind on staying a gentleman that was no doubt her fault.

"Demonstrate in what way?" she asked when he didn't speak, but she instinctively knew the answer. It involved that scandalous bed and liberties she should definitely deny him.

And her heart had begun to flutter in a particularly unruly manner.

When he reached across the small table and took her hand, her pulse began to truly race. His fingers were long, strong, and entirely masculine, and the way he looked at her when they clasped hers made her feel as if she were suddenly transfixed by some magic spell.

Ran said softly, "You are right. No one will ever know what happens here between us. Not what we talk about, not what we do ... You can depart from here with your virginity intact and, meanwhile, we have nothing but time." His voice dropped in timbre. "And I think you are very beautiful."

His libertine status gave her pause, of course, but it was fleeting. The potent pull of attraction he'd described was there. As much as she would like to be known as the one female who did not find the Raven as darkly seductive as everyone else, she did.

From that first moment when she woke to find him sprawled next to her.

She shouldn't.

But, then again, her future involved a dutiful marriage to a man she knew only from stilted drawing room conversations, and the discussion she and Ran had just had didn't present arrangements like what awaited her in the best light.

"I . . . I don't know anything," she faltered.

Rising, he tugged her with him, coming around the small table and drawing her close because he still held her hand, and placed a persuasive palm at the small of her back, bringing her up against his hard body. "You don't have to know." He lowered his head and his breath brushed her lips. "I know enough for the both of us."

That she believed and would have tartly said so, but he kissed her.

There, as the rainbow shadows lengthened, Lord Andrews gave her the first kiss of her life, his mouth firm and warm. The contact was light and then deepened as their lips clung, parting briefly, and he pulled her even closer and kissed her again.

Deeply.

Shockingly.

Perfectly.

When a true rake kisses a virgin, she discovered, it was a moving experience if he puts some effort into it. Or so logic told her, but logic was hardly in charge as her hands tightened on his arms and she let her eyes drift shut. When he lightly traced her lower lip with the tip of his tongue and she stiffened, he murmured against her mouth, "It's just a kiss, my sweet. Relax. I won't ravish you, I give you my word. I just want to taste you. Surely others have tried, but I am honored to be the first to succeed. May I?"

Once or twice she'd been invited for a moonlit terrace stroll, but she wasn't that foolish, nor was her father that permissive. But it was still mortifying he could tell she'd never done this before.

Perhaps this wasn't the time to think of her austere fa-

ther, who would be furious to know of her permissive behavior, clad in only a thin robe, pressed up against the
notorious Andrews.

That thought actually steadied her, made her tilt her
head back and allow her lips to part. Not because she
knew her father would be aghast, but because she understood that no doubt it was just too late anyway. With
each minute that passed, whatever happened with the
rest of her life, this kidnapping had probably already
done the damage it was intended to do.

She was ruined. Her engagement became more tenu-
ous by the moment.

Therefore she should make the most of the evening.

The first brush of his tongue was startling, the intimacy of the moment acute. Her body reacted in a strange
way also, as if every muscle tightened a fraction; every
nerve became more sensitive all once. One hand drifted
to his shoulder and her eyes closed as he explored her
mouth, his tongue alternately lightly licking the corners
of her lips and then erotically pushing back inside until
she was breathless. When Ran lifted his head she realized her arms were fully around his neck.

It was rewarding that when he spoke it sounded nothing like his usual cool drawl but held a raw edge. "There's
a reason lovers usually find the most convenient horizon-
tal surface. It is much easier done lying down. Shall we?"

He might have asked for permission but he didn't
wait for her answer. He lifted her in his arms and walked
the few steps to the bed, depositing her on the linens,
lowering himself on top of her for another long, spine-
tingling kiss. Elena touched his hair for the first time and
found those ebony strands as soft and thick as she'd
imagined. The contrast to his hard musculature was

somehow arousing, and from the tightening in her breasts and the growing heat between her thighs, she hardly needed that.

He'd sworn he wouldn't ruin her in truth, but if he changed his mind he could probably accomplish that task with her eager participation as long as he continued to kiss her.

At that moment there was a glimmer of understanding for all those wayward ladies who succumbed to temptation. *If it feels like this,* she thought as his mouth traveled down the curve of her neck, tasting and teasing, *no wonder.* It was a practiced art, of that she had no doubt, and as he kissed the sensitive hollow at the base of her throat she shivered.

"I need to see what I've been dreaming about," he said, long fingers parting the folds of her robe, pushing it back from her shoulders, fingertips skimming the partially exposed upper curve of her right breast.

"You already essentially have," she responded, but to her chagrin her voice was unsteady. Her chemise hadn't covered nearly enough at that crucial moment when they'd met under the most unusual circumstances ever.

"I remember." His gaze locked with hers. "In the past three days I've remembered all too often. I'm surprised my resolve lasted this long with that image etched in my brain."

She remembered also what he looked like bare chested, flagrantly male, his chiseled features peaceful in repose as he slept.

Same bed but an entirely different situation at the moment. Instead of peaceful he was most definitely awake . . . all of him. Though he still wore his robe, through the thin silk she could feel the press of something long and hard against her thigh.

"This is even better." He shifted her effortlessly in his arms and pulled her robe completely off with facile expertise. "With you willing and wanting beneath me."

Am I really doing this, she thought in response as he lowered his dark head and closed his mouth over her peaked nipple. The sensation was sublime, as surreal as the tower room with the fading multicolored light and the white-hot desire spiking through her body. Was she wanting? Yes, she was, because there was only one first time—and who knew if it would be the last? Her world was in unpredictable disorder after a lifetime of stricture.

When he did something incredible with his tongue along the underside of her breast, without shame she made an inarticulate sound of enjoyment. It was as much the erotic sight of his hair against her white skin, the contrast stark, and the slight rough feel of his beard— he'd made it clear he wasn't at all happy about not being given the means to shave the past few days—against her sensitive flesh.

Skilled fingers stroked her taut breasts, cupping, lifting, testing. By the time he moved to the other nipple she was trembling.

"It's just the beginning," he said, rising to kiss her mouth again with brief, tantalizing pressure.

She had no idea what that might mean but she did know that this bond, this thrill of passion, was infinitely more than she expected, and he was correct. It had been building for the past few days and the pull of it was irresistible on a level she didn't want to acknowledge.

As if sensing that reaction, he nuzzled her throat.

"This isn't the time to think about it overly much. Deep analysis can be reserved for another moment."

She might have responded but his mouth found the juncture of her shoulder and neck, and Elena took in a deep breath, holding it as he traced the valley between her breasts with careful attention and then moved lower to her rib cage.

And lower.

Across the quivering plane of her stomach to the extremely sensitive flesh of her inner thigh, his hands gently pressing her legs open. Allowing it was not easy, but her resistance was overcome when he murmured, "I promise it will be worth it."

If she didn't believe that—believe in him—she wouldn't be in such a singularly vulnerable position. After all, she was naked and in bed with the infamous Lord Raven. Still, she was reluctant until her muscles relented to the pressure of his hands and she relaxed enough to let him spread her thighs.

And he took full advantage of her capitulation.

When he lowered his head she didn't realize his intention until the first paralyzing moment when his mouth brushed her already throbbing cleft. Then he used his tongue. Just a delicate advance at first, a touch, but in such a shocking place she could swear the breath left her chest. Pleasure moved, spread, engulfed, as he pressed closer and began to truly taste and nibble and . . .

There are no words, she thought moments later, captivated in rapture and her fists clenched in the sheets of the bed. Involuntarily Elena opened her thighs wider as he scandalously kissed her between her legs.

The pinnacle of pleasure built, spread, carried her away until she tumbled over the edge into an unknown world and called out his name even as she shuddered and clutched his shoulders and finally went limp.

He lifted his head and his smile was a faint gleam of white teeth. "That, my lady, is your first lesson in sexual pleasure."

It was gratifying to see he could still trust his instincts.

She'd climaxed with the abandon he'd anticipated and her dazed expression reflected what had just happened. Enlightened by their conversation and perhaps a bit more prepared for when she truly embraced her sensual side and gave herself completely to a lover, she'd done it with a captivating lack of restraint..

Beautifully. Everything I expected. . . . But she isn't without a price. . . .

It was something he needed to keep in mind. As delectable as she was, slender thighs slightly parted, long lashes in fans on her cheekbones as he noted the flush on her skin and the soft lusciousness of her lower lip, he reminded himself that neither of them were going to be led to the ultimate mistake. It would be entirely different if he'd met her, been intrigued enough to start pursuit— but it *wouldn't* have happened, as he wasn't interested in that type of permanence—and then chosen this path.

Framed in the spill of her long pale hair, Elena was a picture of temptation, her body shadowed enticingly in the fading light, the rapid pattern of her respiration reminding him this was all new to her.

And therefore should be entirely memorable. His straining erection aside, his purpose was to avoid taking her physical innocence while yet still branding her very soul as the man who first initiated her into carnal pleasure.

Colbert be damned. She's not in love with him; she isn't even enthusiastic about marrying the man. . . .

Analyzing why that was important was not an exercise he wanted to undertake, so instead he concentrated on the satin of her skin under his questing fingertips, the fragrance from her hair, the shimmer in her eyes as she watched him touch her. . . .

The unveiled glory of her body did not disappoint. Slim but curvaceous, the pale mounds of her breasts tipped with pink nipples, the neat triangle at the apex of her legs a darker color than her pale tresses, Elena had responded in small, telling ways to each touch, every caress, and the language was clear.

The sensuality he'd perceived was not an illusion and he wanted this to be a moment of her life she would always remember.

One—he had an uncomfortable moment of reflection—*perhaps we will both remember.*

"That was . . ." She stopped, the breathiness of her voice even more arousing, and it was hardly what he needed.

Ran rolled to his back, the sash of his robe loosened enough to give him some relief from the heat infusing his body, the thin material also not disguising his rampant erection. Contrary to popular opinion he didn't go from bed to bed every night, but the past three days of abstinence hadn't been all that easy with his desirable companion so close by, and he was on the edge.

The very edge.

It didn't help when she rose on her elbows, staring at the outline of his erect cock where it lifted the silk draping his thighs, her lovely face flushed. He didn't expect her to know what to do, and it was evident she didn't have the slightest idea either, which was both refreshing and frustrating as hell.

"The lesson can stop here or we can go on."

"Fair trade?" Her laugh was weak and yet somehow provocative.

"Precisely."

Deliberately he opened his robe and shrugged it off, not exactly surprised at the way her eyes widened at her first sight of a fully aroused adult male. The Greek statues and the sketches of the male anatomy she may have seen did not usually include an erection and he was definitely at full mast. "I can be selfless but mutual satisfaction is more the usual way it works."

Tense, supine, he watched her, the luscious sway of her breasts enticing—and he had no need of further enticement—as she rose to her knees.

"So you said, but what do you mean?"

What the devil *did* he mean? His smile was crooked. "I can take care of it myself or you can help me."

He would have staked his life she was too innocent to have an inkling of what he meant, but to his surprise she reached out, her hand hovering over his stiff cock. "You are going to have to explain to me what—"

"Just touch me." His voice was raspy, his eyes half-closed. "Elena, touch me. It isn't complicated. Touch me and we'll be quite even in moments, I assure you."

Luckily she was perceptive enough to not need a lot of instructions in the attempt. Slender fingers closed over his erection and instinctively slid upward in a tentative glide, and his breath hitched at the gratifying sensation. He kept as still as possible as she explored the rigid length of his hard penis, one finger delicately wiping a drop from the seeping tip, his body quivering at the caress.

It wouldn't take much and he would explode, especially with the taste of her arousal still on his lips. The unskilled glide of her hand had much more effect than it might have under other circumstances; the room was immersed in colored light, quiet except for the rasp of his breathing, and he was so tense he groaned at the next brush of her circling hand. Consciously he let himself travel that crucial distance at her next tentative squeeze.

The hot rush of his ejaculation spilled across his abdomen and chest and her hand involuntarily tightened in startled response, exacerbating the reaction. It wasn't nearly as good as if he'd been buried deep inside her, but in the retrospective haze of much-needed sexual release, it was certainly better than the strain of the past three days. It was inaccurate to say he'd been perpetually hard, but it had happened often enough and he'd wondered more than once if the forbidden-fruit aspect of the situation hadn't contributed to his interest. If so, their captor was exceedingly shrewd and that wasn't a promising sign for a timely release from their little tower prison.

But an extended stay had a sudden rosy glow it had previously lacked.

At least he'd managed to adhere to his purpose so far. Barely. She might not be quite so innocent, but she was still a virgin.

Her fingers loosened when he caught her wrist and he tumbled her on top him in a gentle but insistent pull, regardless of the discharge of his semen slick between them. "Do you understand now why we might need to bathe?" he asked her, their mouths inches apart, his gaze heavy-lidded.

"Yes," she responded and artlessly kissed him, just a touch of her lips—a maiden's kiss. When her long hair brushed his shoulders he fought to not pull her closer and begin again what they'd just almost—*almost*—finished.

God, he wanted to slide between her thighs and bury himself deep, showing her the true measure of what pleasure could be.

He said more curtly than he intended, "You are too damned tempting."

"Am I?"

That vixen's smile didn't bode well for his future good behavior. He told her so in soft whispers, drawing her closer, noting that his erection was already swelling again as a result of her soft body sprawled on top of his.

"I didn't know you ever behaved well, my lord."

Not with her naked in his arms, not in this damned situation. "Remember my brief stint of possessing a modicum of decorum?"

She laughed.

And he found the sound to be infinitely arousing.

Hell.

Chapter 10

"You haven't seen him in how long?"

"Too long." The winsome Mrs. Grant smiled at him with a hint of mischief, pursing full lips. "I rather miss his bonny looks . . . and other parts of him as well."

The innuendo made Ben stifle a laugh, and he thought he understood how Randolph Raine might be attracted to the alluring widow, though she had to be considerably older than he; in her midthirties, at a guess. Brunette and voluptuous, she was a bit overblown for his tastes but her good nature was appealing. Coming out of the shop, her satin skirts swishing gently as her hips moved, she had the air more of a mistress than a respectable matron, and she fit what he knew of the preferences of the missing viscount. Andrews usually kept his affairs light and detached and it was borne about by the fact he chose women who all were unfettered and not financially dependent on their lovers. Which showed a certain sophisticated approach to a libertine lifestyle. Obviously Lord Andrews was amiable to casual affairs but didn't need to pay for the favors of a bed partner. Women put themselves deliberately in his path.

Fair enough.

Then why did he abscond with Alicia's lovely young cousin? It didn't fit at all what Ben knew of him.

"Did Lord Andrews mention why he wished to terminate your affair?" Ben fell into step next to Mrs. Grant, having found her at her favorite milliner, thanks to her gregarious maid and a small monetary incentive. He politely took her parcel, a footman trailing dutifully behind them.

"Are you asking if he left me for Whitbridge's daughter?" Beth Grant arched her brows but her voice was amused.

"I've said nothing about Lady Elena."

"Then you are the only one, my lord. Everyone is atwitter about the earl's daughter's possible elopement with Lord Andrews."

"Is that what you think happened?"

She seemed to consider it as they walked along, but after a moment she shook her head. "I quite doubt it. He's infamously opposed to marriage and nothing he does is secretive. I do not see how they could meet enough times to form an attachment and no one know it. In my opinion it is an unlikely course of events."

His thoughts exactly. However, it had seemed prudent, as he could find out nothing about Elena's disappearance, to investigate the viscount's mutual absence. "Did he ever mention to you anyone with whom he had a quarrel?"

"Believe it or not, for someone whose love affairs garner such attention, he isn't inclined to discuss his private life. Even when we went our separate ways, he didn't really explain why. I think he became bored with me, which was not a surprise. I wasn't offended. We had a delightful time while it lasted."

They'd reached her carriage and the footman hurried

forward to open the door of the vehicle and lower the step. Her diffident attitude surprised him, but Ben was learning he did not know women as well as he thought he did. Drily he said, "Apparently Lord Andrews made quite an impression for you to forgive him so easily."

Mrs. Grant gazed at him with what appeared to be typical directness. "I think you are looking at it the wrong way, Lord Heathton. It is more that he never promised me anything nor did he want that from me. Our interlude was just a dalliance and we both knew it. Had he been serious I would not have been interested, and that is the only reason *he* was interested in *me*. I like being a widow but did not enjoy all that much being a wife."

As he handed her into the vehicle he couldn't help but reflect on the strangeness of the puzzle yet again.

Part of his expertise was drawing conclusions from whatever evidence could be gathered at hand. *If* there was evidence, which in this case was not proving forthcoming. The viscount and Alicia's cousin had seemingly vanished in a wisp of proverbial smoke.

No witnesses.

No request for ransom.

And even more telling, no word even from the extremely reliable community of domestic servants, except the whispers over the disappearances. He'd had Altamont use his resources to ask around the stable lads; there was really very little gossip and none about a possible liaison.

Even Mrs. Grant had hardly proved to be productive. Obviously there was no animosity there between his lordship and his recent paramour. Quite the opposite.

Not an entirely wasted effort, he thought morosely. To an extent the spurned widow had proved quite helpful. Not because she knew anything about the viscount's dis-

appearance but because his former mistress knew quite
a lot about his normal habits. Alicia seemed to be correct
in her conviction that Elena had not run off with him.

Where are you?

Unfortunately, with all the evidence to the contrary,
Ben *still* somehow felt they were together, which might
not particularly make sense, but his instincts rarely failed
him.

Case in point: the first time he'd looked across a
crowded ballroom, bored, restive, and uncomfortable
with the role of earl he'd managed to avoid during the
war, and seen Alicia among the dancers. He'd been
struck by her grace, the glorious contrast of her shining
dark hair and porcelain skin, but most of all it had been
her laugh. Her partner in that fateful waltz had been another man who had said something amusing, and she'd
spontaneously responded with mirth. Ben had to admit
an instant attraction.

She was everything he wasn't. Candid, warm, trusting . . . foolishly romantic.

I definitely *am not romantic,* he thought sardonically
as he walked purposefully up Bond Street. Which made
her ridiculous ultimatum rather difficult, but if he managed to retrieve her cousin maybe she would count that
in his favor, so he wished he were making more progress.

At least after talking to Mrs. Grant he finally had an
idea of how to go about it.

Day Four

*I woke alone, or as much alone as one can be
when trapped in a locked tower room with another
person.*

I am hesitant to put pen to paper and chronicle personal feelings when I am uncertain what will happen to this bit of writing, but at this point I do not have much to lose.

Besides, ironically, my actual virtue.

If Ran decides to read this I can't stop him, but I do not think he is that kind of man. Society hasn't precisely misjudged him, or so I am starting to believe, as much as he is more complicated than he appears on the surface. He's a rake, yes, if that word means "a man who seeks out pleasurable interludes without possible permanence." But if he were as rakish as rumor had it, he would not be so careful not to compromise me in truth.

I am finding the contradiction to be difficult to decipher.

Last eve was an enlightening voyage. A journey, if you will, and I suspect one that no woman ever forgets. I know I will not, nor would I wish to, though I already understand it was not the full measure of the experience.

My father has always told me I have an inquiring mind.

I cannot help but wonder what I missed.

Elena took a bite of bread—some of the best she'd ever eaten, both soft and buttery—and regarded her almost lover with appraisal. Oddly enough she'd been touched by a new shyness.

Beyond a shadow of a doubt, everything had changed.

Not just between them but in her perception of life. It was deeper than she'd imagined, richer, more colorful, more magical, and what she had once regarded as the simple equation of man and woman now took on a new complexity.

All thanks to the man who sat across from her, sharing a meal as they had for the past four days, that errant lock of dark hair hanging over his brow, his robe carelessly open to his waist. He was so easy in his demeanor, she marveled at it after what had happened between them, but she was also sure he had practiced nonchalance like this a great deal. When she'd woken he'd already risen, and by the time she'd taken care of the essential needs—she was getting used to the intimacy of doing that with someone else in the room—he was standing below the stained-glass window, studying it with his head tilted back.

Without turning he had said, "Whoever created this, I've seen their work before. The pattern is familiar and the brilliance of the blue pieces of glass unusual, though I confess I am hardly an expert on the subject."

Then he had turned and smiled.

And for an instant she stopped breathing.

Why she wasn't sure. He'd spoken in an ordinary voice—as if he hadn't kissed her the night before, held her naked in his arms, as if he hadn't brought her shocking, wicked pleasure, as if she hadn't touched him intimately also and later slept in the same bed—but yet her heart seemed to freeze in her chest. She'd woken once to find she was curled up next to him, warm, comfortable, his scent masculine and clean, the circle of his arm a natural fit around her waist.

Had their breakfast not arrived in the usual manner she wasn't at all sure what she might have said, but the boy with the tray and his elderly helper had come in and the smile she found so mesmerizing went tight-lipped as his gaze shifted to the door. There was immediate tension in his broad shoulders and Elena wondered how long it would be before he decided that the rough-looking man with the pistol was not that formidable a barrier after all. Both of them had given up attempting to talk to the two servants. She suspected the old man was stone deaf, or, if not, he gave a good imitation of it, and the boy always just shook his head and darted out the door as fast as possible. Any attempt there was fruitless.

"I was planning on leaving London for the country today." Ran had finished eating before her, which was the usual course of events, his restless energy no doubt accounting for his lean, muscular build. "My family is expecting me. Blast it. I hate the thought that my aunt and Lucy will be worried over my absence."

As she felt the same way about her parents, Elena nodded.

"She never speaks of it but I know Luce misses my father and mother terribly."

Elena suspected his younger sister wasn't the only one. There was nothing in his tone to indicate it, but it was there even in the diffident way he picked up his cup and took a sip and in the slightly haunted expression on his face.

Maybe she shouldn't ask, but perhaps after the night before she could dare the intimacy. "What happened?"

To her surprise he answered readily. "It began with a stomach ailment. Nothing serious, or so the doctors told my father. But my mother grew noticeably thinner and eventually was unable to eat at all. They tried various cures, everything from potions to purging, but nothing helped and in a few months she was gone. He died, if you ask me, of a broken heart. They tried to tell me it was the same illness, but I honestly believe it was grief. He wasted away and perished as well within half a year."

"I'm so sorry." She was, and the hint of rawness she caught in his voice moved her. This was not London's most careless rake but a wounded son. If everyone could see his averted profile and anguished features the perception of him might be quite different.

"They had an unusual love affair."

Elena inelegantly propped her elbows on the table and lifted her brows. "How so?"

He glanced down at his cup momentarily, just a flicker of his gaze before it lifted, but telling. "They met by accident. My mother worked in her father's bakery."

So Viscount Andrews had married a baker's daughter? That was certainly interesting and Elena sensed it wasn't a topic he normally introduced. "He must have truly been smitten." As the daughter of an earl she understood the rigidity of her class.

"Indeed."

"What was he doing in a bakery?" Not an unreasonable question, as most aristocrats had servants to do just about any task, especially one as menial as shopping for bread.

Ran's grin was crooked. "I suppose my sire and I are not that unalike. He had been out carousing and needed something to counteract the effects of several bottles of blue ruin. As the story goes, he was walking down the street, smelled the fresh bread, and stumbled in to find himself facing the most beautiful woman he'd ever seen."

"How romantic."

"Why did I think a female would take that view?"

With due logic she pointed out, "Your father apparently did."

"I must concede that, I suppose, though may I point out that lust is also a powerful incentive to a healthy adult male?"

"You were the one who used the wording *love affair*."

"Hmm. I can't deny that, can I?"

The notorious Raven would know all about lust, though Elena refrained from saying so. "And they fell in love then and there over a loaf of bread?"

"I suppose it could be put that way." Ran quirked a brow. "All I know is my father endured a great deal of familial derision for marrying so far beneath him, but, in the end, he was the heir, he got his way, and they were always happy in my memory."

"They must have been if he mourned her so deeply." Elena set aside her half-eaten piece of toast. "Is that why you are so opposed to marriage?"

The mere mention of the word stiffened his spine, but after a moment he relented. "I don't know. I wasn't in England to see my father suffer the decline after my mother's death. I was in Spain, against his wishes."

No wonder he felt such a responsibility to his younger sister. It was true the heir was not supposed to risk his life and limb, even for the cause against Bonaparte. "Why did you go, then?"

"I'm still not sure." He didn't dissemble but neither did he excuse. "Part bravado, I would guess. The English male can be a stubborn creature. When I first mentioned it my father was so against the idea, I rebelled." Quietly he added, "I wish I hadn't in retrospect, but we cannot relive our lives. It never occurred to me that they were more mortal than I was. After all, I was the one going to war. The irony doesn't escape me."

He was correct. Certainly she could never go back to the woman she'd been before last evening. "Surely reviling yourself is a futile effort. Every experience shapes us."

She should have known he would not let that pass. His tone dropped to a suggestive timbre as he gazed at her, the transformation effortless. "Are we being specific?"

"Perhaps." As if she could ever forget.

"Tell me how."

There was no way she could explain her feelings at the moment over what had happened, so instead of complying she countered. "Tell me about Spain."

He shrugged but his face went shuttered. "I survived. Many others didn't. That is enough said about it, really. War is not a glamorous topic, nor should it be. We laud our heroes, but what it takes to make them such is not pleasant."

It was interesting he did not seem to include himself in the category, but she had already come to the conclusion that whatever Viscount Andrews might be, whether wealthy lord, notoriously skilled lover, or responsible guardian, he wasn't vain. Yes, he had a certain air of self-confidence but it wasn't arrogance. He was undeniably handsome and certainly intelligent enough to realize women thought so, but there was nothing of the peacock about him and he seemed to have no affectations.

"I suppose that is true."

"Take my word." He did something no male *ever* did and poured her more coffee, going so far as to add two lumps of sugar as she liked it, and then handed her a spoon. "Now, then. What would you say if I told you I have a plan to help us escape?"

Elena picked up her cup, inhaled the delicious fragrance of the dark beverage, and said coolly, "I would say that I also have a plan. Feel free to go first, my lord."

Chapter 11

His first real clue to her cousin's disappearance came quite by accident and courtesy of his beautiful wife.

It was humbling, really.

Ben took a moment and carefully guided his gelding around a small puddle from the previous night's rain. "Your grandmother's footman saw what?"

"A strange man loitering by Elena's carriage. The man was chatting with the driver before she came out of the house, and he rushed over and opened the door and lowered the step before the driver could do it and then said something to her. She nodded, so the young footman thought nothing of it."

An eyewitness. At last. The investigation in the disappearance of Andrews was going nowhere at all. Not that Ben had a great deal of confidence that this would solve the case, but at least he could get a description and then maybe query the driver.

"Interesting," he murmured, when in truth he had just stopped himself short of demanding to know why Alicia hadn't imparted this information earlier. His wife—who was delightfully fetching in a dark green riding habit that emphasized the supple slenderness of her body and the

darkness of her lustrous hair—had no idea he had an
outside interest in Elena's sudden inexplicable absence
in the force of the debt he owed Wellington.

"Yes . . . well, I rather wondered about something."
She glanced at him in a quicksilver movement of her
eyes.

The Heatherington affair had been crowded, loud,
and stuffy, and he'd barely seen her despite the sacrifice
of his evening, so he was hoping an afternoon ride might
serve as a substitute if he begged off accompanying her
to the opera. "Such as?"

"Do you think you will find her?"

"Who?"

"Oh, please. We both know my uncle wants you to
find Elena, and so do I. As it happens, I think I can help,
darling, but you have to vow to not be deliberately obtuse in return."

Why had he known that she was going to say exactly
that? Which was not a problem—it actually made it all
easier because now he didn't have to conceal from his
wife that he was looking into her cousin's disappearance.
But the endearment threw him off balance.

Darling?

"Can I point out," he said after a moment, summon-
ing a deliberate smile as they rode side by side, the day
cool enough so the park was not that busy. "I am very
good at being obtuse though I must admit it usually isn't
deliberate at all. Tell me, why do think for a moment you
can help?"

She frowned delicately. "Because you are beyond a
doubt the most intelligent man I know, but women have
different insights. I suspect my uncle, who is not particularly intuitive when it comes to his daughter or he

wouldn't have forced her into an engagement to Lord Colbert, came to see you the other day not as friend but to ask you for assistance. I agree with him that you can find out what happened if anyone can. Surely my help would be beneficial."

Her uncle might not be intuitive but *she* certainly was. Ben was finding his wife had an interesting deductive ability of her own. There had been some female operatives under his command in the war, but the thought of her exposed to such danger made his blood run cold, so he couldn't honestly say he wished she'd been there. But he *could* say he wished he'd had such a promising agent at his disposal. "So, what did the driver tell you when you asked him about the man who helped her into the carriage? And the footman, does he have a description?"

"What makes you think . . ." She started to deny she'd asked such in-depth questions and then sighed, the afternoon sun giving golden highlights to her skin. "Well, I just said you are the most intelligent man I know, so I suppose I can't be surprised you guessed I've been investigating this situation a little. I mean, she *is* my cousin, after all. I love Elena."

"She is family," he acknowledged, his horse dancing sideways enough that his booted foot brushed her skirts. "So, then. Tell me what you learned."

Later he would thank her for the compliment which had been unexpected, but at the moment he didn't have the words. . . . Maybe finding Lady Elena would be his form of gratitude.

His wife thought him the most intelligent man she knew. It wasn't as if he'd ever imagined she'd married him only for his money and title, but it *was* done all the time and he could hardly ignore his recent banishment from her bed.

Still, the sentiment was flattering, and he would endeavor to live up to the expectations of her request.

Alicia cocked her head to the side, her expression thoughtful, the feather on her fashionable hat tickled by the wind. "He didn't recall much. I've found that human beings in general are not that observant, which surprises me. The accent wasn't familiar enough for him to recognize but he did wonder enough to ask the footman if he knew the man. The answer was no."

"But she was abducted from the theater."

"It seems so." Alicia pursed her mouth. "My uncle is being deliberately very vague, though, about the incident."

"He wishes, naturally, to keep it quiet."

"But his child is gone and there seems to be no explanation."

Damnation, the luscious curve of her lower lip was distracting, and he'd just as much as admitted he was looking into the matter. On the other hand, the issue of male-to-male camaraderie aside, to whom did he owe more allegiance—his wife or the often stuffy Lord Whitbridge? "I have some connections still that he thought might be useful in gaining information. And I think he is more affected than you know."

"I certainly hope so." Alicia's voice was firm. "Now, this helpful stranger may mean nothing but surely it warrants further investigation. Perhaps he was trying to make Elena think he works for my uncle and was therefore someone she was supposed to trust."

It was a valid supposition. "Maybe the footman can describe him. I will look into it."

"And don't forget there are other avenues."

"Such as?"

She slanted him a look under the veil of her lashes. "Are you asking me to help?"

That certainly hadn't occurred to him. Cautiously he asked, "How so?"

"Women will tell other women things they wouldn't dream of revealing to a man. I can talk to Elena's friends. After all, we share many of them."

As this was already the fifth day since the disappearance, perhaps he should accept the offer. Then again, he felt a certain trepidation in including his wife when it was possible someone unscrupulous was involved in Lady Elena's disappearance. With each passing day Lord Andrews became more and more the likely culprit in her continued absence, but discreet inquiries had proven the general consensus was that it would have been out of character for him.

Had, for instance, Andrews stumbled on Elena's abduction, been injured or worse trying to help her, and his body dumped in the Thames or disposed of some other way?

White slavery was a profitable business and the young woman in question exceptionally beautiful. How much would a sultan or a foreign brothel owner pay for a lovely blond English virgin? Quite a lot, at a guess. Ben had sent a reliable man to the docks to inquire if any young woman answering Elena's description had been seen boarding a ship within the time period of her absence but it had turned up nothing. Of course, it was possible she'd been spirited on board in the dead of night.

That was hardly a theory he wanted to pose to his wife. He had reservations over involving her at all. On the other side of the coin, she was gazing at him with endearing entreaty, as if a refusal might hurt her feelings. "I think talking to her friends in a very roundabout way to make sure you protect your cousin's reputation as much as possible would be invaluable."

"You needn't worry. I can be subtle." Her mouth curved into a smile. "And tonight is naturally the perfect time as we will be at the opera."

"What opera?"

She sent him a reproving look.

He stifled an inward groan. It seemed he was neatly trapped.

But he suddenly didn't want to leave his adventurous wife to her own devices either.

Alicia took the card, recognized the name embossed on the expensive paper, and frowned. "You say she wishes to see my husband?"

"Quite frankly, my lady, she *insists* on an audience with the earl. She is waiting in the blue drawing room." Yeats added with no inflection, "If I might suggest it, perhaps I could have tea prepared while you change your attire."

She stifled a small inner grimace. The butler was a stately man with white hair and an almost regal bearing, and though he never swerved from proper deference to her role as countess it was clear now and again that he felt her youth meant she needed some gentle guidance. Actually he was correct, for running the households of several estates and the London residence of the Earl of Heathton was a bit daunting at times.

Blast it all.

He'd been correct just *now*, for she was intensely curious to know why one of Lord Andrews's family members was calling and might have gone to greet the visitor immediately, ignoring that she was still wearing her riding habit. "An excellent suggestion," she murmured, moving toward the stairs. "I will be down directly."

A short time later, dressed in a proper day gown of pale green georgette, her hair tidied into a simple chignon, Alicia entered the drawing room to find a dark-haired woman sitting very upright on one of the silk-covered striped chairs. The visitor was hardly in the first bloom of youth but still attractive, with fine bones and a shapely figure, and her gown was modest and not particularly fashionable. That noted, the family resemblance was strong enough that even if she hadn't seen the last name on the card, Alicia would have known the woman was related to the rakishly handsome viscount.

"Good afternoon." She gave a small nod. "I am Lady Heathton. I'm afraid my husband is not here, as he had some sort of appointment. We were out for an afternoon ride and he saw me home and then left at once. I wish I could predict when he was going to return but I do not know precisely. Perhaps we can converse instead."

To say she was wildly curious as to why the woman wanted to see Ben was an understatement. She'd changed so swiftly she hadn't even bothered to ring for her maid and practically dashed down the stairs.

"I am Janet Raine." The woman had risen but sank back down when Alicia settled on a settee near her chair. "Lord Andrews is my nephew."

"And Elena Morrow is my cousin. The disappearances, of course. Is that why you are here?"

"Not precisely, though I am starting to wonder if what I have to show your husband might be related to her absence also. When he came to see me in Essex at our country estate a few days ago I knew nothing."

Ben went to Essex to visit the viscount's aunt?

No wonder he'd been gone all day earlier in the week and arrived home obviously tired and travel worn. Really, the man was too infuriatingly closemouthed. It took some effort to not react. "And what do you know now that brings you here?"

When Miss Raine hesitated Alicia said neutrally, "I have a vested interest also in finding my cousin. She is very close to me. I promise whatever you tell me will go straight to my husband and not repeated elsewhere. You have my word."

Miss Raine took a moment to consider and then she nodded and removed a bit of paper that had been tucked into her bodice. Alicia had always found that an interesting—and obvious—place for women to choose to hide correspondence. "This came this morning. Before this I was at first mildly concerned at my nephew's absence and then more alarmed, but now I am convinced something dire has happened."

Taking the slip, Alicia unfolded it.

Dear Madam:

I believe I have in my possession a watch that is a family heirloom. It has an inscription from the king to the previous Viscount Andrews in which he addresses him most familiarly as Drew, and the date is 1798. If you would like to retrieve this item please send a messenger with a hundred pounds to the address below.

It was signed Herman Crepshaw, and the address was in a part of London where the aristocratic neighborhoods gave way to a less exalted style of living. Not quite a slum but close.

Alicia read it a second time and knew that Ben would be most interested in this unexpected coup. She folded the note back carefully as a maid trundled in the tea trolley, the smell of sweet cakes and lemon tarts delicious, and waited patiently. Alicia had poured two steaming cups of tea when she murmured, "Tell me why this means something dire has happened. Couldn't your nephew have lost the watch?"

"No." Janet Raine spoke with complete conviction. "Ran treasured that watch as a keepsake of his father's life and took it with him every single day. Not to mention that whatever you may have heard about his private life, he is a conscientious guardian to his sister and intensely loyal to his family. My unease with his absence is confirmed by this note. Somehow this odious man asking for money obtained it but it wasn't through negligence on Ran's part, I assure you. I questioned my nephew's valet, who swears it was with him when he left that afternoon five days ago."

Alicia took a sip of hot tea and then said gravely, "You fear foul play."

"Oh yes." The answering smile was thin. "I assure you, my nephew is athletically inclined, quite able to defend himself, and he would not part with his father's precious possession lightly. He is sentimental under that cavalier exterior. Neither would he just leave without word. Something is wrong."

"Did he know my cousin?"

"Not that I'm aware of." Miss Raine took a lump of sugar but no milk and stirred the beverage in her cup, definitively shaking her head. "Naturally, he didn't discuss his private life with me often, but I do believe if he were seriously interested in marrying I would have known. He is very protective of his younger sister, Lucy, and wouldn't have kept a life-changing decision from her either."

It sounded like the viscount was a bit different from what Alicia had imagined. "You seem fond of him," she observed.

"Oh, I am. He didn't want the title so early in his life, but has taken the mantle on with a level of responsibility I did not expect." Janet looked pensive over the rim of her cup. "Such a wild young man in so many ways when he was at university . . . I thought his father was going to have an apoplexy over some of his escapades, but they really were essentially harmless. And I can say Randolph has assumed the role of viscount with ease, whether he wished it or not. The scandalous gossip is somewhat his fault, I do not deny it, but I do not believe for a moment he absconded with your cousin to avoid her father's disapproval. There is no elopement. We need to look past that."

"It *has* been done before." Alicia tried to keep her own inclinations toward fairy-tale romances at bay. An impetuous marriage was a universal concept and she was hoping that maybe that was exactly what had happened to Elena.

"He . . . *wouldn't*. I don't know how to put it any other way but to express my conviction that he is not that sort of man. When he finally marries—and she will have to be exceptional—he will deal with it in an honorable fashion."

Unfortunately, Alicia believed that heartfelt declaration. It made the situation all that more bewildering. "My cousin would never leave and not tell anyone either. She isn't that inconsiderate."

"Then we agree they aren't together."

"Maybe not." Alicia had to admit as unlikely as it was, maybe the disappearances were not related. "However, in the meantime, I think it best if we go visit Mr. Crepshaw and retrieve the watch."

"Before Lord Heathton arrives?" Miss Raine looked startled.

Alicia took a lemon tart for fortitude, since there was no use in embarking on an adventure half-starved. "Who knows when he will be back? He tells me next to nothing about his schedule, and for all we know the chance to interview this Crepshaw will slip through our fingers if we wait. I don't think we should let this opportunity pass us by."

Chapter 12

The plan had promise, and he couldn't take any credit for it. Ran, his pose negligent in his chair, ankles crossed, whiskey glass in his hand, casually watched the boy come collect their trays. An unthreatening gentleman if ever there was one ...

The barefoot English beauty in the room was the real danger.

He should know.

She was certainly a menace to his peace of mind.

"Dinner was quite lovely." Her smile was dazzling enough that despite her age and status as a marriageable young lady even the most seasoned rake might take a second look.

And, Ran thought, I *qualify for that label.* She certainly had him mesmerized.

"Is it possible you could give this to the cook?" With her loose golden hair and delectable form draped only in a thin robe, she was the epitome of seductive innocence, and Ran was not positive that a few more days in captivity together would not overcome the weak restraint he had leaned on in keeping her—only in physical reality—innocent. She tucked a piece of vellum under a plate on the tray. "I just wish to compliment the food and ask that the chocolate torte of the other evening be included again on our menu if possible."

The insidious approach is so much more female, he decided as he sat there and saw the boy's flush and the dip of his head.

She had proposed that since the food they were being served was certainly sophisticated—for instance, the sauce that had come with the beefsteak the night before had been laced with peppercorns and cream and a drizzle of brandy—the chef could probably read. As it was doubtful any of the other staff had that particular skill, maybe, she postulated, they could communicate to the ruler of the kitchen, who might not realize they were being held captive. It could be the kitchen staff did know and was paid enough to not care if they were prisoners, but worth a chance. Elena had suggested that surely it was difficult to find an entire retinue of servants who approved of locking two people up against their will, no matter how well they were treated.

So she'd written the note in French, the choice of language based entirely on the delicate whitefish aspic they'd been served the day before. The only contribution Ran had made was that he mentioned the dish was one he'd had in Paris, and instantly there had been thoughtful speculation in her eyes.

Those lovely eyes that he'd looked into before he'd rashly kissed her and then pleasured her, and then spent a restless night doing his best to not take it to the ultimate culmination.

He needed to stop thinking about it.

His plan had been much more straightforward but it hadn't succeeded, and so, at this point, he was willing to concede that perhaps this was their only recourse, no matter how chafing it was to continue to be confined. He'd decided to do his best to access one of the two stained-glass windows by making a tower of the table and chairs, which proved precarious despite Elena's assistance on holding it steady, not to mention he had no means of breaking the glass, and that once he did gain the somewhat formidable height, the brief glimpse he got through one of the lighter-faceted pieces showed a dizzying vista of trees a daunting distance below. In short, if he did manage to destroy the window and crawl out, he doubted he would do anything but fall to his death trying to descend from the tower.

Not exactly a resounding success.

Their options were extremely limited as far as he could tell, so he was more than willing to hope Elena's plea for help might prove fruitful.

In the meantime it was beginning to get dark, which gave them little recourse but to converse, as the single lamp usually burned out early and wasn't replenished until the next day. Which left them in the dark together and that was a dangerous combination indeed.

He should never have touched her.

But you did. What is done is done.

Bloody hell.

"Do you think whoever owns this estate is down there, maybe even now entertaining guests?" As the bar dropped into place behind the departing servants, Elena turned in a whirl of silk and golden hair. "The walls are so thick we hear nothing. I have done my best to make a mental list of what houses are not that far from London that might have turrets, but I am afraid I'm not widely traveled enough to come up with more than two or three, and I doubt we are in Windsor Castle."

"I've done the same." He tried to ignore the entrancing shadow between her breasts, recalling the warm, supple weight of them in his hands with a clarity that had an unfortunate effect on his libido, making his cock swell. It wasn't that he didn't acknowledge the simple equation of bed, exquisitely attractive woman, and darkness; it was just that the danger of it all had grown, not lessened, after their mutually satisfying encounter the night before. They'd been cautious around each other all day.

He found her virginal embarrassment arousing, and if asked to make odds on *that* at White's not even a week ago, he would have lost his money when he emphatically took the position that he thought innocent misses were dull and to be avoided at all cost.

Unfortunately, she was more intriguingly distracting than ever now and that was entirely his fault.

Or *her* fault. He wasn't sure which and that was disconcerting. Control of his life was paramount because he'd discovered in a painful way long before this abduction that when that slipped all could be lost.

"Do you think you might know where we are?" Elena sat down opposite now that the table was cleared, her gaze inquiring.

"It can't be too far, given how long it was between when I was accosted outside my club and the time I woke up here. Unless I lost a day and a half, and that seems unlikely. We were both drugged but recovered fairly quickly." He'd been pondering it—while trying to not think about her proximity—all day. "I don't think we were taken a great distance. I do know"—his voice hardened—"that I had to be given the intoxicant at my club. It is the only possibility. That's the last I remember of the evening, and I swear to you once again I do not drink too much on a regular basis."

The glass of whiskey in his hand might not be the best support of that declaration, but in his defense he was doing his best to forget she was in the room but her physical presence was impossible to ignore. Luscious in peach silk, her hair was in a cloud of golden disarray that tumbled enticingly down her back. Not to mention the room was darkening and the bed beckoned.

Arousal surged and he negligently adjusted his robe to hide it, trying to define his options.

Abstinence. He could do it. Or could he? He'd spent three nights with her before ever even touching her, but now the dynamic between them had changed.

He wasn't sure that was an option unless she had more restraint than he did, in which case he would take the floor again as a makeshift bed.

"I suppose it is possible I was given something at the theater, but all I had was a glass or two of champagne and nothing else." She glanced up at the window as if she also realized it was getting dark. "My father and mother also had the same."

They'd been over this before more than once. Ran regarded her with as much impassiveness as possible, and she appeared introspective this evening considering what had happened between them the night before. "I think we are going to be in the dark over what happened until we get back to London."

"And when will that be?"

She was almost a decade younger. He could hear the edge of restiveness in her voice and he was hardly reconciled to this captivity either, but the war had taught him the benefits of patience. It was the inactivity that chafed the most for him, and unfortunately he knew how that lack of physical movement could be alleviated. "Whoever is behind this can't keep us here indefinitely."

Elena rose again after sitting for a moment or two, the hem of her dressing gown sweeping the floor as she paced toward the door and stared at it. "One would think so, but I once read a book where a woman was locked in a dungeon by her grasping sister until she was too old to bear children." She turned with a rueful smile. "I know it was simply sensational fiction, but . . . Tell me, who is going to believe *us* once we are freed?"

An excellent point.

She was certainly not too old to bear children, something he needed to keep in mind. Quite the contrary; the fertile-goddess image was striking as she stood there in the flowing robe, her blue eyes dark and inquiring. It was interesting, but he couldn't help but wonder if they had a child, would it have his dark coloring or her golden fairness?

And where the hell did that rogue thought come from, he wondered with a jab of pure male alarm. Not once in his lifetime yet had he thought about conceiving children except in the sense of how to avoid it happening. That was why he chose sophisticated lovers who took precautions to prevent conception, because making love was about the casual pleasure of it, not creating a child.

His delectable roommate was more than a little distracting and no doubt affecting his normal levelheaded approach to life. Perhaps it was time to give them both something else to concentrate on besides their captivity.

*   *   *

Elena was coming to know the notorious Viscount Andrews rather well and something had just happened. A
bit perplexed, she saw his mouth tighten and his lashes
flicker downward, and his face went utterly blank even
though the careless sprawl of his body didn't change.

It couldn't be what she just said. Surely it had occurred to him their story would not be readily accepted
by society. As she stood there Elena reminded herself
that yes, of course it had. He was intelligent and far more
worldly than she was, and he'd mentioned before they
would have to fabricate a more plausible explanation for
their absences, for it was much too incredible for the
jaded *ton* to take as truth.

"No one," he said with measured inflection. "No one
will ever believe I didn't touch you. And in all honesty,
they'd be correct, wouldn't they?" He added softly, "I'd
like to touch you *now*."

A singular warmth coursed through her veins at the
predatory look in his eyes, and perhaps it was the proximity of his rangy body, the dark beard, and his slightly
unruly midnight hair, or his generally overwhelming
masculinity, but he looked quite dangerous suddenly.

The room was also growing dark, the lamp oil never
replenished until the next day, and it must have begun to
rain in the late afternoon, for they'd had to light it much
earlier than usual, which meant it was already burning low.

There was no reason to refuse him. She'd already lain
naked in his arms and, besides, she didn't *wish* to refuse
him. When he'd acted all day as if nothing of significance
had happened between them, there had been a sense of
pique until she'd caught him looking at her several times
in a way that told her instinctively he was not quite as
cavalier about the experience as he seemed on the sur-

face. She cleared her throat and said brazenly, "It appears we are in accord there, my lord."

That brought him to his feet in a single athletic movement. "I was damn well hoping you'd have the sense to deny me, because apparently I've lost my mind."

"I think it is mutual madness," she said unsteadily.

"I usually have more control."

She might not be experienced, but the subtle tension in the air all day told her he was speaking the truth, and the minute he caught her hand, lacing his fingers through hers and tugging her close, heated intoxication washed over her in a slow, rolling wave.

"Kiss me," he whispered, lowering his head, his breath against her lips. "Elena, kiss me."

Could any woman resist that suggestive husky tone? Not many had, according to rumor, and she could understand it at the moment.

The kiss was no doubt a little inept but she obeyed, molding her mouth to his, tasting the heady whiskey he'd been drinking steadily since late afternoon as she shyly brushed her tongue against his in an attempt to seduce him as he'd done to her the night before. It must have been effective, for he gave a low groan and his arm slid around her waist.

The room faded, the darkness no longer important as her eyes closed, and nothing existed but the sensation of his embrace and his mouth moving against hers as he took over the kiss. The heat that shimmered between them was palpable, dizzying, an intoxicant she had never, ever expected.

Their lips clung softly, then a brush of their tongues, then a breathless parting before they joined again . . .

She wasn't a complete fool; he was very, very good at

this or women would not flutter their fans and murmur over him when he entered the room. It was admittedly beguiling.

His hands spanned her waist, then drifted lower. "You enchant me," he told her when he lifted his head, "And we barely began to explore the possibilities of how many ways last night."

It charmed her—as maybe it was intended to—that he just waited then, not importunate but patient, as if giving her the choice, though he had to note her erratic breathing and certainly he knew she was willing. After all, she was warm and lax against him.

"I know." She'd sensed it was just the beginning, the glimpse of a sensual world that was a glimmer of the future. "I cannot wait to learn more."

"Passion and beauty are a dangerous combination, but it seems my instincts for self-preservation are in abeyance at the moment." He nuzzled her neck and lifted her in his arms. "Let us continue your education."

She let him carry her to the bed without protest and wasn't sure if she was disappointed or not when he didn't remove his robe but settled next to her and skimmed her cheek with his fingertips. His smile was endearingly boyish. "I'm not used to this."

"I wish you would define *this*, because I am not quite sure what is happening between us."

"Desire." His gaze held hers. "Don't you feel it?"

"Yes." The stifled laugh caught in her throat. "But I am sure, my lord, you have felt it many times before."

He chose to not address her point. "If I was prudent I would just settle on the cold floor."

"But then I would be cold too, and I don't think prudent describes you very well."

"Your deliberate temptation isn't helping this situation."

She reached up and traced the line of one ebony brow with a fingertip, the gesture bold, but she was feeling fearless and wanton. "I am not sure if I know how to be deliberately tempting, but I am learning from a master."

That he caught her meaning wasn't in question. His dark eyes held a smoldering gleam. "Young women are often too romantic. That is why I avoid them."

"I didn't notice you avoiding *me*."

"I have noticed that too." He kissed her again as he subtly adjusted his position, the action effectively ending the conversation, his hand slipping between the parted folds of her robe and finding her bare breast, eliciting a deep thrill as her body tightened in response to the caress.

He didn't wish to talk. And that was fine with her at the moment because all she wanted was the touch of his hands and the promise of the pleasure he offered so skillfully.

The lamp flickered but it only registered absently as his fingers cupped, caressed, and fondled.

It was all still novel for her but he knew exactly what response he would get, if the slight smile that curved his lips was an indication.

Damn him.

But, then again . . .

His other hand slipped between her legs, the touch shocking but pleasurable as she tried for a moment to hold her thighs together and then surrendered. Exquisite sensation overcame modesty almost immediately as he stroked and her body reacted with wayward abandon, the touch no doubt forbidden but intimately delicious nonetheless, especially when he kissed the hollow of her throat. There was something primal about how his hair brushed her collarbone and the graze of his mouth across her right nipple.

"Sweet," he murmured against her sensitized skin, and she involuntarily shivered as his fingers slowly moved in a sensual circle. *What am I doing*, a vague voice in her brain asked, *allowing such liberties*. Taking what he had to give though she absolutely knew she shouldn't. Had it not been for her growing realization that Randolph Raine was more complicated than people imagined—but entirely as attractive as it was rumored—maybe she would not have. His charm wasn't superficial. Practiced, yes, but not without substance, and it was that realization that drew her more than his striking good looks or easy, seductive manner.

He was . . . afraid of her. Or, more accurately, of his re-action to her, and that alone shifted the balance enough that lying in his arms was a more heady experience.

She rather thought Viscount Andrews, after five days of his constant company, was so much more than his in-famous persona. But at the moment he was being quite devilish indeed and living up to the reputation.

The contrast was intriguing. She had the distinct im-pression the man she was supposed to marry wasn't in the least complex, and with all the hours to contemplate it now she knew the engagement was a mistake and an acquiescence to her father, when she should have been more forthright about her doubts. It was one thing to think a man was nice enough and another to pledge her-self to him for life.

Lord Colbert wanted a pretty, young, submissive wife that would bring a solid marriage portion, advantageous political connections, and hopefully would be fertile and produce an heir. But the intimacy of what that involved told her how little she understood the depth of the agreement and what it entailed.

This kidnapping had very likely ruined her. But maybe her life would have been ruined in a completely different way if it hadn't happened.

"That feels good." It wasn't a question as Ran's fingers made a slow rotation. He licked her lower lip. "I like the way you move when I touch you. Your body is so delectably responsive."

How could anyone help it during such skillful and shameless manipulation? Elena quivered against him, their mutual nakedness an aphrodisiac, his heat and lean length powerful next to her. This time his erection wasn't nearly as daunting because she'd seen it before, but she was still uncertain as to what he wanted her to do so she merely took in a shuddering breath as he leisurely moved his hand between her legs.

The disparity of their experience was so vast that she didn't know what to say, and, in truth, she didn't *want* to say anything. All she wanted at the moment was to feel, and, because this was all so new for her, to learn about wanton pleasure. Could there be a better teacher? She doubted it.

But analyzing the situation was beyond her at the moment as she arched, the gentle rotating movement of his fingers not quite enough suddenly, as if she hung on a precipice, breathless and wanting. As if he precisely understood, he pressed in just the right way, faster and . . .

He kissed her as he pushed her over the edge, a shattering bliss making her cry out and twist away, the sensation too overwhelming.

"You can do that for yourself," he wickedly whispered in her ear as she expired in waves of pleasure. "But I promise you it is better not done alone."

Gasping in the aftermath, she wasn't sure what he meant, but coherent thought was not exactly an option at the moment and languid contentment instead a distraction.

More heated kisses followed and a shuddering moment later the warm liquid of his release spilled across her belly as he said her name with hoarse intonation. Cradled against him she wondered if whoever had plotted to have them abducted and locked in together had changed her life irrevocably, but perhaps not as intended.

It was possible she was one of those romantic young women Ran wished to avoid because, maybe, just maybe, she was becoming more and more fascinated with the dashing, ardent, but carefully distant Lord Andrews.

"I'll bathe you," he said in his signature lazy drawl once the acceleration of their breathing had slowed. "Entirely my fault, but forgive me if I refuse to apologize, for it was also entirely my pleasure."

"Do you usually?" She shouldn't have asked, but there was a sense of loss as he shifted away and sat up. He was entirely right: she was sticky, and no doubt he was as well.

It was dark enough she couldn't see his expression, but in silhouette he seemed suddenly remote yet his voice was even. "With the myriad of other women, you mean."

"I'm not sure what I mean." She'd asked too personal a question, that was clear enough. But was she supposed to apologize with his discharge on her skin? "This is very new to me," Elena said softly, "and it doesn't come lightly. You've forgiven my physical inexperience with the rest of it so far."

For a moment she thought he might not answer, but then his teeth gleamed in the ghost of a smile. "What you are asking me is to define what the emotional part of it is, and that is definitely not within the confines of my expertise, Elena."

"And certainly not mine." It wasn't an admonition as much as an introspective observance.

"No," he had the grace to agree. "Let me see to this."

The lamp finally went out when he sat down next to her and the warm, wet fabric brushed her skin. Her body, still sensitive from the recent spike of pleasure, trembled as he wiped away the residue in the darkness, the muscles in her stomach tightening, and she had no doubt he noticed but he didn't comment.

It was easier, actually, to ask questions if she couldn't see his expression. "That is how babies are conceived?"

His hand stopped moving as if he was arrested by her question. There was enough moonlight outside she could faintly see him but not enough to register his reaction. He said after a moment, "I forget sometimes how sheltered young English ladies are. When a male climaxes inside a female he leaves his seed. If she is fertile she might conceive. It certainly doesn't happen every time but often enough."

It wasn't as if she didn't know there was a process that involved a man and a woman—and certainly she'd become much more enlightened in the past few days, but it was disconcerting to hear it put into words. Elena murmured, "So what we just did—"

"Was for pleasure, not procreation and I didn't penetrate you. Don't worry. There won't be a child."

"I . . . see."

"Do you?" His fingers briefly touched her cheek. "Surely you are not interested in having a babe out of wedlock."

"No." She could say that with all due honesty.

"Then we are in accord."

Were they? She wasn't sure. When he settled into bed he didn't pull her close, but rolled into the blankets and kept his distance. A little bewildered, she listened for his breathing to settle into the rhythm of slumber, but before it happened she found it impossible to fight off her own drowsiness.

At least he didn't sleep on the floor.

Chapter 13

"**Y**ou let her go alone?"

Adams shifted to the other foot. "She insisted, my lord. I wondered at the wisdom of it all, but, no, she wasn't alone. The other lady went with her and your driver, of course. She left this."

Ben liked to think he could usually keep his expression controlled, but when he read the note he was fairly certain he must have looked close to anger because his secretary cleared his throat noisily.

"Is something wrong, my lord?"

Yes, it was *all* wrong. His willful wife was out and about trying to unearth a potential kidnapper and what he wanted to do at the moment was strangle her. The equation wasn't complicated. Alicia's cousin was missing. His wife apparently couldn't see clear to keeping herself out of harm's way despite that obvious fact. Yet none of the fault of it belonged to this young man, so he needed to calm himself.

The spike of alarm had Ben's hand slightly shaking as he set aside the note. An advancing French column on the battlefield had not even been able to accomplish that, and yet one young woman with a penchant for dramatic ultimatums and a sense of adventure he'd been previously unaware of had managed it. "No. I will take care of it. Thank you."

At least she'd left him the address of where she'd hared off to. That was something.

Partnering with Alicia on this investigation is hardly an asset, he thought with an inward curse, *and more of a profound liability*—especially since it paralyzed him at the very thought of danger to her.

And it did. There was no evidence her cousin had come to harm, but there was also no evidence she hadn't either.

"Have them bring my horse around, please," he said crisply. *And I will retrieve my wife myself.*

Perhaps, when they were back safe and sound, he'd explain in private in exact terms why she should obey him, but at the moment he needed to see her whole and unharmed before repercussions came to mind.

A good spanking was not without merit, but he'd never raised a hand to a woman, and he wasn't going to start now, certainly not to Alicia, whom he'd die to protect. Still, there had to be some effective way to make his point . . . for she couldn't do this, couldn't dash off on some whimsical quest with a woman she didn't know . . .

Was she addled or just too trusting?

Or even more adventurous than he'd perceived before this. Who knew she'd be so tenacious in pursuing her goal to recover her cousin? She certainly was not quite as predictable as he'd once thought.

For example, *this* he had not foreseen.

Rather like not knowing her favorite color. Maybe he should have been more observant all along. Swinging into the saddle, he nudged his horse toward a part of

London he didn't consider to be savory and was glad he carried not just a dirk but also a sidearm. His mount, Ambrosias, sensed his urgency, for he danced sideways in the street and usually he was much better-mannered. They were old friends, used to each other, and the stallion was rarely so restive, but neither was he used to the city.

The urge to protect his wife was profound and made him put a heel to his horse's side despite the muddy thoroughfare. Luckily the big horse didn't balk at being guided through streets increasingly crowded with noise and carts, and when Ben spotted the carriage with his family crest sitting in front of the modest residence, Ambrosias was barely breathing hard. He, however, let out a measured exhale as he saw Alicia and a dark-haired woman emerge from the house, both ostensibly unharmed.

His wife caught sight of him sitting there and her smile naturally lit her face as if she had no idea he'd dashed half across London in a state of panic and perhaps even left some muddied pedestrians cursing in his wake.

She even waved with flattering enthusiasm.

God help him, she *waved*.

He was fairly adept at hiding his feelings and dismounted, calmly tugged his horse over to the carriage, without a word handed the reins to the driver so he could tie the stallion to the back of the vehicle, and opened the door for the two ladies himself. "Please get in."

"I see you received my note, my lord. I—"

"Indeed I did."

Alicia might be innocent but she was hardly a fool. Though he endeavored to be as polite as possible, she

caught the edge in his tone when he interrupted her and
glanced up sharply. Her frothy skirts gathered in her
slender hands, she allowed him to take her arm to assist
her into the conveyance. Her companion, Miss Janet
Raine, was a bit older than he was but not by much, and
still attractive in an understated fashion. She also accepted his hand in assistance but kept her gaze slightly
averted as she climbed inside. That told him without
words that this had been entirely Alicia's idea, which he
hadn't doubted in the first place.

He followed, the carriage dipping as he joined them,
his slightly mud-spattered appearance no doubt giving
evidence of his haste. Without preamble, he said,
"Madam, you may now tell me in a very succinct way
why you chose to go out unescorted to this part of London without my permission."

The request came out a bit heavy-handed, but his
pulse was only now slowing, as he could see for himself
his wife was unharmed. If she didn't realize that . . .

But maybe she didn't. One of her points to their recent confrontation was that they didn't know each other
well. Maybe she was right. That needed to be addressed.

So with effort he quickly modified the statement before she answered, "Not that I normally dictate what you
do, but in this case I was worried."

Alicia met his eyes, her chin tilted at what might be
interpreted as a defiant angle. "Miss Raine called with
some rather pertinent information. She was looking for
you, but you were not home. I understand you've met
before."

He ignored the implied question of why he hadn't imparted the information that he'd been to visit Lord Andrews's family. He wasn't required to explain his actions;

it was quite the other way around. "Is there some reason you declined to wait until I returned home?"

"Yes. You didn't deign to tell me when that would be."

"I wasn't aware I needed to do so."

Alicia folded her hands primly in her lap. "You are unaware of many things, my lord."

Had he just been criticized by his lovely wife in front of an audience? Ben lifted his brows. "I am sure I have a myriad collection of flaws, but can we set that aside while you explain exactly why Miss Raine came to see me and then the two of you went haring off?"

"This." Opening her reticule, Alicia produced a gold watch with a flourish.

He took it, their fingers briefly brushing, making his gaze flicker up to meet hers, that contact a reminder of his banishment from her bed. Curious, he examined the timepiece, pressing the side so it opened, the inscription there catching his full attention.

To Drew, Viscount Andrews, in friendship from his king, George III, Sovereign of England, May 1798

"My brother's watch." Janet spoke finally, her tone low. "He was a young man when it was gifted to him. He'd served in the colonial war against America. Randolph carries it at all times. I received a note asking if there would be a reward for its return. That is how I knew without a doubt he had not gone anywhere voluntarily. There are some parts of his life my nephew would not give up lightly, and besides that rare, vile whiskey he favors, this watch is one them. He would never lose it. I've seen his hand stray to his pocket in an absent mannerism more often than I can say to make sure it is in place."

It was a fine piece and Ben gently closed the case, noting there seemed to be no damage. "You obviously paid the reward, so I hope you requested details."

"Actually"—Alicia cleared her throat—"you paid it. I left a note in your name. I did not have quite enough household funds to cover it."

"I see." Andrews was no doubt good for it if he ever found the blasted man, but still a corner of his mouth twitched a little at her audacity. "Very well. As I am holding the watch I purchased back from a man who apparently was keeping it hostage, please do tell me you know how the blackmailer came to have it in his possession."

Really, he doesn't need to use such a condescending tone, Alicia thought with irritation. Or maybe it was guilt, for, to a certain extent, she understood now that Ben was probably correct and she should not have gone off so blithely without even knowing exactly where she was headed. While she wouldn't describe the neighborhood as downtrodden, it wasn't prosperous either, and once they had arrived she wasn't at all sure they should even exit the carriage.

"I wrote it all down," she informed him as the carriage swayed along. "The man claimed he'd found it in the street after witnessing an altercation outside of the club that Lord Andrews frequents. When he saw the engraving he wondered if his lordship would not be interested in getting it back."

Ben weighed the solid-gold case in his palm and nodded. "I am sure Andrews *will* want it. What else did he tell you? What sort of altercation? Did he describe it?"

Disappointingly, the man had seen very little.

"Three men seemed to be dragging another man into

a coach of some kind and he was protesting, but Mr. Crepshaw claimed it was dark and he couldn't see very clearly what they looked like." Alicia was derisive as she added, "Nor did he, it seems, have the courage to come to the rescue of anything but Lord Andrews's watch. If I saw someone—"

For the second time that evening her husband interrupted her, which was very unusual. He was always almost too carefully polite. "I've no doubt you'd do something rash, my dear, but can we get back to the only witness we might have? What else did he say?"

Rash? That was a little insulting, but she wasn't sure she should argue the point at the moment.

"He wasn't all that helpful," Janet Raine admitted. "I think the gleam of gold distracted him, and when he realized who it belonged to, he knew he could extort money for its return."

"What was he doing in front of one of London's most exclusive clubs in the first place?"

Both of them looked at him blankly and Alicia realized that perhaps she wasn't experienced enough to properly interview witnesses. When she thought about it, why *had* the smarmy shopkeeper been in such an exclusive neighborhood?

"It's clear he isn't a member," her husband went on. "And I admit I'm rather surprised he allowed you the watch without the money."

"My pearl earbobs." Alicia tilted her head so he could see her unadorned earlobe.

As he'd given them to her for a gift, he looked momentarily taken aback—or as much as Ben ever looked nonplussed, which was almost never—until she said with a hint of smugness, "Just one of them, of course, as collateral to ensure we'd honor our word. I would never have given him both."

"Clever," he agreed after a slight pause. "I suppose one earring would be difficult to sell. Though the pair is a family heirloom."

He'd never told her that but she shouldn't be surprised. The day of their wedding he'd simply handed her the box and said they suited her beauty. No flowery words of love, of course, but, then, he never had said anything about his feelings except that he admired her looks.

Desire still wasn't enough, but they *might* be making some headway, for he had certainly seemed concerned when he'd ridden up. Her purpose had not been to worry him but instead expediency. She was growing more and more upset about Elena each passing day. "I don't think this particular man wants the jewelry as much as the money," she informed her husband, noting how the shadowed light in the carriage accented his firm lips and lean jaw. Still in his riding clothes, he seemed to take up most of the space, his long legs stretched out enough his boots brushed her skirts.

"It was not a criticism; just an observation." His tone was mild, his eyes inscrutable.

"Then we agree I did what was best under the circumstances?"

She'd asked it a touch too sweetly and he hesitated, but then did what he did best and circumvented a direct answer to the hint of sarcasm. "I agree this was certainly worth looking into, but you should have at least taken along one of the footmen for protection." His gaze shifted to Janet. "There's still no word, I take it, from your nephew?"

"None," she confirmed in a slightly hollow voice. "I

am stymied as what to tell my niece, Lucy, for she is frantic, and I admit I am not easy about Randolph's continued absence either."

"I feel the same about my cousin." Alicia pointed it out quietly, because, in truth, she now felt guilty about the earring. Surely Elena's well-being when measured against something material—no matter how valuable—was more important.

"It has been long enough one does have to wonder." In a mannerism she was coming to know, Ben gazed at the tip of his boot as if suddenly fascinated, his brow furrowed. "At least we have some indication of an abduction; however, nothing to explain why or if it has anything to do with Lady Elena."

"It is not a lack of concern over Lady Heathton's cousin, I assure you, but I would very much like to know what happened to my nephew, my lord. No one thinks he would leave with such callous disregard for our worry. He's a very independent man, though perhaps a bit of a libertine, but he isn't . . . thoughtless."

And maybe I have been just that in my haste, Alicia had to acknowledge, going off to an unknown and, as it turned out, not so safe part of London without waiting for her husband's return. Still, she tried to rationalize her decision as they pulled up in front of the stately house, *he* hadn't bothered to tell *her* where he was going either.

Once Ben had escorted Janet Raine to her waiting carriage, gifted her the watch, and promised he would investigate further, he climbed the steps to the house with athletic precision and motioned for Alicia to precede him inside. "After you, my dear."

She hesitated, an apology hovering on her lips. After all, she had really just been trying to help.

He correctly interpreted her uncertain expression. "We can speak alone upstairs."

There was enough understanding between them that she realized he was still angry under his calm demeanor and privacy did seem to be a good idea. Not that he really betrayed himself except for a tense set to his mouth and a slight glint in his hazel eyes, but she declined to argue and nodded at Yeats as she passed the older man in the hallway, doing her best to look unruffled and unconcerned.

Conscious of Ben right behind her, she climbed the stairs with as much dignity as possible, the slight acceleration of her pulse not due entirely to the exertion. When she reached the top and walked to her bedroom door, she paused. "I—"

"Inside," her husband said with underlying steel in his tone that wasn't easily missed, though he didn't raise his voice even a fraction.

While a part of her bridled at the autocratic order, another part was curious as to what exactly he was going to say. When he politely opened the door for her and stood back, she entered the room and turned around to watch him follow her. He seemed somewhat taller all at once, his dark blond hair ruffled by their earlier ride, his boots a bit muddy, his eyes slightly narrowed.

"What were you thinking?"

"I had no idea I would make you angry." Alicia did her best to not sound defensive.

"I was worried," her husband said with equanimity. "I admit *now* I am a little irritated, for I know you are more intelligent than to go off to meet a man who would stoop to extortion in a neighborhood that is questionable at best and dangerous at worst, but no harm was done. *This time*. I think perhaps it would better if we understood each other. That is what you want, is it not? For us to know each other in ways that do not include our marriage bed?"

"I never said I didn't want to include the bedroom. . . ." She stopped, wondering, from the sudden intensity of his gaze, if she'd just fallen into some trap.

"That is good to hear." He took a predatory step closer. "But we will discuss that in a moment. For now I'd like to ask you to give me your word that you will never do something so foolish again."

"I didn't go alone so it was hardly foolish," she started to object, not sure if she wanted to concede the irrefutable fact it had not been a good idea. The shabby neighborhood had set her aback, but at that point they'd gone that far, so she had brazened it out.

Well, perhaps *foolish* did apply.

"Wasn't it?" Ben moved again and his fingertips brushed her cheek in a ghost of a caress. "I beg to differ, my lady."

The light touch made her unaccountably warm and was unexpected. Alicia could swear he was still not at all happy with her, and perhaps he had a right to be, yet the touch of his hand made her shiver in an interesting way.

She felt compelled to admit, "I might have been a little impetuous."

"Might?" Ben's long fingers caught her chin and tilted it upward.

At that moment she realized he was going to kiss her. It was one of those instinctive instances where no words were necessary . . . if he had spoken it would have ruined *everything*. He didn't, thank goodness, but instead lowered his head and his mouth touched hers—gently at first, their lips clinging, and then his tongue traced the line of her lips and slipped into her mouth. He began to explore in a way that made her tingle in curious places.

Six months of married life and he had never, *ever* kissed her like this.

Not with the palm of his hand warm on the small of her back, not with a change in the slant of his head in which he tasted her more fully, not with such heat and open desire.

It was intoxicating in a unique way that left her breathless when he finally broke it off, her chest lifting against his, she discovered, they stood so close. The tips of her breasts were tight and her lashes lowered in anticipation, but they fluttered up when he said in a matter-of-fact voice, "If you will excuse me, I have another pressing errand. I look forward to seeing you at dinner, my dear."

Then he released her and left her there, standing with her arms at her sides, staring, as he exited the room and quietly closed the adjoining door. Bemused, Alicia wasn't sure whether she should laugh or cry, but there was a glimmer of understanding that they'd just engaged in a subtle battle.

The real question was, *Who had won?* She'd definitely gotten her romantic kiss, but he'd walked away. There had never been any doubt in her mind that Ben was clever enough that he would be a formidable foe with no need of the weapons of his position of power or his wealth or even of male privilege. Not that she really considered this a war between them—it was not a struggle for power either, or at least she didn't look at it that way. It was at the same time simpler and more complex than that.

Which, she was beginning to think, described being in love very well. It was the most simple yet evocative, intoxicating, complex emotion possible.

Thoughtfully, she reassessed her approach.

Maybe she needed a new strategy.

She was still musing over it a half hour later when the knock came, and she was undeniably startled out of her reverie. Alicia rose, straightened her dress, and went to the door. "Yes?"

A footman stood there, an apologetic look on his face. "I'm sorry, my lady, but you have a visitor. He insists on an audience."

She took the card, saw the name with a sinking feeling, then nodded. "Please tell his lordship I will be down directly."

Colbert. Elena's fiancé. She barely knew the man but then she somehow doubted her uncle would give him much information, so even before she entered the drawing room she had a fair idea of why his lordship had chosen to pay her a visit.

"Countess," he said formally, rising politely.

"My lord." She inclined her head, wishing vehemently that Ben hadn't hurried off to whatever appointment was so mysteriously important, so *he* could deal with this.

He had an irritating habit of doing just that.

Blond, tall, and diffident, Lord Colbert cleared his throat. "I'm here about your cousin. As you know we are affianced, and it appears . . . well, that she is nowhere to be found. I wondered if you could give any insight into this confusing matter."

Coming up with an adequate answer wasn't exactly easy. "I wish I could answer," she told him, eschewing the niceties of offering refreshment and deciding that honesty was, in fact, the best approach. "I am worried as well. We all are."

"So you know nothing."

"Nothing. I'm sorry."

He bowed, his expression openly disgruntled. "Thank you, then." With long strides he walked to the door, but then turned. "Does she know Andrews?"

"No. Not to my knowledge."

When he had gone, she sat down and stared abstractedly at the painting above the fireplace.

Elena, where are you?

Chapter 14

Ben heard the little bell ring as he entered the shop. He had to force himself to forget the delectable sensation of having Alicia so soft and willing in his arms and focus on the matter at hand. Time was passing and it would not hurt his cause to please her by finding her errant cousin.

Three ingredients, not obviously connected, combined to make a witches' brew of trouble and finally he had his first real possibility of a lead.

One lovely and innocent young woman. One infamously wicked lord. And their mutual absence all to a purpose Ben was starting more and more to believe had nothing to do with an impromptu elopement. So ... where were they?

As much as he hated to admit it, Alicia's impulsive dash across town had yielded a viable clue. Not from the mercenary opportunist who had ransomed the watch, but in another way entirely.

The shop smelled like old wood soaked in brandy with a hint of tobacco and an overtone of fine claret. Various bottles stood open with small glasses nearby for tasting, and the walls were lined with racks, varying amounts of dust on them. When the proprietor hurried out, he took stock of Ben's fashionable clothing and unerringly said, "May I be of assistance, my lord?"

A skilled merchant knew the beau monde in this district, though Ben had to admit he'd only been in this establishment once or twice. Yeats took care of the wine selection and did all the purchasing. In the past he'd had an operative do this sort of thing for him, but time was an issue, and, besides, he no longer had operatives. Yes, he could call in favors, much as Wellington had done with him, but, truth be told, he was now no more than the Earl of Heathton.

He smiled affably. "I was wondering if you happened to have a rare sort of whiskey from Northern Scotland. I forget the name but I had a glass recently with my friend, Viscount Andrews. I must admit I am yearning to try it again."

Unfortunately, when he'd seen Janet Raine to her carriage and inquired, she had not remembered the name of the distiller but had helpfully recalled where her nephew purchased his stock.

The owner of the shop was a small wiry man with a shock of gray hair and a slight accent. "The Blaven? Twenty years old and smooth as silk, but not for every palate. Aye, my lord, the viscount does do his business here, but I regret to say I sold the last bottles a few days ago."

Before or after Andrews's disappearance? Ben tapped his fingers on the counter and did his best to imitate disappointment. "I see. Mayhaps Andrews will allow me to purchase it from him."

"It wasn't to his lordship, I'm afraid." The proprietor frowned. "Which I'll admit is unusual. Aside from a few ... ahem ... discerning gentlemen like yourself, that particular whiskey does not appeal to many people."

"Do you happen to remember who bought it?"

"Aye, I keep most careful records, my lord. My clientele can expect for me to remember their preferences." Industriously, the shopkeeper bustled to the back and returned with a ledger. "A Mr. Stone came in and asked for it specifically. I noted his address, as he asked for the purchase to be delivered because he was on foot."

It could be nothing, Ben thought later when he emerged from the building, the address in his pocket. Perhaps this Stone was simply another connoisseur of the distinctive Blaven, but the owner of the shop had informed him that usually he went months at a time without selling a bottle to anyone but Andrews. He wouldn't even stock it in his store as it was expensive to have it brought down from Scotland, but the viscount was a regular customer and paid well.

So was it a coincidence someone bought the reserve of this unique beverage right as Andrews disappeared?

Ben was not sure he believed in chance quite that much, and at the least it merited investigation. So even though it was rather late in the day to make a call, he instructed his driver to take him to the mysterious Mr. Stone's address.

Ran had taught her to gamble and apparently he was an excellent mentor. The soft sound made them both look up from their card game, Ran in the act of taking a drink from his glass of whiskey, her fingers letting a card slip to the surface of the table as she discarded a poor one in the hopes of receiving a better draw.

The lamp was at low ebb, and Elena had already

caught the intensity of his gaze more than once, the anticipation of the coming night adding to the ambience of the game. But since their dinner had been served and cleared, the unexpected scrape of the bar lifting on the door jolted them both out of the moment.

Instead of the usual two servants, this time it was a girl, not more than fifteen or so, who opened the door, her eyes wide, face blanched. "My . . . my lady," she stammered. "Monsieur LaSalle sent me."

That proved Ran had been correct about the chef's nationality. Off guard, Elena was unable to respond, but she needn't have worried because the smooth and articulate Lord Andrews had no trouble talking to a female of any age.

"I'm Viscount Andrews." His smile was pure male charm and he'd risen, as if noblemen normally gave such courtesy to servants. "Do you work in the kitchen here?"

The girl nodded, her gaze furtively touching the still-disheveled bed, her cheeks holding a hint of ruddy color.

Elena would normally be more embarrassed but she was too elated over the idea that the note had worked.

"The food has certainly been excellent." Ran's voice was casual, but Elena knew him well enough after these past days in close company that she registered the tension in his tall body. If the guards weren't there . . . his gaze was fastened on the now open door.

Perhaps escape was possible.

"Thank you . . . it has . . . has all been monsieur, of course . . ." The girl stammered again and caught herself, for she said with a touch of desperation, "He invites my lady down to his kitchen."

Absurdly, Elena's first reaction was that she had nothing to wear that was appropriate for leaving their intimate prison. They'd been provided with hot water and clean robes each day, but a dressing gown was still not proper attire for any place besides the bedroom, and at some time in the comings and goings of delivering food and the other necessities, someone had taken her chemise and also Ran's breeches.

"*We'd* be honored. I am her protector and she goes nowhere without me," Ran said with steely inflection.

Protector? The word conjured forbidden images of mistresses and secretive liaisons, and Elena opened her mouth to object in outrage, but she had no desire to actually go on her own so she stifled the response.

The girl hesitated for only a moment as if she would argue and then nodded and acquiesced to his air of authority. "Follow me, milord."

"Thank you." He did Lord of the Manor very well, but it was difficult to resent male privilege when moments later Elena found herself on a set of curved narrow stairs and for the first time in five days out of captivity.

Or at least out of the tower room. The scullery maid lifted the lamp she'd brought and guided them down, and there was another door at the base of the stairs that she gently pushed open. The hinges must have been well oiled, but that wasn't too much of an assumption, because they'd not ever heard the servants approach until the lifting of the bar outside the door.

Elena inhaled deeply as they passed into a darkened corridor. A hint of lemon and beeswax and old wood hung in the air.

"Take my hand." Ran didn't wait but clasped her fingers with reassuring firmness, the low light from the girl's lamp ahead of them not providing enough illumination to make it easy to see her way. "I don't want you to stumble."

He was gallant, but she'd already discovered that—and many other things—about him. Elena obeyed and followed, finding that two long hallways led to another flight of stairs, this one elegantly curved, and then into a great hall and through what was a servant's doorway, obviously. The first hint the kitchen was nearby was a whiff reminiscent of the succulent pork with brandied cherries they had been served earlier, the aroma lingering along with an undertone of bread baking, probably for the next day.

For such a large house it seemed very quiet, which did not surprise her. All along she'd thought it felt as if it might be unoccupied except for the servants there to serve them.

The mystery merely deepened, but one fact she was certain of: Ran was not going back to the tower room in a docile fashion, so while they weren't precisely free, they had one proverbial foot out the door.

"Monsieur?" the young woman murmured as she pushed open a door, pulling a light blue shawl closer around her shoulders, though it was not at all cold. "Her ladyship is here."

In contrast to the rest of the house the kitchen was warmly lit, a large scrubbed table in the center of the space, pans hanging from hooks on the walls, the ceiling low and darkly timbered. A man glanced up from a pot he was stirring on the fire, his face registering nothing as he took in first Elena with her loose hair, robe, and bare feet, and then he assessed Ran in a long, measured look. He said curtly to the little maid, "*Merci*, Beatrice. Leave us."

Monsieur LaSalle did not match Elena's impression

of a French chef, to the extent he was almost slender in build and very fair, even to his eyebrows and eyelashes. His angular features were too sharp to be handsome, but he nonetheless had a presence that had nothing to do with his pristine white apron and more due to a singular self-possession. They were in his domain, of course, so that made sense.

"I received your note, mademoiselle. You enjoyed the pudding *de chocolat*, yes? Tell me what impressed you the most."

Elena blinked. "I suppose I found the texture to be smoother than any other I've tasted," she answered after a moment of a reflection, thinking this was a bizarre way to begin this conversation. "But I—"

"Not too light? The English, they like their food so ... dense." He made a moue of disapproval and set the spoon in a cup by the hearth. "Dessert should be sublime, uplifting, a gift to the senses, not a rock in the stomach."

While under other circumstances she might have taken a bit of umbrage to the insult to English cooking, she didn't think that was wise. "There is something to be said for subtlety, monsieur le chef."

"Exactly." That won her a smile of approval. Then he nodded toward the table. "Though I am sure neither of you are used to sitting in the kitchen, it is a comfortable place, no? Please choose a chair and then explain to me why I receive praise for my food—which I agree is magnificent—and at the same time pleas for help."

Ran politely pulled out a sturdy chair for her but remained standing. "The food has been superb, and, yes, we needed your help."

As Elena sank down she saw LaSalle register the past

tense in that statement. "Ah, now that you have been released—"

"I have no intention of being imprisoned again." That statement was flat and unequivocal. "Unless you also intend to produce a gun and threaten me with it, and even then I am not sure I would comply. For almost a week I have been taken out of my life entirely."

"I see." The chef frowned, his brows drawing in. "I was informed you were two lovers on a tryst, sneaking away for a chance to be alone together.... It was very romantic. However, I did start to wonder at the guard. It seemed to me a manservant and a maid would have been more in order than two armed men who patrol the grounds. And as much as you could play at *Je t'aime*, why would you never emerge from that room? The rest of the house is not used at all, and while I understand passion, even to me, that seemed a bit excessive."

The reference to love gave Elena a moment of disconcerted chagrin. *No, not love,* she thought. Though she supposed those tender kisses and intimate touches were at least a play at lust....

And she certainly understood how a woman might fall for the devastatingly attractive, charming, and erotically skillful Lord Andrews, but she somehow doubted it was a wise idea.

"We were kidnapped." She looked at the chef steadily, hoping he registered her sincerity. "When I woke in the tower I had no idea where I was and neither did Lord Andrews. We'd never even been introduced to each other."

It was slightly irritating that the man's gaze immediately flickered to Ran for confirmation. "Is this so?"

"She is not only distractingly beautiful, monsieur, but absolutely truthful."

The compliment mollified her slightly. "We were locked in."

"That is not what I was told." The Frenchman's voice held a hint of outrage, but she couldn't tell if it was over their imprisonment or the deception practiced on him. "I thought I was preparing food for a rich lord who desired utter and complete privacy so he could enjoy his beautiful lover."

"Complete privacy? Where the devil *are we*?"

LaSalle frowned. "You do not even know—"

"Monsieur, we know nothing." Ran interrupted, the lamplight giving his face planes and hollows. His hands were in the pockets of his dark dressing gown, but there was nothing casual in his stance. "How far are we from London?"

"About two hours by carriage."

So close. Elena let out a small relieved breath. Since neither of them knew precisely how long they had been under the influence of the drug, she had worried they were anywhere from the rugged coast of Cornwall to the Yorkshire dells. "Two hours," she murmured, glancing up at Ran.

"We could be there before midnight." He looked not quite jubilant but definitely lighter.

"No," the chef disagreed, "you cannot. There is no carriage here, I'm afraid. The one that brought me won't be back for two more days, at which time my services are no longer needed, or that was the agreement."

A setback, but if Ran was daunted, it didn't show. "So we were going to be released in two days anyway?"

"I had no knowledge you were captives in the first place, so how can I say?" LaSalle theatrically spread his hands and gave a Gallic shrug. "This is all very confounding, as you can imagine. I would assume you are cherished guests since my instructions were to give you the finest of dishes."

A good point, but Elena had to admit she wasn't anxious to simply stay and test the goodwill of whoever had them drugged, kidnapped, and held hostage for almost a week.

"Condemned men get a last meal also," Ran said with a grim edge in his voice. "I am inclined to leave now, even in the dark."

Chapter 15

Alicia looked in the mirror and adjusted her coiffure slightly, draping a curl over one shoulder. It was flattering because her hair was so dark—unfashionably so—and she had been fortunate to inherit her mother's very English ivory complexion, and the contrast was striking. Her gown, too, this evening was a deep, rich amber shot silk with tiny amethysts sown on the neckline and a deeper-than-usual décolletage. She wasn't at all sure Ben would notice she was being more daring; but maybe she would be proven wrong. A part of her understood he noticed *everything*.

It was what *mattered* to him that was the true mystery. Her attire? She doubted it. His volatile reaction to her absence had been gratifying, so who knew?

She rose, turned, and nodded at her maid. "Thank you, Winnie."

"You look glorious, my lady." The young woman smiled and then gathered up Alicia's discarded dressing gown. "His lordship will be fair struck with your beauty."

Did the servants know she was on a campaign to win more of his attention? She rather thought it possible, as they seemed to be quite aware, and though she could never imagine the upright Yeats gossiping, she suspected he'd overheard her tell Ben he had never kissed her.

But he certainly had now.

And, ah, the difference. Upon reflection, and she'd done quite a lot of it on the subject, maybe a desperately nervous bride would make the initial seduction difficult, no matter how skillful a man was as a lover. After their wedding night she'd relaxed a little, knowing what to expect, but maybe the kiss earlier was an indication her hopes for them were not just a romantic fantasy.

So perhaps later this evening . . . she would find out.

Actually, when considered carefully, she didn't really care so much if Ben was struck by her beauty or not. Oh yes, indeed, she wanted him to *desire* her. Of course. But it was more than that.

She wanted him to fall in love with her.

The memory of that kiss brought a smile. Her stand-offish husband was capable of real passion; he just wasn't anxious to admit it.

Perfect.

"My lady?"

Alicia turned in the act of reaching for her slippers, a half smile on her face. "Yes?"

Her maid offered a slip of vellum. "This was under the door."

Alicia took it and saw the seal, and all feeling of jubilance fled. She had a premonition that the missive might not be the best of news and she was expecting too much of the evening. "Thank you," she said to Winnie in dismissal, and the minute the girl was out the door she broke the seal and read the note.

Will not be able to join you for dinner but will do my best to see you at the rout later.

Respectfully, your husband,

Benjamin

"Ooh." The disappointment was acute enough she sat down abruptly on an embroidered chair, taking in a deep breath.

The dress, of course, was a wasted effort now. She fingered the material and shut her eyes in frustration. This battle was like swimming upstream fully clothed ... possible to make progress, or so she hoped, but hardly easy.

With as much dignity as possible, she rose to her feet again and prepared to go and have dinner alone.

If he was right about the location of the estate, he could travel there, check the premises, and perhaps be back in time for a waltz with his lovely wife.

His beautiful, beguiling, and currently *unavailable* wife.

Damnation.

Ratcliff Castle was thirty miles south of London and the only reason he knew of its existence was that a friend had an estate nearby. This acquaintance had mentioned that he'd heard it was for sale and then bought by a mysterious owner through a third party. That would not be so remarkable by itself—many wealthy landowners chose to keep their identities secret—but the servants had immediately been dismissed, a small new staff hired in London, and the owner, as far as anyone could tell, had never been in residence. At the time Ben had only half listened, counted it as an eccentricity on the part of the man who wanted the property, and then dismissed it as unimportant.

But was it?

Case in point: one of the main distinguishing features of Ratcliff was a single tower, once designed to hold prisoners of the highest rank, usually those who were more inconvenient than dangerous. Cromwell and his infamous Roundheads had in particular used it to secretly house political enemies they didn't dare outright murder.

Just the sort of place, Ben mused as the carriage rattled forward, *that might be used to keep a notorious viscount who enjoyed a very rare whiskey.* When he'd gone to the address where the shopkeeper had delivered the liquor, it had turned out to be a small company that handled finding employment, and with some monetary persuasion the agent had told Ben he'd been hired by a solicitor to find a fine chef and arrange for transportation for him and the case of whiskey. Their destination was Ratcliff Castle.

The entire situation was a paradox. Why did someone hire an agent to purchase expensive libations if there was harm intended to the victims of a kidnapping? On the other side of the coin, what had been gained by Lord Andrews and Lady Elena's disappearance?

The answer to the latter was rather simple, actually.

Scandal.

Ben had been coming to that conclusion all along once he accepted that they hadn't run off voluntarily together, so he wasn't sure he really needed to hurry to save them, as the damage had already largely been done. However, he had weighed the option of not rushing out and decided that Alicia would prefer her cousin's timely rescue to dinner and polite conversation.

Hopefully, he was correct. With her, it seemed, he was wrong often enough. A humbling realization, that.

"Do you really think," Adam Altamont asked him, his long legs crossed at the ankle, "that some toff who owns a castle would kidnap a lord and a debutante and then take the time to serve the viscount his favorite spirits?"

When venturing into a duel with an unknown enemy it was usually best to have a second, and as Altamont was aware he was searching for Andrews already, not to mention they hadn't had time this week yet for their routine meeting about his racers, when ordering his carriage around Ben had asked Adam to accompany him.

The man had a point. Ben lifted a brow. "I think that the only person in London who enjoys Blaven whiskey has disappeared and someone else bought several bottles of it and had it delivered to Ratcliff Castle. There seems to be a straight line from one point to the other."

"Or some eccentric bloke also likes the blasted stuff."

"By all accounts it is quite an acquired taste that very few actually acquire, except some locals on the Isle of Skye. The distiller makes only a few cases a year. I have no idea how Andrews found it in the first place, but he goes through some not-inconsiderable expense to keep it on hand."

"That's curious, I admit." His trainer looked thoughtful.

"What if," Ben pointed out, "you wanted a normally wary man to act in a reckless way?"

"His favorite liquor would be a logical choice," Adam agreed. "Rather a backhanded strategy, though. Don't you think?"

"Yes, in fact, I do." It gave some insight to the way the villain's mind worked.

"So what precisely is the plan, if I might ask, my lord? I cannot see you walking briskly up to the door, knocking, and asking if Andrews and the fair lady are being held in chains in the dungeon."

"No, I suppose that wouldn't do." Ben stifled a laugh. "I was more thinking that perhaps we might take a look around for ourselves. No house is impenetrable."

"Broke into one or two, have you?" Altamont looked openly amused. "I'm actually not all that surprised, if you don't mind me saying so. You've the air of a man who knows what he's about. That is why I took on your stable. If you were so convinced I could train your horses, then I wasn't going to argue."

"I thought you were cocky enough for it."

Adam laughed, his dark eyes alight. "I was nervous as Hades, my lord, to be truthful."

"A win at Ascot with Hermes in your first season? I'd say you proved yourself quickly enough. It seemed to silence your detractors nicely." It had been the highlight of the summer before and Ben was not likely to forget that Adam had trained that horse since he was a colt. Even the most promising foal might amount to nothing in the wrong hands.

His trainer said emphatically, "Raphael will beat his time."

"Do you honestly think so?"

"He already has." Adam nodded, his smile holding a hint of self-satisfaction. "I wasn't going to tell you for a few weeks because he isn't reliable in the stretch yet, but since the subject has come up, why not now? Just in case we spend the rest of the evening hauled up in front of a magistrate, you should know. They are only likely to toss you in a posh cell in Newgate for a night or two. I might hang from a gibbet."

"I would never let them hang a trainer with such promise," Ben said drily. "But let's not get caught, shall we? All I wish is to know is if Andrews is at the estate. If he is there voluntarily, then so be it. But the question will remain about Lady Elena's whereabouts. It doesn't seem to me he'd forfeit his responsibilities in London in such a cavalier fashion, but often enough the measure of a man is a mystery if you don't know him well, and sometimes even if you do. Either way, he seems to be the only man in England to like that particular whiskey, and just a few days ago those bottles were delivered to Ratcliff. The possible connection intrigues me."

"Or maybe a hearty Scot from where the stuff is distilled has rented out the castle," Adam pointed out with due logic, his good-looking face reflective. "But I suppose if a man disappears like a puff of smoke, there isn't much else to go on, is there? His stable master said he didn't even take his favorite horse."

Ben stifled a laugh at the disbelief in his companion's voice. When a man lived and breathed horses, that was obviously unthinkable. "Or his carriage. So if he did whisk Lady Elena away, how did he do it? He could have hired a hack, I suppose, but what would be the point when he had a perfectly good vehicle of his own at his disposal?"

Besides, the story from the man who tried to ransom back the watch didn't support a voluntary absence from London. If he was to be believed, he'd witnessed a kidnapping.

The trip was less than two hours and passed quickly

as they discussed Ben's bloodstock. What Ben had told Alicia was true. He had a passion for watching his horses race, and even more so, was competitive enough to want them to win. The stable he'd inherited from his father had been a fine one but he intended to make it the best in England. He was almost surprised when the carriage came to a halt.

Even though it was dark there was a rising moon. It wasn't difficult to discern the correct location of the estate, for the single turret rose in silhouette on one end of what appeared to be from the distance a sprawling country house with a forested park surrounding it and an ornate gate that was firmly shut.

It really wasn't all that remote, the village only a few miles on, but it *was* quite private. Ben clambered out of the carriage and instructed his driver to wait with the vehicle in the shadows of a nearby copse of trees. "We'll go on foot," he told Adam. "Or you can stay here if you don't wish to participate."

Adam gave him a level look. "I didn't come along to back out now, my lord."

"I believe Lord Andrews was abducted. As that constitutes a breach of English law, I am not sure just what we might encounter. If, indeed, he is here at all. Just a word of warning."

Altamont gazed toward the mansion. "There's only one light I can see in the windows, which is surprising in such a large house. Even for the country, it is early for everyone to have retired."

"But also convenient for us to have the place so dark." Ben slipped a set of picklocks from his pocket and deftly went to work on the gate under Altamont's amused stare. Moments later they were slipping through and quietly shutting it behind them. His trainer was right: there was only one light in the house in a downstairs window. Almost instantly Ben was aware the grounds were not deserted no matter that the house seemed so quiet. Grateful for the moonlight, he heard the crunch of boots on the crushed stone of the drive and caught Adam's arm, drawing him to the left where a venerable elm spread majestic branches and cast deep, inky shadows. Luckily, as a man used to dealing with skittish horses, Adam understood the need for quiet when it was warranted.

Interesting. There appeared to be a man walking the grounds as if on patrol, in a manner Ben recognized from the war, a musket hanging loosely in the crook of one arm, his gait nonchalant and unhurried.

At least it was a musket, not a rifle, and the patrol looked perfunctory at best.

What a choice of words, he thought with an inner wince. The last time he'd heard that word it had been applied to the way he kissed his wife. Hopefully, she no longer felt that way, but what happened next was going to have to wait until this current drama was resolved.

Locked gate. Armed guard. The whiskey . . .

That all was promising, but without Andrews, he still knew nothing. Truthfully, while he was curious as to what might have happened to the viscount, Elena was his true concern.

There was an advantage to having experience with reconnaissance but he had to admire Adam for his ability to stay absolutely still as the man walked past, neither of them so much as moving a muscle even as the waft of tobacco and ale drifted to them on the night air and his breathing was audible, he was so close.

As soon as he was far enough away they silently moved toward the house in unspoken agreement, skirting the tall trees, staying to the depths of the shadows, and, if Ben had ever entertained the notion of walking up to the door and knocking politely, that was long gone. Instincts were invaluable, but considering the patrol he didn't need his gut to tell him this was enough out of the ordinary that further investigation was necessary.

"I think we will go to the back garden," Ben murmured, leading the way past a willow near a pond that was no doubt very picturesque in the daylight. "In my experience those windows are the easiest to access."

Adam laughed in response, his chuckle suppressed but still audible enough to cause a twinge of alarm. "I bow to your expertise, my lord."

Perhaps Ben might have said something caustic in response, but at that moment he caught a glimpse of something pale under the trees, just a glimmer in the moonlight, a flash that might have been a trick of the illumination, but he stopped dead by the side of a bush that held a plethora of fragrant white flowers and waited.

It seemed they weren't the only ones besides the guard creeping about the grounds, because he realized in the next second that there were two figures moving forward under the trees, going from tree to tree much as they were, and one of them had long golden hair and was dressed in some sort of light flowing robe and the other was tall and dark and unmistakably male.

It took a moment to assimilate. While he'd wondered if he might find the *ton*'s most notorious couple together after all, he hadn't really expected it. There was also the question of how to approach them quietly without alarming them and therefore the armed guard.

This entire evening, he decided at that moment, *is hardly going as planned.* He'd missed dinner with his wife, no doubt losing whatever ground he might have gained. Now he was not just hungry and ankle deep in dew-soaked grass, but also about to risk being shot at if the fleeing couple was startled enough to alert the guard.

"My lord," Altamont said urgently, pointing.

"I see them," he replied drily. "This will be the tricky part. Follow my lead."

Chapter 16

Ran put out a cautionary hand behind him, making sure he was far enough in front of Elena that if there was actual danger he would be the first in harm's way. After all the trouble taken it was unrealistic to think they could just walk away, and just as he suspected, that possibility appeared unlikely.

However, he had to admit he was puzzled.

The guard—the bewhiskered one with the belligerent attitude and the pistol, stepped into the slanting moonlight as he strolled, unconcerned, back up the path toward the house. He was armed now as well. For the first time in five days Ran could smell the grass and the sweet night air, and hear the ordinary call of a night bird, which on a normal basis would not be something he even acknowledged but would never take for granted again.

As satisfying as it was to have escaped, he did wonder who the devil the two men were standing in the shadows, also watching the guard walk away. It was too dark to see them properly but he had no doubt they were aware of his presence and Elena hidden behind him.

There were times when a man could simply feel danger. It was there in the prickles along the nape of the neck, a sudden sweat on the palms, and even a deep twist in the stomach. None of that was happening, though, because he sensed the interlopers were just as anxious as he was to not be discovered.

Both were tall. At least his height, and one could be a few inches more. They were very still, not speaking, but he'd already discerned they were simply waiting.

For what?

"That looks like remarkably like Ben."

He turned, admittedly confused by the soft whisper. "Ben who?"

Elena's lips brushed his ear as she stood on tiptoe to whisper in response, which was quite a pleasant sensation. "It is difficult to tell in the uncertain light, but I have fairly keen vision . . . I think it is my cousin's husband, the Earl of Heathton."

Benjamin Wallace? Ran might have pointed out he thought it was *impossible* from this distance to discern the features of either of those two indistinct figures, but then one of them stepped forward, the clouds tore open for a moment, and he also recognized the earl with a singular jolt in the fleeting light.

Hadn't Heathton worked for the War Office? He thought that was true, and what that might have to do with his presence on the grounds Ran wasn't sure, but perhaps this was not the time to debate the whys and wherefores but to leave as quickly as possible. He'd wondered all along just how he and Elena were supposed to return to London with no coin whatsoever and clad only in their dressing gowns. He'd counted on his ability to improvise, but this was much, much better.

Surely, if Elena was his wife's cousin Heathton would help them. . . .

Yet he was reluctant, he decided, to risk her safety in any way. As the entire kidnapping had been beyond the realm of normal experience, was it logical he should trust a man he only knew in passing?

This needed to be handled quite carefully.

His arm circled Elena's waist and he drew her to the side. "I want you to stay here."

"Lord Heathton knows me."

"And perhaps that is good—or bad," he argued quietly. "We have no idea who was behind the abduction."

"You can't think he—"

"I don't know," he said in a steely voice. "Why is he here? Who is that with him? Let me go talk to them. Stay right in this spot. If it doesn't seem to be going well, run back to the house. LaSalle will keep you safe." He smiled crookedly. "Or at least well fed."

"I am hardly going to run off," she said with vehemence, even though she was speaking in nothing but a hushed whisper. "You aren't even armed, and, besides, I may not know him well, but Heathton is *not* behind this. If anything, he is here to help. Alicia adores him and she is not a fool."

Trusting the judgment of romantic young women was hardly a prudent choice, but Ran found himself not having much latitude, especially as the earl and his companion were now coming toward them, soft-footed across the grass.

Not to mention the delicate fragrance of Elena's hair was distracting and he was loath to let her go, her body warm where it rested against him, the familiarity both comfortable and arousing. He was used to contact with women, but it occurred to him even as he tightened his arm protectively around her that this felt very . . . right.

All of her, from her head to her dainty toes. And it wasn't just the perfect size of her full breasts or the dip of her waist or the length of her slender legs. When this was over, which it possibly was at this moment, he would miss her company and not just in a physical sense.

He'd never felt quite such a sense of companionship with a woman.

Not the most opportune moment for that sort of revelation.

"Elena. Lord Andrews. I hoped I'd find you here." Heathton nodded formally but his voice was so low the words were barely audible.

Considering the circumstances it was a rather calm statement, not to mention they were both wearing dressing gowns and nothing else. Ran responded urgently, "Shall we discuss this elsewhere?"

"A capital idea," Heathton's companion agreed. "It isn't like our friend with the gun won't be back. His lordship has a carriage waiting."

The earl looked at Elena. "Are you well? Alicia has been very concerned."

Under other circumstances, Ran might have taken umbrage since Elena had been with him the entire time, but he understood. They'd been missing for nearly a week and, in truth, they were essentially undressed. Elena nodded. "I'm unharmed. Do not worry."

Thus reassured, Heathton seemed to agree action was the best course. "This way. I've already unlocked the gate."

"Unlocked how?"

The tall, dark-haired one said with a cheeky smile, "With a picklock. Like his lordship had been raised in the gutters of London his whole life. Took him about a wink of an eye. I admit I was impressed."

Ran didn't actually care about the earl's questionable talents, but that was interesting, and still not *as* interesting as being able to decamp as soon as possible. "The guard is armed."

"So we saw. Are you that dangerous, Andrews?" Heathton at first sounded flippant, but then Ran realized he was more posing a contemplative question out loud. "And as for armed, so am I."

"I was in the war," he answered quietly, "and I'm a good shot."

"And you like Blaven whiskey, which led me here."

That was certainly a point to ponder, but at a later time . . . when there wasn't a man prowling the grounds with a gun.

"Lead us out of here now," Ran muttered, "and I will be forever in your debt."

It was almost too easy.

After being locked in a tower for the better part of a week to simply be ushered through the gate and to a waiting carriage seemed absurdly simple, though it was ominous to think her cousin's husband was carrying a weapon, not to mention the guard she'd clearly seen patrolling the grounds was also armed.

If anyone was hurt . . .

Not to mention she should be embarrassed. After all, there she was with three men, clad in nothing but a dressing gown, her hair loose. Never mind if she was politely handed into the carriage as if they were departing from a formal ball; the fact remained the situation was highly irregular.

The Earl of Heathton's companion suggested, "I'll ride up with the driver in case there is pursuit."

Ben nodded. "Good idea."

Arranging her skirts demurely, Elena tried to ignore that two very tall males took up most of the space as they lurched away and considered the requisite explanation for not only her absence, but also being in the company of Randolph Raine at some obscure estate, wearing nothing but a dressing gown.

Nothing glib and believable came to mind.

The surreal effect of the past week was like a residue she couldn't wash off, but Elena heard the swift clop of the horses' hooves on the road in an echo that reflected relief as they started away.

Home. She was on her way home.

Five days. She'd never even thought about how much five days might change someone's life. In her case, *irrevocably*.

Her bare toes were visible. Hardly the normal venue in a young woman's life, but neither of the men seemed to notice. Instead they eyed each other with wariness and a strange sort of calm, male adversarial acceptance that she caught but didn't quite understand.

The dynamics were tense, she realized that.

Why was another matter.

"You traced me through the Blaven?" Ran quirked a brow, lounging back on the seat next to her, unshaven and rumpled, his presence protectively close.

Ben took a moment to respond. Elena had never been sure what to make of her cousin's standoffish husband and this moment was no different. He was actually quite handsome, with even features and a pair of truly vivid hazel eyes, but he tended to not put himself forward, and before now she'd not thought of him other than as an aristocrat who was unremarkable aside from his title and fortune. However, a glance at his set face belied that assumption, and when he spoke his words were weighted.

"It is an unusual choice in drink, I'm told."

Ran's mouth curved into a smile. "So I understand. Don't ask me why I favor it but I do. How did you hear of it?"

"Your mutual absence along with that of Elena's was noted."

"Yet I doubt, no matter how bored the *ton* might be, that my taste in whiskey was ever fodder for the gossip mill."

"Your aunt mentioned it."

"Janet?"

"Yes. She was also adamant you would never leave your sister voluntarily."

"She's perfectly right. Lucy is very important to me and I take my responsibility as her guardian seriously."

Elena knew it was true. Through conversation and his concern over what his sister might be thinking over his absence that had become very clear to her.

It made him rather more attractive and that was not needed in the case of the magnetic Lord Andrews. Even now, in contrast with their companion, who was not formally dressed but certainly wearing more than a dressing gown, he seemed comfortable with himself, which might be, she acknowledged silently, a great deal of his charm. He didn't apologize for who or what he was. She would never say he considered it beneath him, but she might venture that he was not bothered with protocol.

All fine and well if a person was male, privileged, and wealthy, but she had more stringent parameters on her behavior. "We are both concerned over our families,"

Elena said firmly, bringing their focus her direction. "What has my father told everyone?"

Benjamin Wallace regarded her with his usual enigmatic expression. "He hasn't said much publicly about your sudden absence, but I can tell you personally that he's been quite beside himself with worry."

"That doesn't surprise me." She smiled but had a feeling it was a bit wan. "He appears much more detached than he actually is."

"I agree. Now, then, we've two hours back to London barring any interference in our departure. I'd appreciate it if you would recount to me what happened step by step."

"We were both drugged and kidnapped," Ran answered with unswerving vehemence. "It was meticulously planned, if you ask me. Neither of us recalls any of the actual abduction." He then proceeded to briefly outline the general tedium of their captivity—leaving out those memorable moments spent in each other's arms—and concluding with LaSalle's aid in their escape.

When he finished, Ben said neutrally, "I would guess it would have to be a clever plan to take you off guard, but you wouldn't be expecting it. Would you?"

It took a moment for Elena to register the barely veiled accusation. It wasn't precisely unfriendly but it wasn't cordial either. Next to her Ran didn't move a muscle. "If you are inferring that it might have been due to a personal dispute, I am going to say to you what I said to Elena right after we realized our predicament. Why would anyone seek to punish me by locking me in with a very beautiful young woman?"

That didn't seem to faze Ben, his brow merely elevating a fraction. "Because they know you better than most?

Because they realize that if the circumstances warranted it, you would marry her rather than ruin a young lady's reputation? Let us keep in mind that the same person knew an intimate detail such as your preference in whiskey."

Would he marry me? Elena was not as sure, and from the expression on Ran's face he wasn't either. He'd flat-out said he wouldn't but that was when he'd thought she might have been party to his abduction. Responsibility was one thing; coercion another. In a hard voice he said, "I cannot think of someone who knows me that well who would ever put me in this position."

"Then we need to explore the possibilities of who you might *not* know so well—or think you don't—that would want to remove you from the whirl of London society for a short while. Though we actually can't be sure how long your stay at the castle was planned, you tell me the chef was due to be released after a week, which gives us a time frame of sorts. Tell me, what was supposed to happen in your life during your absence?"

Ran narrowed his eyes. "Nothing significant that I remember."

Elena chose to put in. "Lord Andrews seems to think this was more directed at me than him."

"Yes, I get that impression," Ben murmured. "It is possible, of course, that some sort of retaliation against your father is involved. He has been under some considerable emotional duress not just over the possibility his daughter might have come to harm but the general implications of your disappearance. And, if you will forgive me, at times he can appear a trifle pompous, especially when it comes to his political views. And let us not forget your fiancé."

The roundabout way of mentioning the impending disaster that lay ahead did not escape her. "My father seems much more haughty than he actually is," she told her cousin's husband with a glimmer of a smile, because, in truth, social ruin might be imminent but she was so relieved to be free that she refused to worry over it at the moment.

"So Alicia assures me," he said drily, but he returned her smile, which was rather rare for him. "And since this has happened, I believe it to be true. When he first came to see me, he was quite emotional."

Why her father had immediately turned to Lord Heathton she wasn't sure, but as they drove along in the dark toward home, it had obviously turned out to be a fortuitous choice. "Did you tell him where you were going this evening?"

"No. I wasn't at all sure that my deductions about your location were correct or, in fact, if the two of you would be together. What about Colbert?"

"What about him, in what way?"

"I think he's asking if he could have anything to do with the abduction." Ran didn't look at her. "Since I am going to conjecture that everyone thinks we have been together for the past five days."

It wasn't like she didn't know their mutual disappearances would be linked together. "With all due honesty," she said quietly, "I don't know him well enough to answer about any speculation in that quarter. I can't see why he would have any motivation to have me compromised unless he wanted to cry off for some reason, but surely he could simply sever the marriage agreement."

Ben's gaze seemed to hold a measure of new respect. "I see you understand the gravity of your current position."

"There has been little else to contemplate, my lord."
She demurely folded her hands, though a tiny shiver
touched her. Her newfound freedom was hardly perfect.
There was a scandal to deal with and she could sense
that Ran was thinking along the same lines.

"Colbert could have a vindictive enemy." Ran's voice
held an edge.

"It's possible," Ben said slowly, settling back in his
seat.

*There is nothing quite like alighting in a fashionable
neighborhood clad in a dressing gown and nothing else,*
Ran decided with a twinge of wry humor as the vehicle
rocked to a halt. Hopefully most of the *ton* was out and
about for the evening, but the servants would whisper
and that was just inevitable.

At least Heathton had loaned Elena his evening
jacket, not that it covered everything, but it did afford a
semblance of propriety. Unfortunately, it emphasized
her femininity, her fair hair spilling over the dark lapels,
her slender form dwarfed by the size of the garment.

Ran hesitated for a moment as the door to the vehicle
opened, the earl's assistant in their strange rescue standing back after lowering the step. Elena gazed at him with
shadowed eyes, her expression hard to decipher.

Very aware of Heathton sitting across from them, he
said formally, "It has been quite an adventure, Lady
Elena."

"Indeed it has." There was the slightest tremulous
note to her voice.

Why the devil he hesitated to exit was a mystery even
to him. "I feel confident we will see each other soon."

With a hint of the humor he admired in her, she murmured, "Perhaps we can even be properly introduced, Lord Andrews."

To his surprise, what he wanted more than anything was a good-bye kiss. Maybe that was what kept him in his seat, unmoving, when escape was in his reach. His past love affairs had involved mutual pleasure but also mutual detachment, and this had been, needless to say, entirely different.

Or maybe *she* was different.

That possibility was what pulled him convulsively to his feet and toward the door.

Chapter 17

The ballroom was something to see *en fête*.

This was one of the premier events of the season, which was why Alicia had insisted they both attend, but as she was announced she had a sinking feeling that the Countess of Heathton would be attending this particular event alone. Placing her gloved hand on the banister she descended the stairs and did her best to smile graciously. Luckily, since this was such a fashionable event her sister was in attendance, and at once she sought her out.

"Hattie."

Harriet turned, her eyes a similar dark blue to Alicia's own, questioning. "I heard you'd arrived. Where is Benjamin?"

That was certainly the question of the hour. Alicia answered, "Detained, it seems. He sent a note. Goodness, it appears all of London is here. I must say you look splendid this evening."

Fingering the fabric of her deep rose taffeta gown, Harriet laughed lightly as she eyed Alicia's daring neckline. "Thank you, but not half as stunning as you. I love the gold silk. So dramatic. And bold for you."

And worn possibly for nothing, but she refused to dwell on it so Alicia said brightly, "I was assured it would set off my unusual coloring, though being referred to as unusual was actually not that flattering. I assume you were luckier than I and Oliver accompanied you?"

Her sister's husband was a young baronet, his knighthood granted because of his service as a minister to the king in some vague capacity that Alicia had never questioned but suspected had something to do with his very influential grandfather.

"Yes, he is here somewhere." Harriet companionably linked her arm through Alicia's. "The card room, probably. Shall we get some champagne? I'm anticipating questions I can't answer about Elena's continued absence all evening and could use some fortitude."

"That is an excellent idea."

And it was, for the first glass. The second was a bit cloying, and when almost two hours later Alicia accepted a third from a passing footman with a tray, she was truly irritated. It wasn't so much being left without an escort. That was common enough in English society as to be unremarked. It was Ben's *promise* to join her and choice not to that rankled. He was infinitely more of a gentleman than that, not to mention his cryptic note had told her nothing about why he was so conspicuously absent. Yes, he'd had a tendency to not accompany her often in the past, but usually there was not a broken promise involved.

How ironic, since after that soul-satisfying kiss, she'd been so encouraged.

"Lady Heathton, how lovely to see you."

Oh, Lord, she thought crossly. Really, this was not the time to run into the very silly Tillitson woman, but what choice was there than to offer as gracious a smile possible? "I feel quite the same. Are you enjoying yourself this evening?"

The older woman waved a hand in dismissal. "I am never sure why I attend these events other than it is such bad form to refuse all the invitations."

Flighty as Mrs. Tillitson was, maybe that was a valid point. Alicia considered it and then nodded. "I suppose you are right. In our quest to stay admitted to the inner circles we all do things we perhaps would not do if given a choice."

Over the rim of her glass the other woman gave her a knowing look. "Your husband does not suffer from that malady." The tilt of her head was reminiscent of an inquisitive bird. "Well, that is not accurate. He goes his own way."

"I didn't realize you knew him so well." It was unintentional, but Alicia's voice was cool.

"I don't. No one does. But wait. Here he is after all, I see."

What might have been said next would forever be a mystery because suddenly a hand touched Alicia's waist and she heard a familiar voice murmur, "I am unforgivably late."

Benjamin.

How true.

The warmth of her husband's breath against her neck made her entire body go taut. Rarely did he touch her in public, which made the caress even more meaningful. It was almost mortifying how Mrs. Tillitson smiled knowingly and wandered away in her vague fashion, but it was outweighed by the shiver of anticipation that shot through her. "Well, perhaps not unforgivably, though I was starting to feel somewhat neglected."

"I had to run a small errand that took longer than anticipated."

He had a certain way of smiling that did not involve his mouth. She wasn't sure how it happened but she did recognize it. It was obvious he'd stopped to change, for he was in full evening kit, the stark formality of his tailored attire strikingly masculine.

"Did you, now?"

"Can I purchase some amnesty if I tell you that my absence involved recovering your lost cousin?"

"Elena?"

"Please tell me you don't have another missing relative. I was hoping we would be able to waltz at least once this evening. Shall we?"

The orchestra *had* struck up a popular tune, she realized, and she was much too off guard to resist when he took her hand—not that she would have resisted anyway. He was actually a very competent dance partner. That was hardly a surprise. If he made an effort he was competent at just about anything.

Except the intimacy she craved, but it was apparently not a lost cause. He'd just kissed her neck in public, which had shocked her. That would not go unremarked. Not that she cared so much what everyone else thought, but as a gesture it was effective. A display of affection was hardly the normal course of the lives of most married couples of their class.

"Did you really find Elena?" she asked as she placed her hand on his shoulder, looking into his eyes, the vivid hazel color mesmerizing.

"Indeed." Ben swept her easily into the first turn. "It is an interesting story, but I will let her tell you if she wishes it. For now all I will say is that she is safe and she is home, and I made all due speed to get here so we could share a dance."

"She's well?"

"It certainly seemed so."

That was reassuring and a relief but she desired to know more. Alicia's skirts brushed his boots as they moved fluidly to the music. "How did you find her?"

"Whiskey."

That made no sense whatsoever, but she was frequently in the dark due to his cryptic nature. She narrowed her eyes. "What?"

"Never mind." His hand was strong at her waist, his mouth faintly smiling. "Shall we leave it that I did find her, as per your request?"

Did he actually think she'd just accept that? "I am grateful, my lord, but that is hardly an explanation. Where was she? Why did she leave no word? Were she and Lord Andrews together after all? How did—"

He interrupted her. "Why are women always so inquisitive?"

"Why are men always so vague?" she countered, but her heart really wasn't in the argument. Elena was safe, even if he wasn't willing to tell her just what had happened, and at the moment he was holding her—what might even be considered a fraction too close for propriety—and had just intimated that he'd hurried so he could waltz with her.

He leaned forward and whispered in her ear. "On the contrary, we can be quite direct if we wish to be. For instance, may I say you are the most beautiful woman in attendance this evening?"

His wife stared up at him with those glorious dark blue eyes, her glossy dark hair done in a style he never recalled her wearing before, the décolletage of her gown showcasing her glorious breasts in a fashion he was sure — to his annoyance — every man in the ballroom had noticed. The topaz color of the material set off her porcelain skin and emphasized a beauty that he felt didn't need embellishment, and a delicate fragrance of roses drifted from her hair as he tightened his arm around her waist and brought her just a shade closer.

"You are trying to distract me, but thank you." Her voice was hushed. "I confess I hoped you'd admire this gown."

"It isn't the gown I admire." It was a reckless statement but he was in that sort of mood. The mission to find Lady Elena was done — not as expediently as he wished, but satisfactorily. It was also already evident that Alicia had forgiven him for being late and he had high hopes that a successful seduction was in his immediate future.

It was remarkable to realize that he'd even lost his sense of affront over having to exert himself to gain an invitation to her bed. It was proving to be an enlightening challenge. When he'd courted her it had been a matter of both practicality and physical attraction, but he was beginning to admire her in other ways also, which was, at a guess, exactly what she wanted.

His beautiful wife was clever as well as beguilingly attractive.

Perhaps unknowingly he'd met his match.

The music came to a stop and he didn't realize it right away, which was disconcerting in and of itself. Alicia demurely slid her hand from his shoulder and allowed him to escort her from the floor, and he was never so grateful as when he heard her say, "I know you have just arrived, my lord, but it is quite late."

"Extremely so," he agreed at once, though it actually was early by *ton* standards.

"Will you forgive me if I ask you to take me home?"

He'd kiss her feet for the privilege—*which might be an enjoyable undertaking,* he thought, picturing her dainty instep—but instead of pointing that out he merely said, "Whatever you wish from this evening, it is yours."

"I am not sure yet what I wish."

That is a disappointing response, he decided, but it could be interpreted in several ways and he chose to remain optimistic. In his adult life he'd certainly been abstinent for longer stretches of time than this one, but, then Alicia had not been so tantalizingly close by yet off-limits.

He *could* point out his tardiness was due to his quest to retrieve her kidnapped cousin.

He could also mention that he'd been extraordinarily patient where other husbands might not be so tolerant.

But the truth was, he found he wanted her to *want* him, so he was willing to take responsibility for the inauspicious start to their marriage. He'd evidently wasted half a year.

"That is fine," he said neutrally, rewarded when his wife sent him a sharp look.

"You aren't upset over . . . waiting?"

Was she piqued or just asking? "I'm obviously not willing to ask you to do something that you don't wish to do."

A man could not be more fair or concise, in his opinion.

"It isn't I don't wish it. I've already told you that."

It was a start. He liked the very slight suggestive tone of her voice and the way her gloved fingers tightened on his arm.

"I'm gratified to hear it."

"Ben," she said reproachfully.

"Alicia," he responded with as much composure as possible, "you were the one who extended the ultimatum."

"It wasn't—"

"Oh, indeed, it was."

She said quietly, "We have been over this before. It wasn't intended as such."

"Perhaps we should discuss it at home in private."

She understood the insinuation—or he was fairly sure she did, because she nodded and allowed him to guide her through the crowd. When they reached the doors, she accepted her cloak with a gracious smile, and though he'd only stayed for one dance didn't comment on the already waiting carriage, which he had to admit was not very subtle.

Once he'd handed her in, she gazed at him as he settled on the opposite seat.

"You came for me and never did have the intention of staying."

That direct declaration took him off guard. Yet it was true. The thought of her dancing with other men—and, even worse, thinking he'd not bothered to attend when he'd said he would—had driven Ben to change his clothes in record time once he'd delivered Andrews and Lady Elena home. His wife was disconcertingly right. He'd come for her.

"I said I would attend and I did feel a sense of responsibility to attend." The moment the words were out he felt ridiculous. Even more so like he'd cheated her in some way. As if it had been more about his pride in keeping his word than a desire for her company, so he quickly amended, "But, yes, you are correct. I came for you."

Whatever his wife wanted it must have been close to what he'd just said, for she smiled at him then, leaning back against the squabs in her vivid golden gown, all glorious female beauty, her ankles lightly crossed under her silken skirts. "I find it difficult to ever know what you are thinking, so it is hardly a given to assume I understand your motives. I came this evening because we'd agreed to the invitation, not because it was a test of some sort. You needn't look so wary."

Ben elevated a brow. "You wanted your cousin returned and I obliged."

Alicia brushed a silky dark curl off her enticingly bared shoulder. Her exhale was audible. "I am grateful you were successful. Infinitely so. My entire family will be, but—"

"Your entire family will not know. I'd just as soon keep it between you, me, Elena, and your uncle."

His wife just looked at him from across the carriage, one hand going to the strap by her seat as they rocked around the corner. "Why?"

For whatever reason, in his life he'd always found that a difficult question to answer. *What, where, when,* and *who* were all a great deal more simple. *Why* involved motivation and other complex human emotions and he was not interested in dissecting his own mind. "It will make me uncomfortable to receive thanks where none is really due. I merely drew a few conclusions."

"I doubt it was that simple at all."

It had involved a bit more; that was true. He shrugged. "What is important is that she is unharmed."

"But not unscathed."

Alicia was not a fool, and despite her age, not naive either. He acknowledged, "I doubt you are the only one with questions. Andrews will also not escape this easily."

"So they were together after all?" Alicia's eyes widened. "I cannot imagine it. He is the last kind of man my cousin would choose to run off with. She is already engaged, after all."

The viscount's air of familiarity with the beauteous Elena begged an argument on that point, but they had been imprisoned together and adversity could make for friendships—or more—that might otherwise not come about. Ben chose to not pursue the line of conversation. "I am sure she will be much more forthcoming with you over what happened than she was with me."

The corner of his wife's mouth tilted upward in unconcealed amusement. "You didn't ask, did you?"

"Do I think they eloped or he coerced her? No."

"Darling, you have a unique way of never answering a question in a direct manner."

And *she* had a unique way of firing his blood—perhaps that was why of all the debutantes and eager misses he'd encountered since he'd come into his majority Alicia was the one who had caught his interest.

"Perhaps," he said softly, "you aren't asking me the right questions."

Chapter 18

He had lain down a challenge.

It would be more of an incentive to best him, but she was too vulnerable to play this unfamiliar game much longer, and, quite truthfully, she was coming to the gratifying conclusion that as experienced and clever as Benjamin might be, he wasn't proficient at it either.

Neither of them had played for these stakes.

Perfect.

Suddenly her palms were damp. Her breath caught, and as the carriage rocked to a halt Alicia was not at all sure how to respond. He had made an open attempt for the two of them to find a level field on which to joust, and she was unskilled at the sport.

The offensive seemed best. "The right questions? That is a quandary. What would you ask if you were in my position?"

There was a glimmer of approval in his eyes. Or was it just a hint of respect? Maybe a subtle recognition that she was not so easily dismissed. . . . Whatever it might be, she was fascinated.

He got out of the carriage in his usual effortless fashion. In his dark evening wear he was impressively elegant as he offered his hand. "What would *I* ask? Can we discuss it upstairs?"

Yes, indeed they could. And she had a feeling she understood exactly where the discussion would lead, but she was determined to maintain some control if possible.

If possible . . .

"I'm no longer an uncertain bride," she said for his ears alone as she clasped his fingers, lifting her silk skirts in her other hand.

"I think you have made that quite clear." He was obviously amused. "However, you might not be as sophisticated as you think."

Her very fear. Still, it was best to brazen it out since she'd come this far. "If not, it is up to you to educate me, my lord."

"An intriguing proposition. This has been a somewhat trying evening so far, but unless I am mistaken you have just offered me an opportunity to vastly improve it."

By making love to her. It was there in the clasp of his hand, in the intense look in his green-gold eyes, in the way his hands lingered at her waist as he lifted her from the conveyance.

For whatever reason she was suddenly more nervous than she had been on their wedding night. This would be different. She knew it as surely as the sun would rise the next morning, and since that had been her goal all along, it would be unfair for her to decline now. It wasn't accurate to say she'd accomplished all she wished in her marriage in just five days, but they had certainly made progress and that was what she'd asked of him.

"You are not mistaken."

"I concede that I am most happy to hear that."

Had the words not been so softly spoken maybe she

would have discounted them as mere rhetoric, but as Ben guided her toward the house, she sensed in him an unusual tension, which was oddly reassuring. *He* should *be nervous also,* she decided as they ascended the steps, because if this was the new beginning she wanted, he needed to guide her.

Certainly her mother's instructions for her wedding night had not helped. *Just lie there and shut your eyes.* A woman could passively allow her husband his conjugal rights—she had, in fact—but surely there was more to it. She'd come to the conclusion that perhaps he didn't realize how much she *wished* to enjoy it more and that was entirely her fault for never telling him.

Tonight, she vowed silently, she was going to be more honest. It was what she asked of him, after all, so only fair she should make an attempt as well.

Yeats had long since retired but a footman whisked open the door for them and Ben thanked him, his hand warm at the small of Alicia's back. The hallway was only lit by one lamp and the stairs elongated by the dim illumination, and the steps she'd walked up so many times suddenly were daunting.

"Don't falter now." Her husband leaned closer, his mouth brushing her temple in a light caress before he lifted her in his arms in a sweep of amber silk, ignoring her gasp. He carried her up the stairs with seeming ease, his lashes throwing shadows on his cheekbones, his expression difficult to interpret. This time he didn't seek her room but his, and took her directly to the huge bed in his bedchamber, deposited her without ceremony, and straightened. Long fingers went to his cravat. "You won't need your maid. I'll undress you. Completely."

The emphasis on the last word did not escape her and

Alicia could feel her pulse accelerate, the choice of using his room instead of hers significant, and she watched him shrug out of his coat. His shirt went next and the sleek musculature of his naked torso was a bit imposing, the lamp his valet had left burning throwing shadows across his chest and the flat plane of his stomach. He sat down to remove his boots, jerking them off and tossing them carelessly aside. "I'm not going to douse the light."

"Whatever you wish, my lord." Was her voice really that husky? And she was trembling. Not from fear but from something else she couldn't quite define. Alicia took in a deep breath.

"No."

"No?"

"Why don't we make this evening about what *you* wish?"

"Me?"

"You are the one who seems to have reservations over the romantic aspect of our marriage."

True enough, but the trouble was she wasn't sure what exactly she wanted. More intimacy, yes, but . . .

"Another kiss, perhaps?" Clad only in his breeches, Ben slid on top of her, balancing lightly on his elbows, his body heavy on hers but in a pleasant way. "You seemed to enjoy the last one."

She touched his hair, the strands thick and surprisingly soft considering the rest of him was hard—especially the rigid length she could feel through the fabric of his breeches. "I did."

"Let's see, shall we, if I can make this one even more memorable."

It was, she discovered, when he lowered his mouth to hers. Not because it was more tender or even more passionate, but because he very much took his time, tasting and teasing, his tongue doing a leisurely exploration, his arms braced and his hands otherwise not touching her. Still fully clad in a formal gown and even her slippers, Alicia wondered how it would be to have him kiss her this way if they were both naked—a rather scandalous speculation—but this was very nice also.

Extremely nice.

Not perfunctory at all. He lingered over it, nipping at the corners of her mouth, lightly tracing the curve of her lower lip and then capturing her mouth again ... and again. At some time he loosened her hair, but, caught up in the moment, she didn't remember it. *This,* she thought, running her hands across his shoulders, *is much more like what I'd imagined before we married.*

And then he did something entirely shocking. He deftly unfastened her gown and before she really knew it had happened, eased it down over her shoulders to bare her breasts, bent his head, and licked her nipple.

Of course he had touched her like that before, but it had always been under her nightdress, and in a room so dark she really could not see it, but it was startling how the vision of him, his mouth on her breast, brought a rush of heat between her thighs and the pleasure of it made a sigh she didn't intend escape her lips.

And her husband smiled. It was slight, just a curve of his lips, but against her sensitive flesh she felt it. He murmured, "You are entirely overdressed for this, my love."

The languid enjoyment stopped at the endearment and she went very still.

My love?

Was she his love?

*   *   *

He'd shocked her, but maybe not as much as he'd shocked himself.

My love. He was not one for endearments and had never employed that one before.

The slip had not been intentional and Ben paused, hovering over his wife's extremely delectable body, her dark hair spilled over the pale bed linens in a shining mass, her eyes gazing into his with a poignant sincerity that left him at a loss. One pink-tipped breast was still moist from his attentions, and, frankly, he wondered why he hadn't ever done this before.

Tonight he was going to strip her bare and enjoy every minute of making love to her, and duty to his title be damned. But he did wish he hadn't made that accidental slip.

It was possible he'd been looking at this the wrong way all along.

Love he was not ready yet to address but it needn't be discussed now, not with Alicia in delicious dishabille beneath him, receptive and ready. Or almost ready.

It hadn't been all that long since he'd shared her bed, but, then again, it had never been like this. He had unquestionably married out of obligation to his family because he'd inherited a title he'd never wanted all that much and the war was over. It was necessary to do what was expected and he had—as always, he realized— faced the situation with due resignation and gone forward.

However, there was nothing very logical about how soft Alicia was beneath him or how the tantalizing sweetness of her mouth caused a sheen of sweat over his whole body, or, for that matter, how delicious she looked half-dressed, her rich gown around her waist, the fullness of

her ivory breasts moving slightly with each audible in-
hale.

Physical desire was a predictable entity. The sexual act
itself was pleasurable, so it wasn't a surprise that he
wanted her, but what was a surprise was the intensity of
not just his arousal but the possessiveness that accompanied it.

Mine, he thought as he smoothed his hand over her
shoulder, downward, skimming his fingertips over the
curve of her breast and lower to catch the material of her
unfastened gown so he could completely remove it. He
lifted her and slid off her gown and chemise, leaving her
in just her stockings and slippers, the sight so erotic the
throbbing in his cock took urgency to a level that he
could never recall before. "You are incredibly beautiful."

She quivered when he touched the dainty dark triangle of her pubic hair, the color in her already-flushed
cheeks deepening, but she didn't try to turn away though
her slim hands flexed as she obviously resisted the urge
to cover herself. "I'm glad you think so," she whispered,
the words holding a feminine throatiness. "But I am hoping that is not all you admire about me, my lord."

"No," he said, taking off each slipper before unfasten-
ing a garter and easing a silk stocking down her smooth
thigh and calf, tossing it aside, "but I do admit I can't give
a list of your other admirable qualities at the moment. I
want to be inside you so badly that apparently my mind
has ceased to function."

Did she have any idea how glorious she looked, fully
naked when he dispensed with the other stocking, all
pale satin skin and lustrous dark hair, woman incarnate
and readied for her lover . . . ?

He doubted it. Most gentlemen treated their wives

differently than their lovers and so far he'd been no exception, but more and more he was starting to think that had been a grave error on his part. Yes, she was a lady—an innocent one when he married her—and despite that she had pointed out earlier she was no longer a bride, it was entirely his fault she was still inexperienced in the bedroom.

Tonight would be different.

Ben smoothed his hands upward over the sensitive flesh of her inner thighs and gently pushed. "Open for me."

"I—" She started to speak, stopped, and he guessed he'd never know what she was going to say because she took in a deep breath that made her breasts rise seductively and parted her legs.

The leap of faith would not go unrewarded. Ben lowered his head, parted the soft folds of her sex, and pressed his mouth in exactly the right spot. The first flick of his tongue stifled her initial stiffening in objection, and the second slow whirl brought her hands to his shoulders.

"Ben!"

The manner of address was almost as surprising as when he called her his love. She rarely used his given name, much less the shortened version.

He rather liked it, especially at the moment when he was licking, tasting her arousal, hearing the heightened cadence of her breathing.

Slowly he set about bringing her to climax, urging her higher and higher, his hands firm on her hips as he played upon her confusion and rising sexual tension, each small sound and gasp giving him a sense of satisfaction. To his gratification, when it happened she did not hold back but cried out and shuddered against him, her legs wide open now as the orgasm overtook her receptive body in quiver after quiver until she went limp.

Only then did he rise to unfasten his breeches with clumsy hands, shove them down his hips, step free, and join her again on the bed. "Call me Ben again," he told her, touching her cheek lightly, marveling at the incredible indigo color of her eyes. "Remind me that Lord and Lady Heathton are not in this bed."

Alicia wasn't positive she would ever quite recover from the glorious thing that had just happened, but before she had time to contemplate the matter, her husband was positioned between her legs, the pressure of his entry causing another shimmer of pleasure so acute she made a very, very unladylike sound of enjoyment.

His eyes closed, the lowering of his lashes slow and the rigidity of his muscles under her palms betraying more than the dusky hue of his flushed face or the obvious care he took to push his hard length into her body inch by inch. He'd always done so, every movement slow and measured, and now she realized that some of the disappointment of the past was that she'd caught glimpses of that rapturous burst he'd just given her in the most scandalous way possible—but it had been elusive.

In that single moment she'd understood a great deal more about the dynamics of the world of men and women.

She'd also learned something very important about her husband.

It had never occurred to her that he separated the man from the earl and his fortune and privilege.

"Alicia." He began to move in and out in long slow strokes, his gaze holding hers, his breath warm against her lips as he lowered his head to kiss her again. Under her hands his skin was hot and damp and it wasn't long before he shuddered and went still, the flood of his release forceful and deep inside her as the air left his lungs in a low groan.

Languid, enlightened, content to lie beneath him, she waited for what he might say next, because what had just happened had been . . . perfect. She did not wish to break the spell.

Neither did he apparently, because once their breathing had calmed, he simply eased free, rolled to his side, and put his arm around her waist.

At least he hasn't carried me to my room, she thought with philosophical jubilation, though it was no mystery as she drifted toward sleep that he was still wide awake, their bodies nestled together, his seed sticky between her thighs.

Without a doubt everything had changed for her this evening. Her last coherent thought was to wonder if it had changed for him? His silence could mean . . . anything.

Chapter 19

All conversation stopped so it was utterly quiet at the breakfast table when she first entered the room and sat down. She should not have been surprised, but Elena was fairly sure she was not the one who needed to speak first. It was unfortunate her grandmother was in residence now that the season was in full swing. The night before had been more the tearful reunion; now, in the light of day, it was time for the reckoning.

She and Ran had discussed what they would say when they escaped—if they escaped—but the finer details had not been ironed out. Since they had no idea why they'd been abducted, who had done it, or even how it had been orchestrated, even inventing a story was impossible. Now that it was over she was starting to realize that though getting away had seemed to be the most important thing just yesterday, this morning the who, how, and why were the least of her problems.

"A disaster." Her mother took the initiative and broke the silence, a piece of fruit from her compote on her fork, which she waved in the air as she obviously continued the discussion they'd been having before Elena's arrival. "Of monumental proportions."

"Gargantuan." Her Castilian grandmother agreed with appropriate emotion, motioning for more coffee with an imperious hand. "Enormous."

"And a good morning to you too." She picked up her spoon to stir some sugar into her coffee.

"I'm sorry, darling. Did you sleep well?"

She hadn't, actually. It was surprising how quickly a person became accustomed to sharing a bed. It wouldn't be very productive to point that out so she said instead, "It's good to be home."

"What do you think Lord Colbert is going to do?" Her grandmother looked at her pointedly.

As far as Elena was concerned he could cry off and she would not be in the least upset. After all, he did not have midnight silk hair and a quicksilver smile. He certainly never would have taught her the finer points of cheating at cards, nor, she suspected, would he have done such wickedly delicious things to her body. . . .

And this was not the time to sit around dreaming of the nefarious lord who never actually ruined her but who might possibly have ruined her contentment with a safe, orderly marriage.

"I admit I have no idea. I really don't know the man all that well." Which, she had to ponder as she tried to take a bite of coddled eggs, was ironic. Wasn't it?

God bless her aunt Margaret, who spoke up staunchly. "Elena is back safe and sound. I would think that, rather than bemoaning the possible whispers, we would all be celebrating."

"Of course." Her mother still gave Elena a reproving

stare. "But a person cannot ignore the future because the present has worked out in a satisfactory fashion. This is no longer a crisis"—her gaze did soften across the table—"but I am still concerned."

In general they did get along well, but Elena was well aware her mother held very strict views of the role women played in society. Becoming a wife and mother was the only option, and marrying well the ultimate goal.

"Elena and I will discuss this in my study later," her father said with his usual brusque authority, his quelling glance sweeping the occupants of the room. "Until that time I suggest we change the subject."

She couldn't help but wish that interview could be postponed, but with a sense of inevitability she did her best to eat, rather missing LaSalle's incomparable chocolate croissants, of which she'd become inordinately fond. When the meal was over she rose and followed her father down the hall to the hallowed sanctuary of his personal study, where she'd last been, she recalled, the day he'd informed her that he and Lord Colbert had come to an agreement on the marriage settlement and the engagement was official.

This promised to be a different sort of conversation.

"Please sit down, my dear." Her father motioned toward a chair. When she sank down, he took his usual spot behind his always tidy desk, the papers stacked in perfect piles, not a drop of ink on the blotter and his pipes lined up in an immaculate row next to the tobacco jar. When he folded his fingers together in a mannerism she knew well, she braced herself for a lecture, though, in this case, she could honestly say she was blameless.

Well, *almost*. Blameless for the abduction, blameless for being locked in a tower with London's most notorious womanizer, and blameless for arriving home the evening before in a state of undress. But while she still was technically a virgin, she wasn't blameless for the interludes spent in Ran's arms.

And curiously enough, she didn't regret it one bit.

"Last evening," her father began, "in the emotional aftermath of returning home to find that you were unharmed and restored to us, I was too overjoyed to ask probing questions. I am still overjoyed, but please understand that your mother is correct. Your safety was my most pressing concern; you seem well enough, and for that I am eternally grateful."

As far as she knew she'd never been in any real danger, though she had to admit that if it wasn't for LaSalle and Benjamin Wallace it was hard to say what their ultimate fate might have been. "I'm also happy to be home," she said neutrally, fingering the skirt of her pale rose muslin day gown. All the requisite garments were actually confining after a week's reprieve.

"Tell me exactly what happened."

Not an unexpected question. She'd debated how to answer it, and she and Ran were both well aware their story might not be believed, but nothing else would work either. How could a person—two persons, in this case— explain their mutual absence for five damning days? She still didn't know what they would say, but to her father she would give the truth.

She did, as succinctly as possible, explaining how she had awakened first, taking care to mention Ran's outraged accusation that she had possibly instigated the situation, and then going on to the guard, the silent servants, and finally the note to LaSalle and Lord Heathton's timely arrival. Her father listened without comment, though he drew his brows together once or twice, and when she finished, he looked at his clasped hands for several moments and then glanced back up. "I confess I am perplexed."

"So was Lord Andrews. He seems to think this might have more to do with me than him."

"Does he, now? You swear to me he did not persuade you to run off with him?"

She looked back steadily. "I should not have to swear. I just told you the absolute truth. If I were going to lie, trust me, I would make up something more believable. I feel ridiculous recounting the story but that is what happened."

For a moment, by her father's scowl she thought he might argue, but then he sighed, leaned back in his chair, and rubbed his forehead. "Even when you misbehaved as a child, you did not deny it. If you say that is what happened, I believe you."

She'd definitely misbehaved as an adult recently, but hopefully he would not question her about that directly. "What is it you suggest we do now?"

It was much more her father's provenance to take charge, and he was obviously grateful to assume it. "I will talk to Colbert. I am not positive what I am going to say quite yet, but he is a decent sort. As unhappy as he is over this turn of events, he is hopefully reasonable enough to see it isn't your fault. If only Andrews weren't the other party, this might not be of such interest to all the gossipmongers. When you first were missing and it was rumored he was gone also, that was Colbert's concern. He wanted to know if I was aware of a connection between you. I told him of course not. I would not allow that libertine anywhere near my daughter."

The other party. An interesting way to put it. As for being a libertine, perhaps the description fit but she knew Ran was so much more than the rakish picture of him that was often painted.

She already missed the hint of perpetual laughter in his eyes, the easy companionship, the teasing power of his smile, the way he looked at her as if she were the only woman on the earth. . . .

She missed *him.*

And had the sinking feeling that was not going to change.

Elena shook it off. "Speaking of Lord Colbert, I've been thinking . . . what if this was directed at *him*? What if someone wished to ruin me because of our engagement?"

"Colbert? I can't really imagine it. He's far too upright and honorable."

Unfortunately, that might just be true. Boringly so, she could add, but doubted her father would appreciate it. "I think it is very difficult in this life to go through it and not have an enemy or two, no matter how sound your character. Whatever the motivation, it remains that now he is forced into a somewhat difficult decision."

Her father rubbed his chin. "I suppose that is true and puts a different slant on it."

"I thought so too."

"But Andrews is a much more likely candidate. The man is a notorious philistine."

"Who avoids marriageable young ladies as if they carry the plague," she argued reasonably, doing her best to not leap to Ran's defense. "You cannot have this both ways. This will not affect him other than the speculation. He is immune because he doesn't care about gossip and never has. He didn't instigate what happened and he will not be ruined by it either. Other than his utter frustration at being locked away for five days when he has obligations, this will not significantly affect his life."

It took a minute or two of deliberation but then her father slowly nodded. "Actually, as confounding as it is to admit it, you are right. Given his propensity for vice I would have guessed the viscount to be the target, but maybe that is not logical."

"He is off for Essex this morning to see his sister because he is her guardian and most worried about her concern over his unexplained disappearance. He told me if you wished to discuss with him how to explain it all, he would be amenable to a meeting when he returns."

"Sporting of him, I suppose."

Then the dreaded moment happened, but she'd been braced for it all along.

"While the different angles of determining why this all happened might be valid, Andrews was still in that room with you for nearly a week. Did he touch you?"

It was unthinkable to have to discuss this delicate subject with her father, but the abduction had irrevocably changed her life. Her face heated in a furious blush but she said emphatically, "I can assure you I am still a virgin."

Having to defend that was one of the most embarrassing moments of her life.

"And if Lord Colbert wishes confirmation?"

As she had absolutely no idea what he'd just asked her, she merely stared at him.

"A physician," her father elaborated, his own face turning a slight dusky hue, "to examine you. He might request it. I am not going to try to dance around the subject. When a fortune and a title hang in the balance, most men wish to make sure both go to their direct heir."

To examine her? She had a much better idea what that might entail now, but was not about to explain how she learned it.

Elena stood and said with deliberate cool intonation, "If he does not take my word, please inform his lordship I do not wish to marry him."

Blackstone Hall looked the same—ivy-covered walls and the elegant fifteenth-century façade familiar, mullioned windows shining in the morning sun—and Ran had to admit to a different sense of appreciation as the carriage rolled up the drive. It was one matter to assume that life would move forward in a certain way and another to realize it might not. Privilege had benefits, but no man was immune to circumstance.

Fate had certainly visited him in the form of the memory of days—and nights—with a very beautiful, alluring, passionate young woman who could only ultimately be attained by marriage.

Damnation.

The vehicle rolled to a halt and when he alighted, properly attired for the first time in days, he stepped out, thanked the footman who rushed over to greet him, and inquired about the whereabouts of his sister.

Lucy was in the garden, sitting on a bench between a rhododendron and a bank of fragrant roses, where he expected she would be on a lovely day like this one. A book was perched pages down on her lap instead of held below her face, as usual. He took in the neat braid in her dark hair and her pensive expression, her gown still childish but not entirely concealing that womanhood was not far away.

It struck him then that the weight of his responsibility had never come home so much as when he'd worried he would not be able to fulfill it.

"Luce."

His sister turned at the sound of his voice, her head whipping around, and the instant, utter joy in her face humbled him. Her beloved book—all her books were beloved—tumbled to the ground as she jumped to her feet. "Ran!"

He caught her as she hurled herself into his arms, an unprecedented event, noting to himself that while they were not usually so affectionate, maybe they should talk about their relationship more often. Certainly his first worry when he realized he was being held prisoner had been her well-being in his absence, and apparently she had missed him.

This entire experience had given him a slightly different perspective on his life. His throat tightened.

"I wasn't gone intentionally." He lifted her chin so they could look at each other. She reminded him poignantly of their mother, even much more so as she matured, with the same slightly curly hair and dark eyes he'd inherited as well. "I'll explain later, but surely you do realize that I would *never* leave without telling you."

Like their parents had done. A spontaneous and carefree trip to Bath with friends, the note left with her governess, and then the tragic accident that had cost them their lives when a bridge collapsed during a raging storm and they had drowned. Ran had gotten the letter months later in Spain, his shock complete. Resigning his commission immediately and sailing for home, it still had taken him weeks, his parents long since buried upon his arrival, and if it hadn't been for Janet, the situation would have been untenable for a bereft child.

"I hadn't thought so. I was sure of it, really, but that made it worse." His sister's voice sounded shaky but was resolute enough. "Still, when your solicitor took the time to come from London and said you were gone, and we had no idea what to do. . . ."

Ran gently disengaged her clinging arms and smiled with as much reassurance as possible. "It is over now and I'm here. Where's Janet?"

"She's been in town, trying to discover your whereabouts. She just returned last evening. I think she's in the conservatory with her flowers." Lucy blinked rapidly, her eyes still liquid. "I would never say she was overwrought because you know she does not believe in dramatic displays of emotion, but she was certainly not very happy. Did you know someone tried to sell her back Father's watch?"

He did, actually, thanks to Heathton. Ran was fairly sure he'd have eventually gotten both himself and Elena back to London somehow, but having the earl show up so conveniently had been timely and efficient. And a relief. In retrospect, as badly as he'd wanted out of their tower, how the devil would he have protected Elena with no weapon and both of them only half-dressed? She was far too beautiful to be wandering dangerous roads, clad in nothing but flimsy silk, and had something happened he would have never forgiven himself.

He owed Heathton a great deal.

Elena. Try as he might, he could not stop thinking about her. Oh, she was desirable enough to keep any man's riveted attention, but that was the least of it. He was used to a much greater level of detachment, and especially in their case he should be able to walk away as he had so many other times.

In the cold light of day or, in this case, the warmth of a lovely afternoon, he needed to face the truth.

He'd been kidnapped and dragooned.

She'd been just as helpless.

Had he taken advantage of her or had something else happened?

Well, to start, without question he needed to admit he'd seduced her even if her physical innocence was still intact. "I heard about the watch." He touched Lucy's face again, as if to ground his world back in the reality of Essex and the estate. "I'm going to go talk to Janet now. I'll be staying overnight, but then I need to return to London."

"I'll tell Cook," Lucy said, turning in a swirl of simple, soft material, her long braid swinging, the happy gleam of her smile giving him pause. "She'll be so delighted you're back she'll make all your favorites."

"I assume that means all of *your* favorites," he countered drily, marveling at how at not quite sixteen she already knew males liked to be indulgent, because she just laughed and ran down the path toward the house.

He found his aunt—they weren't more than ten years apart so it was difficult to think of her that way at times— among a blooming bank of white blossoms in the glassed addition to the back of house. Her profile was remote, her dark hair gathered as usual into a demure chignon, the gown she wore too severely cut in his opinion, the brown color not in the least bit flattering. The understated approach she took to life might have been due to her unmarried state, but, his father had remarked to Ran once that Janet had never seemed all that interested in suitors. As close as she was with Lucy, he had wondered before if she hadn't at least wanted children of her own, but all along she had respected his privacy and so he showed her the same courtesy. Perhaps if she had graying hair and a cane, he might have dared ask, but she hadn't even yet seen her fortieth year and was poised and elegant, and they had always gotten along on a mutual consensus of paying attention to their own affairs.

Actually, *he* had affairs in a sexual sense, and she didn't, to his knowledge. Surely a woman her age might have done so or still did ... but her past had never been a subject open to discussion and this certainly wasn't the time.

"Janet."

"Randolph?" She whirled at the sound of his voice, her face showing relief. One hand went to her throat. "Oh, goodness ... I thought it was one of the gardening staff, but it's you ... really you ... Oh, my ... I can't tell you ... We've been so frantic—"

"You weren't alone," he interrupted. "It was a rather long five days."

"I'm *so* glad you're home." She did look flatteringly relieved.

He smiled and went over to take her hand. "Thanks in part to you. I owe you more than I can say. Heathton told me you came to see him. Who knew my eclectic taste in liquor would one day do me good? Somehow he managed to trace the trail of the last purchase of the Blaven, but only because *you* mentioned it to him. Very clever."

"I'm not at all certain what you are talking about."

"As unlikely as it sounds Heathton tracked down my favorite whiskey and, as a result, found me."

"He found you *that* way?" Janet took a moment, but then shook her head. "It was accidental, so I hardly deserve any credit. I really only told his wife about the watch. He did get it back for you, by the way."

"So he told me on our journey back to London last night. I didn't even know it was missing—well, I knew it was gone, but, then, so was just about everything else. Including my clothes, dignity, and freedom."

There was a small stone bench by one of the sunny windows and she withdrew her hand and sank down on it. "Randolph, please, don't be cryptic at a time like this. Where on earth have you been?"

"It sounds a little like a fairy tale of the sort you used to read to Lucy, but I can honestly say I was locked in a tower with a beautiful maiden."

His aunt looked nonplussed. "I don't understand. From our conversation with the man who tried to sell back your watch, we gathered already you were abducted in some way, but there was never a request for any ransom. I feared you might have been impressed to service on a foreign ship. One does hear of such horrible things happening."

"I don't think money was the objective." There was a grim note of conviction in his tone because he knew down deep it had never been the motivation.

"Lady Elena, I take it, is the beautiful maiden. I went to see her father first and when he heard your watch was being ransomed, he directed me to Lord Heathton, in case your disappearances were linked together. Heathton's wife and Lady Elena are cousins."

A bee droned at one of the white flowers and Ran watched it for a moment, marveling at how the simple act of standing in the conservatory had taken on a magical quality. He'd always been an outdoorsman, athletic and full of restless energy, and that had certainly been the most difficult part of his captivity. But here he was in his own house, free to leave or to stay or do whatever he wished again.

Elena had, of course, been compensation for that hardship.

Meeting Janet's gaze squarely he said, "There's going to be a scandal over this. I don't see how it can be avoided. The truth sounds too implausible. If we say nothing speculation will be rife anyway, and I can't think up a convincing lie for our disappearing at the same time and then the mutual reappearance. If her father wishes to keep her return a secret and whisk her away to the country and invent some suitable story at a later time, I will naturally support that plan. But I need to be in London for the next parliamentary vote, not to mention I have business affairs to tend to. I'll stay here tonight but I am going straight back in the morning."

"I just returned myself last night because I couldn't bear to leave Lucy to worry with no one to talk to but the servants, but now that you are returned to us it is different. Her governess is a capable young woman. I think I should accompany you."

And lend him a much-needed air of respectability. She didn't need to say it out loud.

"I don't need your protection." He was amused even under the circumstances. They'd never discussed his status as one of England's leading rakes.

"Randolph, I think, blameless or not you are going to have to face one irate father and a disgruntled fiancé, because whatever the truth may be, by your own admission you were alone with an unmarried woman from a prominent family for five days." She straightened her spine. "And five nights. I think you need someone from your family to defend your scruples should they come into question. I try to not follow the gossip about your personal life, but naturally I have still heard some of the whispers and none of them involve innocent ladies engaged to other men, so that is to your credit. I am certain you were a complete gentleman and will say so to anyone who insinuates otherwise."

Ah, the crux of the problem. Claiming total innocence was a falsehood, and though he had his flaws he disliked liars, which was why he wanted Whitbridge to invent the story. He would support it for Elena's sake—he was starting to think he'd do quite a lot for her sake—but lying was not his forte.

If asked directly if he'd touched her, he was not sure he could in good conscience deny it. Unless *she* asked for him to lie about that particular question, and, curiously, she hadn't.

Actually, it isn't curious at all, he reminded himself as he contemplated that dilemma. Elena would never ask him to lie for her. After all those long, lazy conversations, he knew her in a way that did not involve their lovemaking but a different level, and he had no idea how to feel about it.

In retrospect, Janet's idea was sound. He nodded. "Come to London with me, then, in the morning. If need be you could talk to Lady Elena, whereas I suspect I would be skewered if I placed a foot on Whitbridge's property. I have no idea why someone decided to make us the victims of their bizarre joke or who is behind it, but I don't want her to suffer for this."

No, he wanted the *culprit* to suffer. Their rescue was

all well and good, but who the devil had turned his life upside down? Luckily, he had wealth and influence, and he planned to engage an investigator.

"Don't you?"

Had he just betrayed too much? He wasn't sure but a hint of softness in Janet's eyes told him he might have. So he answered coolly, "Of course not."

There was a subtle rustle of silk as she stood, composed, her hands folded in front of her in a ladylike fashion. "You do realize that Lord Colbert might challenge you."

If he knew the truth he certainly should.

"And I," he said, recalling the tale of Elena's objection to her engagement and how it was ignored, "am an excellent pistol shot, so if that becomes an issue, then I will deal with it at the time."

Chapter 20

B en realized the visit was inevitable, but he still didn't welcome Alicia's uncle particularly on a day when he should be enjoying the aftermath of a personal triumph.

His duty was done, Lady Elena was back with her family, and though as of yet Ben still had no idea who had perpetrated the crime—he wasn't even certain it would be considered a crime by a magistrate, since both parties were unharmed and back with their families—he had fulfilled his promise. Wasn't that enough?

So he merely motioned to a chair. "Whitbridge," he said, inclining his head. "I understand you wish to see me, and I can guess why, though I doubt I have many answers."

"Who did this?" The petitioner was gone. The Earl of Whitbridge was gracious enough to not be downright surly, but he was still an unhappy man. "My daughter told me what happened. It seems fantastical to me that someone would deliberately seek to imprison her with a known rakehell like Andrews, but that seems to be what has occurred. What can you do?"

Ben admitted silently he was convinced he'd already

done quite enough. He wasn't necessarily eager to get back to his duties as the stodgy earl again, but neither was he obligated to go out seeking errant viscounts and missing maidens. "With all due respect, my lord, I found your daughter, just as you asked, and as far as I am concerned my participation stops there."

"Someone is behind this."

"I agree."

"I want the culprit caught and punished. Who would want to bring scandal upon my daughter?"

Deliberately Ben folded his hands. "I suggest that you take the necessary steps, but I am not a detective for hire, even if the payment is fulfillment of family obligation. Alicia is very fond of Elena, so I did my best, but that is over."

"You have no personal curiosity?" The earl lifted his graying brows and leaned back, his laced fingers over the front of his waistcoat. "I was told you would be most intrigued."

Damn Wellington, Ben thought darkly. The man was a crafty general.

"I have personal obligations," he countered. He was intrigued, true, but he was also busy.

"Alicia will agree with me. My niece is a most intelligent young lady. I assume that is why you married her."

That was difficult to argue, unfortunately. Picking up a long, engraved letter opener, Ben toyed with it as he considered his next comment. "I married her for myriad reasons. That aside, if vengeance is what you seek, I could perhaps suggest a few names of some people who might be able to help you ferret out the culprit. I think Andrews would also be more than willing to contribute both funds and energy. It was not his choice either to be locked up for five days against his will."

Whitbridge gave a derisive snort. "So he says."

"He is not behind this." Ben had already given it a fair measure of thought and was convinced. "Do not waste your energy in that direction. Even setting aside the evidence of a family heirloom that I know he treasures ending up in the hands of a common thief, it is my opinion that if he'd wanted to seduce your daughter, he would simply seduce her. All the publicity surrounding their disappearance puts social pressure on him and paints him in a bad light. Whatever you've heard, please think back and admit there aren't rumors about him preying on unsuspecting debutantes. He isn't interested in marriage, but he is interested in protecting his younger sister. If he is a libertine, he is a selective one, and all his staff, from the lads in his stable to the upstairs maid, swear he cares for his duty to family and country above all else."

At the end of that long speech, Whitbridge stared at him. "How do you know all this?"

"How did I find your daughter in the first place, sir? I thoroughly looked into him."

That courteous—or Ben thought it was—reply was met with a blink. Alicia's uncle had the grace to clear his throat apologetically, but his hand curled around the arm of the chair so tightly the knuckles went white. "I'm not certain how you managed that, but I am very grateful."

"Then take my word about Andrews."

The Earl of Whitbridge nodded grudgingly after a moment. "I suppose you have a right to ask that of me, so I agree. If he wasn't the one who masterminded it all, then, who was it?"

"I have no idea. Who are your enemies, my lord?"

"Mine?" Graying brows shot up.

"Yes. You might want to make up a list."

"That is ridiculous." His wife's uncle frowned fiercely. "I can't think of anyone who would be so cowardly as to seek to harm me by striking at me through my daughter."

"You might take the time to ponder it if you intend to investigate."

"You have no intention of discovering who might have done this?"

Ben picked up a pen, jotted down a few names, and handed over the slip of vellum. "My Lord Wellington will confirm these are all sound trustworthy men and most of them have experience along the lines you seek."

"I want *you*."

Now, that was damned inconvenient. Ben had done this in the first place for Alicia, to repay a favor second, but he wasn't haring off to castles in the middle of the night on a regular basis, much less retrieving ransomed watches or even lending his coat to semiclad young ladies. "My lord," he said with as little inflection as possible, "I have other obligations. You are also a busy man. Surely you understand."

"I understand you are my niece's husband, and, therefore, family. Please tell me you realize my daughter has been irrevocably ruined. You and I both know it. Since it was done with malicious intent, I would, as her father, like to know why she was targeted and, most of all, by *whom*."

It was a difficult argument to resist, especially since Ben had the feeling he might have to participate in the same discussion with his wife later. He could tell Whitbridge to go to hell, but Alicia was another matter. An inner groan was only barely stifled.

Just when it was all going so well ...

Once he'd heard the story, he'd wondered if getting the lovely Elena home was going to be only part of the chore. Whitbridge's request didn't really come as a surprise. "Should I hear anything I will let you know at once."

The earl proved more wily than anticipated. "Picture this, Heathton. A tiny child, *your* child. The first time you hold her in your arms makes you acknowledge the world actually is full of miracles. A child you and your wife created together and is part of you irrevocably, and as this child grows and matures you can see your features in her face, your mother's eyes, the same temperament as the father you lost far too young. . . . She is *yours*. Not in the same way you own your estate or the title you inherited or even the money that came with it, but this is you. Understand? It is life."

Ben took in a deep breath. "I do think I understand where you might be going with this, and—"

"Not until you are a father." Lord Whitbridge stood. His gaze was piercing. "Someone deliberately destroyed my daughter's future. I need to know *who*. Please keep me informed on the progress of your investigation."

To her utter surprise, her husband joined her.

When the door opened Alicia was absorbed in a discussion with her maid about what gown she might wear, and both of them looked up, startled beyond measure as

Ben entered the room. The unprecedented event made them both stop midspeech, and she nodded when her maid hastily excused herself. The Earl of Heathton didn't usually arrive at this hour . . . or really at any hour.

The night before had certainly left an impression on her. *Maybe on him as well?* She could only hope. Boldly, she asked, "Since yours is the only available opinion now, what do you think, my lord? The aqua silk or the midnight blue?"

"What?" Ben abstractedly seemed to register she was dressing for the evening and eyed both gowns. "I'm partial to green, as you have pointed out."

A typical nonanswer. "It isn't one of the choices."

One eyebrow went up. "You don't possess a green gown? How remiss of me to not have purchased one for you. That aside, can I speak with you for a moment or two about something much more important?"

As she was sitting at her dressing table, clad only in a chemise, her hair still tumbled down her back, she had to suppress a laugh. "I'm hardly in a position to get up and dash from the room. Not that I would anyway. I'm beyond fascinated as to why you are here."

"My motives are pure enough." His gaze skimmed her décolletage. "Or at least they were before I walked in that door. Don't distract me, please."

He was a bit distracting himself in just a white shirt unbuttoned at the neck, dark breeches tucked into polished boots, and his hair uncharacteristically rumpled. He was usually impeccably dressed and it was getting late.

"My apologies." She wasn't truly sorry her partial nudity distracted him; quite the opposite. It felt wonderfully intimate to have him in her bedroom while she was not fully dressed. He'd certainly seen every bare inch of her anyway, and she was rather enjoying her newfound freedom now that she understood better the potent power of desire as opposed to simple marital duty. "What is it we need to discuss?"

His gaze lowered to her bared calves and thighs, where it lingered before he looked her, with obvious effort, in the eye. "You are a very beautiful young woman."

The compliment was nice, of course, but she looked back at him a little nonplussed. "I . . . well . . . thank you, my lord. You are hardly unattractive either."

There was a glimmer of amusement finally in his eyes. "I am glad you think so, but that isn't my point. I mean that you are beautiful, gracious, a success in society, and the daughter of a titled wealthy man."

She was well aware her uncle had called earlier, and she finally realized this had to do with Elena. "I take it my uncle did not just spend an hour in your study this afternoon to thank you."

Ben lifted his brows. "Were you not going to also ask me to discover who is behind the deliberate and malicious destruction of your cousin's debut? I am merely facilitating the process by giving you an opportunity to do so now."

Not that there weren't leagues of distance to go, but she was finally getting to know him better and as such had become used to the indirect way he approached a question. Alicia paused for a moment as she decided how to respond. "Well, my lord, aren't you also curious? You have bested much more cunning opponents, I'm sure, and while you did recover my cousin—for which my entire family is grateful—the villain remains at large. It hardly seems fair for such a vindictive person to get away with what may not be precisely a crime but certainly a wrongdoing."

He regarded her with unsettling directness. "Yes, I'm curious, but in an abstract way only. I've a full schedule as it is, and even more so lately, as my wife now likes to take rides in the park and walks in the garden."

Alicia lifted a brow. "Do you find those activities tedious?"

"That isn't what I am saying at all."

A part of her sensed he was testing her resolve to hold fast to her ultimatum, but after the delicious interlude of the evening before, she wasn't sure she still had the ability to resist him anyway. Had she accomplished all she set out to do? No, not yet, but the progress had been most satisfactory.

"I will be happy to help you. Seeking out the perpetrator of Elena's kidnapping could be something we do together on an intellectual basis."

It took a moment but then he laughed softly. "Touché. I was hoping you would say that after last evening I was no longer required to court you to gain entrance to your bed."

"Last night was wonderful." There was no helping it; she blushed when she thought of the wickedly pleasurable sensation of his mouth between her legs. "But I still believe we have quite a lot to learn about each other, my lord."

"I see." His masculinity was a stark contrast to the pale blue and rose in the patterned rug, the faint smile curving his mouth telling her he remembered the night before also. "I suppose, as there is no one better to question your cousin, you could assist me in that capacity."

A bit surprised at the easy acquiescence, Alicia merely nodded. "Of course I will talk to her. I planned to visit tomorrow. Harriet is going to go with me, but I am sure I can get a few minutes with Elena alone."

"As I mentioned, she is very beautiful and was popular this season. There are other women who also have those same attributes, but why is it your cousin was kidnapped? There's a key." He walked across the room, his brow furrowed. "She holds it. I'm afraid I don't have the slightest idea what it might be. If it lay with Andrews, the man would have deciphered it already. I saw his face on the carriage ride back to London. He had five days with nothing to do but think about it and couldn't come up with a solution. The more I contemplate it, the more I am convinced he's right. This isn't about the viscount. When a man has a foe that is potentially vindictive he generally knows it."

No one wished for Elena to escape this unscathed more than Alicia. It would be nice if she could at this moment produce a brilliant thought that would solve the entire problem, but if Ben was puzzled, she was even more so. "I appreciate the earlier compliment but I am also the *wife* of a wealthy, titled man," she pointed out, admiring the way the linen of his shirt clung to his broad shoulders. "There would be absolutely no point in ruining me. I assume it has occurred to you that the person behind this could have targeted Lord Colbert. After all, he is Elena's fiancé. Or still is, as far as I know anyway. There is every chance he will cry off, I suppose. How would you feel if I were locked away with the notorious Lord Andrews for almost a week?"

"You would never be unfaithful to me."

The lack of hesitation and the conviction in his voice

warmed her. "No," she agreed with soft emphasis. "I wouldn't. But not all men are as insightful as you are."

"A stunning compliment from a woman I could swear has inferred more than once before that I am somewhat obtuse." He raked a hand through his hair. "But, yes, getting back to the actual discussion, Colbert is a distinct possibility as the catalyst. But we must ask ourselves what the underlying motivation is. An attack on his pride or his heart? Our villain is counting on something specific happening from the sequence of events. Once we understand what that is, we can narrow our focus to a motivation. If someone wanted to make sure the engagement was severed, then they will benefit in some way or they wouldn't have gone to such trouble."

She hadn't thought of it in quite those terms but he was right. Of course. Ben was no doubt frequently right on this sort of topic, but he didn't share his opinions with her often.

What a nice change in their lives that he'd done so.

"I can't say." She lifted her silver hairbrush and ran it through her hair, thinking. "This entire scandal has affected any number of people, now that you put it in that fashion."

When he watched her idly use the brush, something in his demeanor changed. It was subtle enough she might have even missed it, but with this heightened awareness between them, she caught his honed-in attention to the languid movement of her hand.

Yes, he'd largely ignored her for the first six months of their marriage, but for the first time she wondered how much she'd ignored *him*. Ben was not easy to understand but she'd expected *him* to understand *her*, not the other way around.

Maybe she hadn't been entirely fair.

"Since we are going to be colleagues, in a manner of speaking, perhaps," she suggested, her tone dropping a notch, "we could forgo the festivities this evening and stay home and discuss this."

Chapter 21

His wife was a siren, complete with flowing dark hair and a tempting smile.

Ben had sat for two unproductive hours after Alicia's uncle had left and done what had worked for him so well during the war. He'd used solitude like a friend, like an ally, and taken time just to think.

Infuriatingly enough, though, he hadn't really given much focus to the problem at hand. Instead he'd wondered what Alicia might be doing, what the evening might bring, and he'd be damned if in the end he hadn't actually gone to her room.

And now she wanted to stay in and . . . talk.

In delectable undress, with her long-lashed eyes shadowed and the lace of her flimsy chemise barely covering her oh so perfect breasts, she sat at her dressing table and looked at him as if she had no idea just what she was doing to him.

Bloody hell, he hadn't wanted to go out in the first place, so her suggestion was appealing.

"It is a clear evening and the temperature pleasant. Shall I order dinner up?" He could hear the lower timbre of his voice but couldn't help it. "Alfresco on the balcony, perhaps?"

An inspired idea. She smiled in a way that sent a jolt of intense desire through him, a dimple appearing in her smooth cheek. "That is very romantic, my lord. *Much* better than our previous plans."

Romantic? Should he point out that if they ate on the balcony, the bed would be conveniently nearby?

No, probably not.

He didn't have the slightest idea what their previous plans were except they no doubt involved evening wear and a play, party, or opera he didn't want to attend. Though he doubted her idea of romantic matched his exactly, he was interested in finding out how close they could come to a mutual perception of the word.

His involved her naked beneath him or on top of him, for that matter. Now that the ice between them was broken, so to speak, he was more than anxious to explore just how adventurous his lovely wife might be coaxed into being in bed. After all, she was the one who insisted they follow a less traditional path than most couples of their social class. The usual course of it all was that a wife was a duty and a mistress a pleasure.

How convenient if she could be both.

"I'll make the arrangements." He hesitated, reluctant to reveal he had absolutely no idea what her favorite foods might be, and settled for saying instead, "Do you have a preference as to the menu? I am certain the cook would oblige any request."

"Have you *met* our cook?"

"Come to think of it, no." Before his marriage he had left all that to Yeats, and now he supposed Alicia had some hand in managing the household. He had enough to do as it was.

Alicia shook her head and he couldn't help but notice how it sent her shining hair sensuously brushing across her pale shoulders. "We arrange the menu for the week every Monday and changing it is a very dangerous proposition, I assure you. She is a force to be reckoned with and rules the kitchen like a small tyrant. Whatever it is you can be sure it will be delicious, but do not risk your life by asking her to change it for me. She will be delighted, though, I must say, that you will be home." She added softly, "So am I."

"I suppose I am guilty of eating at my club fairly often, but it never occurred to me that anyone cared one way or the other, much less the staff. Less work for them, one would think."

"I believe more people care about what you do than you realize."

"I'm the earl." Which translated to a great deal of people depending on him and on the success of his estates and business ventures, even on his influence in the political arena of Parliament. That was why he was so busy.

"Not what I am referencing at all, but we will leave it at that, shall we?" Alicia's mouth twitched. "If you will give me a few minutes with my toilette, I will join you shortly."

It probably would have been more gallant to go kiss her hand or give some similar gesture, but instead he merely nodded and left the room, not trusting himself to keep from hauling her into his arms and carrying her straight to the bed. A unique sensation, since he'd always prided himself on his self-control, but lately that had been severely tested.

Downstairs he encountered Yeats in the hallway and conveyed his request, and he'd be damned if he didn't think he saw a slight glimmer of satisfaction in the older man's face as he nodded. "Very good, my lord. Er . . . may I inquire, on her balcony or yours?"

"I doubt it matters."

The butler cleared his throat. "May I suggest yours? Assuming, of course, this is a gesture on your part, or otherwise Lady Heathton would be making the arrangements."

Earl aside, he suddenly had the feeling a great deal of his household was paying more attention to the nuances of his marriage than he had been himself. Drily, he acknowledged, "Yes, it was my idea, so my balcony it is."

"Excellent choice. I will have a table brought up and all arranged."

"Thank you." He stopped in the act of turning away and asked, "Tell me, is the cook truly temperamental?"

Yeats smiled, which he did not do very often. "Very much so, my lord, but she is worth it, and there are some things in this life one must weigh on a scale of gain or loss. I believe you've had her roast capon. Extraordinary. Now, then, shall I have wine ready to be served in say . . . an hour?"

The gown she selected was a soft green but not appropriate for dinner, with a modest neckline and small bits of white ribbon; much more suitable for the afternoon. However, they were eating outside at home, and it was perfect for the clear evening and soft breeze, and for once she wasn't subject to society's close scrutiny. Alicia had her hair swooped into a casual twist at her nape and left it at that, and when the knock came on her door she rose with a singular anticipation.

This was the first time Ben had suggested they spend time together alone. He'd chosen the venue, and her heart was beating fast as she moved toward the door adjoining their rooms.

He stood there, and though he'd changed his clothes also he had eschewed a cravat, which she found she liked. Her austere husband could be too formal as it was, and the casual look made him more approachable. When his gaze swept over her, she experienced a small tingle of anticipation at the gleam of appreciation in his hazel eyes.

Or maybe it wasn't all that small.

"I see you possess a green gown after all."

"Well, not an evening gown, but I see that informal is the tone of the evening."

"A nice change." Ben offered her his arm. "I admit to not having a fondness for stuffy ballrooms."

She allowed him to escort her through his bedroom to where French doors opened to the balcony and was rewarded by the sight of a small table covered with a white cloth lit with candles that flickered in the light breeze. Crystal glasses and a bottle of wine awaited them, and someone—she doubted it was Ben, but still a romantic touch—had brought up a spray of roses from the garden.

"Nice, indeed," she agreed as he politely pulled out her chair. Stars were just beginning to appear as dusk waned into twilight, and she settled her skirts as he deftly poured her a glass of wine and accepted it with a smile. "Thank you. This is a lovely idea."

"Actually, I think staying in was your idea, my dear, but I will take credit for it if you are willing to give it to me."

Well, *my dear* was not *my love*, but Alicia had the impression her husband had not meant to say that endearment in the first place. It was unrealistic to be disappointed, so she took a sip of wine and didn't comment. It was a beautiful night, the man she loved was sitting across from her giving her his full attention for once, and it would be ungrateful to not appreciate the moment. Just a week ago she would have counted this scenario as highly unlikely.

"I don't give credit such as that easily," she murmured over the rim of her glass. "Just remember that, my lord."

He caught her teasing tone and the corner of his mouth lifted in an attractive quirk. "Yes, I've noticed. And here I thought we'd come to a meeting of the minds, so to speak."

She had to laugh because she thought it was possible Ben was actually teasing her. "I don't believe our minds are precisely what you want to meet."

"A compromise is always nice."

The arrival of a footman with a tray stopped her from having to comment. The first course proved to be a delicate broth with floating tips of asparagus and was deliciously light and fresh. Ben ate with enjoyment, which was a bit different from his usual abstraction, and one bite into the next dish, a fillet of sole stuffed with tiny shrimp and topped with some sort of creamy sauce, he murmured, "I believe you about the cook. I am not sure why I never noticed before. By all means, let us keep her happy."

"She worked for a French chef as a scullery maid but showed enough aptitude that he began to train her, or so she said when Yeats hired her."

He took another bite with appreciation, chewed slowly, and swallowed, then asked, "That is somewhat of a coincidence. I don't suppose you know his name."

The candlelight flickered again, giving shadows to his cheekbones and the straight line of his jaw. Alicia had always done her best to not think about the women he'd known before her because her husband truly was a very handsome man.

A passionate lover.

She'd lost track of the conversation. *What did he just ask me?* "Whose name?"

"The chef's."

Perplexed, she stared at him. "No, I don't. But I have never asked either. Why would I? Isn't it easy enough to believe she is telling the truth because the evidence is on your plate?"

"The food is superb," he murmured in agreement. "And I imagine there is more than one French chef in England, but still it would be interesting and it is one of the aspects that confuses me."

She didn't have the slightest idea what he was talking about. "Aspects of what?"

"Why did your cousin's kidnapper make such an effort to treat her and Andrews so well? Whoever it was hired a talented French chef and took the time and trouble to get Andrews his favorite whiskey."

Well, they had ostensibly stayed in to discuss that very topic, though she had to admit to being distracted by both his proximity and the intimate implications of a moonlit dinner on the balcony off his bedroom. She did her best to concentrate on the subject at hand and not notice how the breeze slightly ruffled his hair. "It is rather a contradiction since one would assume the kid-

napping itself was an act of malevolence. I confess part
of the reason I wished to stay at home this evening is to
avoid all the questions over my cousin's absence and
now reappearance. The *ton* can be relentless when there
is a hint of a juicy scandal to be had."

"And here I assumed it was a desire for my company."
Ben picked up the wine bottle and refilled his glass.
"How arrogant of me."

"I do desire you." The moment she said it, she hastily
amended, "I meant, I do desire your company at all
times."

"I liked the first way you put it better, for I most definitely desire *you*."

A flush touched her skin at the meaningful look he
gave her. Had not the next course arrived, with another
footman discreetly whisking their plates away, she was
not at all sure how she would have responded. The entire
point of confronting him had been to make him aware of
her as a woman, not just the wife he had acquired. It
seemed she'd accomplished that goal.

Be careful what you wish for. . . .

There was a somewhat predatory gleam in his eyes,
and she had a feeling that the control she'd taken when
she'd insisted he not bed her unless he made some effort
in other aspects of their relationship was slipping away.
That was demonstrated when they finished their dinner
and he declined port, dismissed the staff with his compli-
ments to the cook, and regarded her across the table. "I
suppose, as you have set the rules, what happens now is
entirely up to you."

To be fair, she understood his stance—after all, she'd
counted on his honor in the first place when she'd decided to take a gamble and confront him. And yet was it

too much to hope that her husband would be swept away by the romantic setting?

It *had* been a gamble to lay down her terms in this intimate war. She wondered if he fathomed how much she'd risked. He had options, plenty of them, if she denied him. "Do you have a mistress?"

Ben looked more than a little startled. After a moment he did his usual and didn't answer directly. "Why would you even ask?"

"Many men do."

"Alicia . . . many people do many things . . . and that does not mean all gentlemen of our class keep a mistress just because some of them indulge in that behavior."

It was rather nice to hear the exasperation in his tone. But, she noted—now with a relieved sense of humor—he didn't deny or confirm, just gave her a generality. "Is that a denial? With you it is always hard to tell."

"I'm confounded over why you would even suspect that was possible when I have made it so abundantly clear I wish to share your bed very much."

He still hadn't answered. Not directly. She said quietly, "I ask because I care about the answer."

Her husband rose then, his chair scraping back. "Shall I demonstrate how much I want you and no one else?"

The woman was driving him to madness.

Completely.

Without question.

If she had no idea how tempting she was in that soft green dress that draped her curves, her dark hair loosely gathered, her lovely face softened by the moonlight, she was not paying attention to his riveted interest.

Did she really have the naive misconception that he might be even remotely interested in anyone else?

Well, it would be his pleasure to prove to her otherwise. Alicia eyed his outstretched hand and then offered her slim one in response, letting him pull her to her feet. She was still more maiden than seductress, for she lowered her gaze and her cheeks held a hint of color, but her fingers did curl around his and she willingly followed his urging into the bedroom.

When he eased her gown off one shoulder she didn't object, but instead gasped when he lowered his head to lick her bared breast, the pink tip of her nipple taut under the swirl of his tongue.

He wanted to get her with child. For the first time it was not an obligation to his title or an affirmation of his birthright, but he wanted to see her ripe with his son or daughter. Maybe it was the intrinsic femininity of her body that prompted that sudden realization, or maybe it was his acclimation to a marriage that was becoming more and more a reality when he'd done his best to set it aside.

Either way, at this moment he was very aware that his wife had become part of his life. Her methods hadn't been the easiest to accept, but he had to admit she'd accomplished that part of her goal.

When her hands caught his shoulders and she took in a swift breath, he took that rigid nipple deep in his mouth and sucked, and was rewarded by her answering moan.

Not a bad start to what he hoped would be a very satisfying end to an already enjoyable evening. He'd had a most delicious meal, and now he intended to indulge himself with his wife in the most carnal way possible.

Much better than a boring soiree or an insipid fête populated by shallow people he didn't like all that much to begin with, the false gaiety all too often a symbol of their empty lives.

He wanted so much more.

"Turn around." He urged her with his hands and then unfastened her gown with an astounding swiftness, even to him. Alicia wore only a simple shift underneath, and he divested her of that too as fast possible, and then undid her hair. "The bed."

Maybe later the autocratic tone of his voice would give him pause, but not now, not when he'd wanted her all evening, not when he remembered exactly what it was like to have her in his arms.

She obeyed—not necessarily a given considering her recent streak of independence—and moved toward the bed with her long hair brushing her luscious buttocks. As Ben took off his shirt, boots, and breeches with alacrity, he wondered if his current state of need was unprecedented because of her approach to the situation or because of his reaction to it.

Either way, she was winning. Not that this was a war but it was at least a skirmish, and the arsenal at her disposal far outweighed his weaponry.

He was fully aroused and ready to take her, but it was hardly as if he was engaging the enemy. More like a battle between forces that might not be exactly opposing, but certainly did not see eye to eye. "So," he said in a whisper as he lowered himself next to her and smoothed a lock of silken dark hair off her brow, "what is it you want next?"

"That is suitably vague, my lord." She looked back at him, her eyes luminous. "We are naked in bed together. I assume there is a certain expectation on both sides."

"I want to make love to you."

"Do you?"

"Oh yes."

Alicia reached up and touched his cheek. It was light but the brush of her fingers sent fire through his body. "Well put, for I do love you."

He wasn't ready for it.

Every muscle went still, locked into place.

Not ready for innocent declarations of love, not for the implications of it all, not for his own tumultuous feelings. Instead Ben kissed her when he could take a breath, parted her thighs with his knees and tested her readiness with fingers that found warmth and a gratifying wetness. He adjusted his position and entered her, not slowly with his usual restraint but in a swift thrust, and through the pleasure as he fought for an apology for his abruptness, she said breathlessly, "Oh."

Such a simple syllable that held so much meaning. It wasn't enough that she was delectably tight, her arousal fueling his own, and when her arms wound around his neck and she arched closer, he came undone.

Completely.

"Move with me," he said persuasively, his eyes closing. "Lift your hips."

Her acquiescence was perfection. Her slender body undulated with his, taking his cock as he moved in quickening need, her thighs tightening around his hips, her breath warm against his shoulder, and when he reached between them and touched her between her legs, she made a soft sound of pleasure, the betraying tremble giving him the affirmation that she was also enjoying it.

A soft bed, his beautiful wife in his arms ... what could offer more satisfaction in this life?

Arousal built, rose to a pinnacle that couldn't be denied, and he rotated his fingers in just the right spot. As her inner muscles tightened and she cried out, he lost control and orgasmic release rushed in, the pleasure so acute he groaned and stiffened as he poured into her, rapture slamming through him, making the world spin.

He went lax for a few crucial moments until he came to the realization that his weight might be too much and rolled to his side. He held her in the panting aftermath, his cheek against the fragrant spread of her hair, and wondered what to say.

Did a man need to say anything just because he'd pleasured his wife—and been pleasured in turn? The protocol of it escaped him, and he didn't really care, because she seemed as content as he was to lie there as their respiration came back to normal and the clock on the mantel ticked into the resulting silence.

Until she shattered his world by whispering again, "Ben ... I ... I love you."

He had no idea how to respond. Love was not a foreign concept, but the commitment involved in saying the words....

She saved him then. Alicia had a unique way of doing just that. "It doesn't require an answer." Slender fingers raked through his hair and dark blue eyes held his gaze. "It doesn't actually require anything, and regardless of whether or not you feel the same I love you. I thought I might say it at a more formal time but this seems more appropriate."

It was. *Perfect.* With their bodies still joined, his thigh over hers, his hold close and possessive.

"Alicia." He kissed her, but it was different from the earlier passion, instead gentle and tender, their lips clinging, her hair tangled in his hands. Later when she'd drifted to sleep, he lay in the darkness just listening to her breathe.

And it gave him joy.

Chapter 22

It wasn't as if he'd ever expected to escape this debacle easily, but when almost every conversation stilled when he walked into his club, Ran swore inwardly.

Maybe he should have taken another day in the country.

Not that it would have diminished the scandal, but at least he could have put it off. It was midafternoon, but there were still a fair number of members, all of them at the moment gawking at him.

If it was like this for him, he wondered how Elena would do her first time out in public.

"Good afternoon, my lord." The steward was infinitely more polite than the patrons he served, for he greeted Ran with his usual courtesy as if nothing at all had happened. "Are you meeting with someone in particular?"

"No. Just stopped by for a drink."

"There is a table in the corner if you would like it." The young man kept his expression scrupulously neutral.

"Diplomatically put." Ran smiled sardonically. "Perhaps that would be best."

"Right this way and I will have your special whiskey brought at once."

It occurred to him then that perhaps his fondness for Blaven was better-known than he imagined. Surely all the staff here knew of it since he had to order it and have it kept in reserve for him only.

Hell. "Thank you," he said somewhat grimly. "Lord Heathton doesn't happen to be here, does he?"

"No, I'm afraid we have not seen his lordship today."

That was unfortunate, as Ran wouldn't mind talking to the earl in private, but it looked as if he'd have to call on him at home, which he'd rather have avoided. Though he'd provided a timely means of transport back to London, Heathton hadn't seemed at all like he wished to be associated with their rescue and Ran really couldn't blame him. His own current state of notoriety was evident as heads turned when he walked past.

Damn all.

While the one person he'd hoped to see was not there, a moment later it was evident the person he'd hoped to see the least *was* there. The avid interest in his arrival made sense when he heard a voice say with cutting directness, "Andrews."

He glanced up. Lord Colbert stood by the side of the table, his mouth a tight line. Basically, Ran had always liked the man well enough, though they weren't particular friends. Wary but not wanting a confrontation, he said with as little inflection as possible, "Would you like to sit down? I think that might be best under the circumstances, or else I suppose we can discuss what I know you wish to discuss outside. Let us not make an unfortunate situation worse."

To give him credit, Colbert considered it for a moment and then took a chair. His nostrils looked pinched and he nodded at the waiter when asked if he wished his drink brought over but he didn't speak, leaving it to Ran to start the conversation.

Where *to* start?

I never touched her.

No, not true. He'd kissed her, brought her to climax, shared intimate afternoons, slept in the same bed; in short he was guilty as hell even if he had left her virginity intact. However, since he had no idea yet what Whitbridge had told his potential son-in-law, Ran chose to say, "I count you a lucky man. Lady Elena is very beautiful and gracious."

"Odd, that, coming from you." The man across the table gazed at him in open animosity. "Or are you speaking from personal experience?"

Very close to a direct question. Ran nodded gratefully at the young waiter who discreetly set down his whiskey and not just because he needed the fortification, but because the distraction was also welcome as he contemplated his answer.

"Is this going to be an altercation, or do you wish to discuss what happened?"

That was straightforward enough.

Colbert took a moment to visibly compose himself. He inhaled deeply, and when the waiter delivered his drink he ran his fingers down the side of the glass and his hand was not quite steady. "To be honest, I'm not certain. You must admit I am in an awkward position."

Ran said quietly, "There isn't a man in this room who isn't paying attention to our conversation. They may not be able to hear us speak, but they are watching. Keep it in mind. I'd prefer that Elena suffer as little as possible. I assume you feel the same."

"I haven't spoken with Lady Elena yet."

"Oh?" That hardly helped the situation. What precisely had Whitbridge told him? Ran settled back and picked up his glass. "We could resolve this with pistols at dawn or we could be more civilized. Which do you prefer?"

"Which one should I contemplate?"

I have to give the English credit, Ran thought as he sat there, *for their understated approach to violence. Tread lightly,* he reminded himself since he didn't know yet how Elena's father wished to handle the matter.

"I've never even been formally introduced to her," he informed his guest, his gaze wary.

That was true and neutral enough.

Colbert stared at his drink but then looked up and his eyes were shadowed. "Be that as it may, were you together?"

The dreaded direct question. It took a moment, but then Ran said, "Not by choice."

"What the devil does that mean?"

It was difficult to fault him for asking or for his male outrage. "I'm sure Lord Whitbridge told you what happened."

"Actually, he was rather evasive about it all, saying he wasn't quite sure what transpired but that Elena had not left London voluntarily with you."

A muscle in his jaw tightened. How nice of Whitbridge to leave it so vague he was vilified. Ran responded as calmly as possible, "If the implication is that I had anything to do with her absence, that is untrue and had best not be repeated. For whatever reason, we were both abducted. At different times, by different means, and as I just said, I had never even been introduced to her. I'd never asked. Unlike you, I am not interested in marriage at this time."

"Abducted? That's ..."

"Ludicrous. I agree. But it happened. On my honor. Neither one of us knows who or why, but it is the truth."

"May I take that as an assurance that you kept your distance, then?"

"You may take it any way you wish." It required some effort to keep his voice even. This was not the time or place for an argument, but he supposed it was as good as any if it had to be.

"Don't be testy, Andrews, when I am the wronged party."

"I'm afraid I don't completely agree on that point."

"Did she speak of me?"

As it was the last question he expected Ran had no idea what to say at first. "What?"

"Speak. Of me."

"Some," he admitted. This new direction could be more dangerous than an armed meeting on the field at first light. "She talked of the engagement."

"What did she say?"

"I don't recall specifically, Colbert. I was kidnapped and somehow that unusual occurrence was foremost in my mind."

He didn't want to mention Elena's misgivings. It wasn't his place, he had no right, and that was that. If she wished to discuss severing her engagement with her fiancé, it needed to come from her.

And if she declined to marry him, then she would be free. . . .

For?

Lord Colbert stood, nodded in as civil a fashion as Ran guessed he could muster, and turned to walk away.

She'd declined all visitors so far; how could anyone expect her to entertain the morbidly curious? But when Alicia and Harriet were announced, Elena nodded at the young maid and set aside her correspondence.

The interview would still not be easy. None of this was going to be easy. But it would be very nice to be able to just tell the truth. To someone.

They were both in the yellow salon, and when Elena entered, Alicia, who was the far more impulsive of the two, rose and came over to give her a sound hug. Harriet followed, and then the three of them settled down in a sort of unspoken agreement that this was all awkward. She knew they were there in support of her. At some point she would have to tell her story and perhaps they were the best place to start.

She would welcome, especially, the chance to talk to Alicia. They were not far apart in age and had always been good friends, and, after all, she owed her cousin's husband a great deal. Including the need to return his coat.

"I was kidnapped."

Alicia nodded. "Ben told me. How awful."

It really hadn't been all that awful because of Ran, but Elena declined to point that out. Had it been someone else trapped with her in that tower room . . . it could have been far worse. She was glad she didn't have to debate that matter. "I'm fine, as you can see."

Harriet had always been the direct one. "Locked in with Andrews? That had to have been interesting. Any inkling as to why? One of his paramours bent on revenge?"

Elena smiled wryly. "He was the one to point out to me that it was doubtful anyone who sought revenge on him—and he couldn't think of anyone readily—would trap him in with a young lady. He has honor, but if it isn't his fault, no obligation to me. That is difficult to argue."

Harriet muttered, "Or convenient. For him."

It was difficult to explain that even with his notoriety she'd grown to trust Ran, and while his good looks and facile charm were compelling, there was more to him. Much more.

"In any case, he wasn't behind it all." Alicia nodded. "Ben agrees. So what can we do for you to help?"

Trust her cousin to get right to what mattered. "I don't know." Elena watched the tea cart being rolled in, her voice subdued. When the footman exited the room she added, "How would anyone know how to deal with this situation?"

"True enough." Alicia, looking lovely in a cream day dress with small yellow tulips embroidered on the sleeves, picked up the pot and poured even though she wasn't the hostess, her expression thoughtful. "Though one does wonder over the motivation."

"Motivation . . . pffft." Harriet accepted a cup, her gaze inquiring. "Tell us about Andrews."

It was simply impossible not to flush a little. "He's actually quite pleasant," she said, hopefully with composure. "Polite. Cultured. Considerate."

"Undeniably attractive," Harriet provided, one eyebrow lifted. "Notoriously charming. Rakishly infamous. Legendarily virile ... I'm trying to think of more euphemisms but sadly failing." She turned to her sister. "Any suggestions?"

Alicia laughed lightly. "Stop it, Hattie. We are here because we want Elena to know we support her as a family without question. Though I suppose I might add *gloriously handsome*."

It was just the needed bit of levity to ease the situation.

Elena took an éclair and accepted a cup of steaming tea. "I adore you both. Have I ever mentioned it?"

"No need," Harriet said airily. "We know we are infinitely adorable. Now, then. Andrews?"

While Elena was blond, they were both dark-haired, though their skin had the same ivory hue, and all three of them had the signature indigo eyes that were a familial trait. She glanced at both of them and then set her cup aside with a sigh. "He's very ... cordial."

"You've mentioned that." Harriet pursed her lips. "I assumed he *could* be cordial, or else women in general would not like him, but it is not a word I would expect in description of the viscount."

"Well, he is," Elena said defensively, aware that the general repercussions from their captivity and his already disreputable reputation were not just going to affect her. "He protected me."

"From?" Alicia's question was delicate and quiet.

"There were armed guards that threatened us with pistols."

"What?" Harriet looked properly horrified.

"It was not a lark." Elena still recalled that moment

when she realized just how serious their predicament might be. "We were locked in, and though well treated, our liberty was not in question. Ran— er . . . Lord Andrews tried to escape the first day and was most effectively convinced his personal safety was at stake if we did not cooperate."

"That is rather barbaric."

"I agree."

"What did they want?"

The question of the hour, certainly. Elena said slowly, "We have no idea. Trust me, we had time to discuss it at length and did so, and neither of us could come up with an answer."

It was probably best to leave out the details of what else they had done. She could still recall the feel of his lips on hers, the skilled touch of his hands, the bursts of decadent pleasure . . . but more so the quickness of his smile, the way his gaze would catch hers, the brush of his long fingers as he handed her something, how he laughed . . .

She could not decide if she couldn't wait to see him again or if she dreaded that fateful moment. Whatever their captivity had been for him, it had profoundly affected her life, and she didn't mean just in terms of her new social notoriety. If he merely greeted her politely and acted as if they hadn't slept—among other things— in each other's arms, she had a sinking feeling she was going to be deeply wounded. However, if she was logical about the situation, it was certainly best if that was exactly how he handled it.

A devil's own dilemma.

She found she thought of him constantly. It could be,

she kept telling herself, that it was a comrades-in-arms sort of an attachment since they had shared such an unusual adventure.

But maybe it wasn't—though it would be a supremely foolish notion to fall in love with the very attractive but inconstant and detached Viscount Andrews.

Wouldn't it?

Chapter 23

Alicia rapped smartly on the door and smiled apologetically at her uncle's butler when it opened. "I'm afraid I forgot my gloves."

"I will retrieve them for you, my lady."

"There's no need. I know the way." She walked past him and went back down the polished hallway, turning to gift him with a gracious smile. "Besides, there is something I forgot to say to Lady Elena."

Luckily, Harriet had an appointment of some kind, so Alicia had deliberately left her gloves and sent her sister on her way, saying she would take a hackney home. She loved Harriet dearly, but Elena was much more likely to speak frankly to her alone.

Her cousin was still in the salon, looking somewhat pensive, her cup of tea—no doubt tepid by now—set aside. At Alicia's reentrance she looked up in slight surprise.

"I forgot my gloves." Alicia pointed them out, neatly almost hidden under a small embroidered pillow on the settee she had earlier occupied. "On purpose. Do you mind if I stay a few minutes longer?"

"No . . . of course not."

"Excellent." Alicia closed the door and went over to take her seat again. She gave her cousin a direct look. "Please trust me when I say I am not prying, but I need you to tell me the story of your abduction and the time you spent with Lord Andrews again, but this time in much more detail."

Elena looked bemused. "Of course I trust you, Allie, but may I ask why?"

It seemed only fair if she was asking for trust, she give it back in turn. "Ben is going to catch whoever did this to you but he was certain you would be more comfortable talking to me."

Her cousin's voice held a resigned note. "I suppose my father asked him. He is quite bent on revenge of some sort. I am not convinced personally that won't just draw more attention to what happened."

That was a valid point but Ben was one of the most discreet people Alicia had ever met, and if and when he found the culprit they could then decide how to handle the situation. Her uncle, no matter how pompous he could be at times, would not seek further scandal either.

"You know we all want to protect you, not cause more problems, but it is rather hard to know how to do that if we don't understand who went to such lengths or why this happened in the first place."

Elena's perfect complexion took on color, a delicate blush suffusing her cheeks. *She really is very beautiful,* Alicia mused, *with her pale hair and dark blue eyes. Surely Andrews was* not *immune.* Elena said quietly, "I think I know exactly what the villain wanted. A person would not have to have great detecting skills to deduct the intent."

"To create a scandal . . . yes, I agree."

"A bit more than that."

That was intriguing. Alicia lifted her brows. "Oh?"

The blush deepened. "Your husband is correct. I would not tell this to anyone but you. My father doesn't even know the particulars, but I am quite certain the entire purpose of the abduction was for Lord Andrews to ruin me in truth, not just by our mutual disappearance. We were locked in a room, our clothes gone, and besides a table and two chairs there was only a bed we had to share. We were given romantic dinners and fine wines each night, and silk robes but nothing else to wear."

It was her turn to blink. "I see."

"It was very much like a calculated seduction, or at least the perfect setting for one."

Did he seduce you? The question hovered on the tip of her tongue, but she didn't ask it. Instead Alicia said, "Start at the beginning and remember that no detail is unimportant."

"I don't remember the beginning," Elena said flatly. "I was at the theater, and then I woke up in a strange place next to a man I knew only by reputation, and most of my clothes were gone. All I was wearing was my chemise."

"That *would* be disconcerting." Up until lately, even as a married lady, she'd never been that undressed in front of a man.

"When he finally woke—it was obvious he was drugged either more heavily or after me—Ran was so furious at first that he accused me of orchestrating the entire thing."

Ran? Well, Alicia did suppose that being locked in together for that many days might make for some informality and especially under the conditions just described, but still . . . *Ran?*

"Surely he realized quite quickly you would have never taken part in such a scheme to trap anyone. Not to mention that you could have your pick of the gentlemen of the *ton* and are engaged," she said with true indignation, because her cousin was not only genuinely lovely on the outside but also good-natured and intelligent.

"Keep in mind he was as confused as I was. Neither of us understood what was happening. "

Well, if that was true, Alicia was not sure she could blame the viscount, for titled men had been trapped into marriage before. That noted, Elena was hardly a likely candidate for that sort of maneuver. Her dowry was no doubt generous, she was the daughter of a powerful man, and she was, of course, a beauty. "Hmm. It is all very curious. What else? What can you tell me that might be helpful? Think hard and leave out nothing."

"There really isn't much." Elena leaned back, slender against the elegant chair. "We played cards, ate together . . . he was restless at being imprisoned but so was I. We conversed, of course. What else was there to do?"

Alicia was more enlightened than previously as to what else there might be to do, especially with the licentious viscount, but she quelled the impulse to mention it. "That had to be . . ."

"Awkward? Yes, at first, but he is very easy to know."

Apparently Andrews had lived up to his reputation for smooth charm. Alicia tried to concentrate on what she thought Ben wished for her to ask. "Did he have any ideas about who might have arranged the kidnapping?"

Dark blue eyes regarded her with a hint of wry humor. "He was convinced, and I assume nothing has changed, that it had more to do with me than him."

"Is that so?" Alicia murmured the words, trying to assimilate the information. "So if I am correct, someone incarcerated you with a handsome, legendary lover and made sure you could not escape, the entire time treating you basically well."

"As ridiculous as it sounds, that sums it up quite nicely." Elena rose then and walked to the window. This side of the house faced the street and through the lace panel of the drapery she watched a carriage roll by. Alicia could hear the clatter of the wheels. Without turning around she asked, "Can you arrange a meeting, do you think?"

It was her turn to pause, but she'd caught a certain undercurrent to their conversation. Cautiously she ventured, "With Lord Andrews?"

"Colbert has not yet canceled our engagement. I dare not do it openly."

Alicia hesitated, but then said, "I have come to believe my husband can do just about anything. I suppose I could ask him to speak to the viscount, but may I ask just what it is you wish to discuss? Does it have anything to do with the investigation?"

When Elena turned, her smile was tremulous. "No. But it might have to do with the rest of my life. I don't want to, but I'm going tonight to the Perrington ball. I know it is going to be a trial, but a public appearance now might be better. The longer I wait, the more people will whisper."

The rest of her life?

That raised interesting questions, but Alicia didn't ask them. "Consider it done."

*   *   *

Ran picked up the note, dropped it, and then picked it up again as he uttered a foul word. It had arrived earlier via an anonymous messenger, but he knew in his gut that Heathton was involved. It was in both the wording and the stealthy manner of delivery. Very rarely did someone leave a missive on his pillow slip and no one in the house had the slightest notion as to how it got there.

Rather showy of the man, if you asked him.

I will be at the Perringtons' this evening. E

He was glad she'd given him warning. At least he could approach politely, murmur a commonplace greeting, and retreat. But what he thought they should do was eschew words at all, lie naked in the same bed, this time with complete freedom to explore each other's bodies, and complete the final act of love. . . .

Love?

Damn him to hell. He'd thought the word more than once. It was ridiculous. A person did not fall in love so quickly. Or did he? His expertise did not fall into that category. He'd had affairs that had lasted for months and his feelings had never been so engaged, so that was all he could base his assumptions on.

But, then again, he'd never felt quite *this* way either.

Elena was affianced.

He was a blackguard.

Enough said.

Love.

This was lust, certainly, that was undeniable. And why wouldn't it be with the Earl of Whitbridge's delectable daughter? Unless he stopped breathing and the blood froze in his veins, he would want her.

In the act of tying his cravat, he stopped, that realization causing his fingers to still.

That had never occurred to him before. He viewed women usually as a passing distraction. A pleasure, certainly, and a necessary part of life, but not in an individual way.

"My lord?"

Distracted, Ran glanced up, realizing that his valet was at his elbow, holding up two different jackets. As if he cared if he wore the blue or the gray. "Either one," he said more shortly than he intended, and then amended with a crooked smile. "You usually know best. I'm woefully blind to color unless it is the specific hue of a certain lady's eyes, in which case I seem to be able to remember that very well."

"In this case?" Gorman was ever polite but handed him the gray.

"Indigo."

"I see." He took the jacket back. "The dark blue might be better."

"Because you wish me to match her eyes?"

Gorman had the grace to laugh. "No, my lord, but maybe it would be best if you didn't clash."

"I have no desire to regulate my life to her wardrobe or coloring."

"Then it is clear you've never been married, my lord."

Was Gorman married? He didn't even know. Ran cleared his throat. "I suppose if there is wisdom to impart, I am open to it."

"Anything you can do to please her." Gorman helped him into his superfine jacket. "Such a small gesture, but . . . it is appreciated usually. They keep note of the smallest concessions."

"So she will notice my jacket matches her eyes?" His voice was full of amusement because never in one million years did he think that to be true, and supposedly he was notoriously seductive.

His valet said with composure, "You might be surprised, my lord, what women notice."

Arrested, Ran took a moment, thought about it, and then asked, "Like what?"

Young, personable, and generally attentive, Gorman paused in the act of picking up Ran's discarded shirt. "*You* are asking *me*, my lord?"

"I actually think I am." Ran grinned then but it was an afterthought. "No offense meant in the way I worded that either. So what would you do if a young lady who might be unavailable to you caught your attention?"

"How much of your attention?"

"Quite a bit." It was a telling admission but he was beginning to think it was true.

"How unavailable?"

"Very. Short of marriage."

"Then . . . why not marry her?"

The simplistic answer made him freeze. "I beg your pardon?"

"And have her all to yourself, sir. That is the point of it all, isn't it?" Gorman stepped back as if he hadn't said something so catastrophic and nodded in approval of his appearance. "You look very fine, my lord."

Have her all to myself. It was frighteningly appealing but he still argued, "I've only known her for a short time and, besides, I'm not interested in marriage."

"I'm unconvinced that the measure of time in which one knows the right young lady matters, and if you pardon me for pointing it out, sir, few men are interested in marriage until they meet the woman that changes their mind."

Ran stepped over to the glass to check his cravat, more as a distraction than anything, because had it been askew his valet would have instantly corrected the problem. His voice was unsteady. "I had no idea you were a philosopher."

"And I had no idea, my lord, you were a romantic."

The first impulse was to deny that, but he was beginning to realize his interest in Elena may not just be casual. He, who had bedded countless beauties, could remember with precision the exact texture of her silken hair and the smoothness of her skin, and he'd be damned if he wasn't wearing a jacket very close in hue to her gorgeous eyes.

This was extraordinary in his existence, but, their courtship so far—if one could call it that—had been of a *most* extraordinary kind.

All he knew was that he wanted to see her.

Desperately.

And an hour later he did.

The ballroom was crowded but it wasn't difficult to spot her, as all heads were turned that way, plus her signature pale hair was unmistakable. Ran had an idea already that if Elena was going to make her first public appearance—men gossiped as much as women, in reality, so he knew she'd been in seclusion—it would be at a crowded function like this one. The Perringtons were known for their largesse and this was no exception, for the ballroom was crammed with well-dressed people, most of who were gawping at the Earl of Whitbridge's daughter.

Waltzing with her fiancé.

Hell.

"As soon as people notice you are here, this insipid entertainment might actually get interesting."

Ran glanced up and registered the lazy smile of Jack Ferguson, his slight Scottish accent subdued by an education at Cambridge, which was where they'd met. They'd been friends for a decade and had both fought in the war, though in different regiments.

"Didn't know you were in town," Ran said conversationally, though his smile was genuinely warm. "You usually send word."

"I had some business in London, and for your edification I did send a note, but you were not in residence, which seems to be the topic of the hour. She's a lovely lassie, I must admit."

"I'm a bit behind in my correspondence."

"So I'm told."

Dark, with almost startling green eyes, Jack was not really the quintessential Scot in appearance, but intensely loyal, not just to his country but to his friends. Ran didn't mind saying quietly as possible so he wouldn't be overheard, "I have no idea what people are saying . . . Well, maybe some idea. Tell me."

Jack considered, stroking his jaw. "They seem to think you made off with Whitbridge's daughter, though there is dissention over how you could possibly have managed it and returned alive, because he isn't a benevolent man."

"Good to know," Ran muttered. "We've met but not since the abduction."

"So you did take her off for nearly a week?"

"No, of course not."

"Care to explain?"

"Later." Ran offered it in as even a tone as he could manage. "The finest brandy money can buy will accompany the story. But for the moment could you please excuse me?"

Chapter 24

He was there. Everyone knew he was there. *She* knew he was there and ignoring it wasn't working.

Elena accepted a glass of champagne, smiled, and did her best to not look in the least interested in what Viscount Andrews might be doing, but she had no illusions. The evening had been awful so far—more awful than she had imagined.

People watched them. Both of them, which was better, maybe, than when everyone was just watching *her*, but there was also the new challenge of not even glancing his way.

When she very, very much wanted to observe what Ran was doing, maybe even go over, talk to him like they'd done on those long, lazy afternoons, and then ...

She was, in a word, hopeless.

He might know more about her than anyone else. It was startling to realize, but their unusual circumstances had prompted some soul-baring confessions she hadn't even told Alicia. Not that any were earth-shattering, as her upbringing had been fairly conventional, but she'd confessed a few things she might not normally tell anyone.

So the seductive Lord Andrews knew all her secrets but one.

That she'd fallen wildly in love with him. Well, who was to say it wasn't just a romantic backlash of their adventure and wouldn't pass quickly?

Except she felt sure that was not true.

"It is a lovely party, is it not?"

Distracted, she almost didn't catch the question. "Yes. Absolutely. Of course. Quite . . . lovely." The stammer wasn't elegant.

Lord Colbert said in measured tones. "He's here."

"Who?"

"Andrews."

"Oh yes, I noticed he was present." She smiled with what she hoped was aplomb. They'd just finished their dance and exited the floor, his hand at her elbow, and he'd immediately signaled a passing footman and gotten her some refreshment. So far he'd done nothing more than inquire after her health and comment that he admired her gown. She'd been perversely glad that he hadn't said more but also anxious to simply get the inevitable discussion over with rather than putting it off.

"And I noticed you noticing." Her fiancé's voice was still almost too even considering they hadn't spoken yet about her disappearance.

The odd aspect of this entire debacle was she liked her possible-but-unlikely-now husband more than ever for his efforts to make it seem as if all was well between them. Perhaps he'd been doing it as much for his pride as for her, but she still appreciated the public display of support. Elena exhaled softly in a rueful laugh. "I am sure you have questions and I will do my best to answer them."

"Good. I prefer we be frank with each other."

"And I am grateful for the effort you have made to make it seem as if nothing has happened and not immediately repudiate the engagement."

Her fiancé regarded her steadily. "I am hoping nothing *did* happen."

She said nothing in response but neither did she look away. This evening was not going to be about making excuses. Had it been, she might have stayed home.

"Yes," he murmured eventually, turning enough he could seem to casually survey the room. His tone took on a hint of resignation. "That is what I thought. I've talked to Andrews also, and while he didn't admit anything, he seemed . . . involved, though he denied culpability. So, what do you wish to do now?"

Involved?

Was he?

Since the beginning of this, no one had ever asked *her* what she wished to do, so that was at least refreshing. "I understand and support a severing of our arrangement."

Lord Colbert reflected with visible contemplation before he spoke. "I am going to tell you I would not like an heir that does not resemble me in the least."

That was irrefutably frank, but given the conversation, understandable. And, after all, her father had prepared her for this moment.

At this point she had a clear choice. "You wouldn't have one," she told him, because he deserved that much. "But considering the circumstances I don't blame you for the concern."

To his credit, his gaze softened. "Someone did this deliberately to you."

"Or perhaps to us? You cannot believe there were not

some disappointed young ladies when you proposed to me."

He didn't answer, deny, or even look surprised. Elena had to smile, though she suspected it was shaky. She went on. "Surely that is as possible as anything else? Men in your position, with money and power, have enemies."

"Good evening."

Her breath caught then. Subtle, but there was something unique in the way the words were said, and when she slowly turned, champagne in hand, the gaze of the man standing behind her was so intense it took her breath away.

Ran. She knew him. Knew that quixotic half smile. Knew the straight shape of his nose, the length of his lashes, the way he woke in the morning, his beguiling smile when he was teasing her . . .

"Lord Andrews." She didn't quite succeed in being completely serene, but she was at least close to seeming calm, her smile faltering only for a moment. "How nice to see you."

"Lady Elena." He took her free hand and raised it to his lips.

Theatrical and immediate. In that way he had.

In that very special way he has.

And the tension was suddenly palpable. All across the ballroom. All across London as far as she could tell, as if the entire core of their social world was avidly attuned to this meeting.

And she could not help but respond in kind to the power of his deliberately charming smile. *Which is why women fall at his feet, and why you shouldn't be one of them.*

Such a compelling point.

But looking into his dark eyes, it wasn't quite so easy of a decision. She murmured, "I was not sure what to expect when we saw each other again."

"You and everyone else. They are currently dying to know what we are saying to each other." He turned to Colbert. "And how civilized this will be."

"That is up to you."

However, when her fiancé slid his arm around her waist, Ran visibly tensed. She did as well since it was not particularly a gesture of affection as much as possession, and an irreverent voice inside her damned all men and their pride straight to Hades.

No. She was not a prize meant to be won or lost.

Elena gave both parties a polite smile. "I am going to tell you what it will not be. I am not interested in being a spectacle for the entire *ton* to whisper over even more than it is already. None of the three of us is at fault over what has happened, so let us not punish each other."

"That is a reasonable suggestion." Ran took a moment and his handsome face was tight. But then he said, "I know this might not be greeted with a great deal of enthusiasm, but perhaps we could meet and discuss it."

"You and I?" She recalled all the times they'd sat and speculated together. Unless he'd discovered something what would be the point?

"The three of us? I think that is reasonable." Colbert said the words with cold precision.

The declaration made her glance up sharply at her fiancé. There was something about his expression that made her wonder if he had something to hide. Not guilt, precisely, but he was certainly being very decent and she suddenly had an inkling he might not be as innocent as she thought.

Startling, that.

The man who had offered to marry her, to give his name and protection, actually looked uncomfortable.

"Do you know something we don't?" she asked sharply, and maybe she should have not been so abrupt considering there were people hovering everywhere, no doubt trying to eavesdrop. But usually his manners were impeccable, the fluid grace of his bow and easy smile affable, and there had to be a reason a small sheen of sweat covered his brow.

"I might," he muttered.

This was rather interesting. If he had expected anything of this evening, it wasn't to be standing with his former fellow victim and her fiancé in a far corner of a ballroom, a bevy of matrons and other guests ogling them as they conversed.

However, of the three of them, Ran was fairly sure he was the one most versed in being the center of all eyes, and he advised quietly, "We should have this conversation elsewhere."

"Not the worst idea I've heard," Colbert agreed tersely. "Our club, later?"

Ran inclined his head.

"No." The declaration was flat and unequivocal. Elena, gorgeous as ever in an elegant gown that matched her eyes as much as his jacket did—he didn't miss the irony—lifted her shapely chin. "No. I'm sorry, my lords, but not *without* me. This isn't between the two of you but among the three of us, and I will not be left out. I am uninterested in being informed later of the decision the *two* of you have made. It seems to me entirely too much of my life lately has been controlled by the actions of other people, including whoever decided it would be a fine idea to have us abducted."

It might have been right then, at that moment, in front of hundreds of other people intent on trying to overhear them, not to mention in front of the man she was promised to, that Ran knew he was in love with her.

Her beauty aside, her spirit *captivated* him.

And he really couldn't agree more with her reasoning. "It will feed the gossip mill for weeks, but shall we step out onto the terrace? At least we won't be overheard."

There was a split second of hesitation when he considered publically offering her his arm. Partly because it was a natural reflex to do so and partly because he was jealous as hell of Colbert and wanted her to choose him instead, but in the end he just stepped back and let her precede him to where twin sets of doors let fresh air into the stuffy ballroom. The crowd parted as Elena made her way across the floor and the two of them followed her, Ran admiring both her composure and the very feminine sway of her hips. The whispers rose, and Ran had no doubt that the guests expected violence of some kind was about to ensue.

Oddly enough, he didn't anticipate any physical altercation, the assumption borne out once they stepped outside and walked to the balustrade. Elena turned to look at her fiancé with inquiring eyes. All Colbert said in a brittle voice was, "I like to think I'm a fair-minded man, so I am not sure between the two of us who owes whom an apology in this situation." He shot Ran a quick look that wasn't precisely friendly but not lethal either. "Though I *am* certain, Andrews, that you owe me one."

He did. To an extent anyway. However, since he had not instigated any part of what had led to the abduction, he was disinclined to split hairs at the moment. "Obviously you have a theory. Care to share it with us?"

Colbert looked out over the gardens and tugged at his perfectly tied cravat. "It could have been Maria. She has the means and the motive. Once I sat and truly thought about it I admit I had a certain suspicion." He glanced over. "Beret. I've been told you are old friends."

Maria Beret. Ah, now this started to make a bit more sense. The lady in question had a penchant for younger men and there was no question she was a bit volatile. If Colbert was her current lover . . . It was almost amusing, or it might be later, but for now it was plausible. "I know Maria," Ran admitted slowly. "But it was years ago. I take it you are more recently acquainted."

"Who is Maria Beret?" Elena cast them an askance look, and she certainly was entitled to both the question and an explanation. He noticed that in the starlight her hair glimmered gold.

The theater would not be a good career for Lord Colbert. He looked distinctly guilty.

Damnation.

This entire conversation would be easier if she wasn't an innocent victim, but she was, and obviously he and Colbert were not. If he could change the course of what had happened, he would . . . or would he? While being taken prisoner and kept from his family was an infuriating experience, he would never have met her otherwise and that would have been a life-altering omission.

Maybe he owed the passionate Mrs. Beret his sincere gratitude.

He was the one who answered her question in a dry tone. "A mutual friend, apparently."

"Oh." Elena took in a breath. "I think I understand how you both *know* her. Let me take a guess. The current hypothesis is that she decided to take revenge on one of you or both of you, by destroying me socially, because you have *both* been her lovers. How absolutely delightful."

His past was not something he was inclined to apologize for, but she was different and Ran couldn't bear to see the disillusionment in her eyes.

He caught her shaking arm as she turned away. "There was no intent to hurt you. Ever. I hate to support Colbert in any way, but I don't think so on his part either and I can vow that there never was on mine."

"I second that and offer my apologies," Colbert said earnestly. "I don't know if this is an excuse but gentlemen are granted some license while waiting to be married."

Apparently she didn't agree. "So this happened *after* our engagement?"

Colbert might have done better to keep that inadequate explanation to himself. All excuses between them were waived when Ran stepped into the breach, since her averted profile tore him apart. She deserved anything he could tell her to mend this unforgivable moment. "Darling . . . there is no comparison between you and her."

If he hadn't felt her tremble again he might not have done what happened next, but she did.

And he did.

It was the shimmer of tears in her incredible eyes. She

had asked nothing of him, yet as all of fashionable society—or at least all curious ones who were spying out the windows—watched, he took her hand and brought it to his lips, kissing each finger with care, taking his time.

Effectively declaring his intentions for a woman engaged to someone else.

This was the time for Colbert to interfere if he wished, but it seemed he didn't. Either too ashamed of himself or too worried he might say something to provoke an argument, he turned then and walked back into the house, leaving them alone, yet hardly alone at all, since most of London proper witnessed that public abandonment.

This was not how it was supposed to be. Ran didn't fall for the lovely lady that had provided him with a pleasant distraction—he forgot her.

He rarely explained himself; he just moved on.

He didn't equivocate or apologize.

Most certainly he didn't usually tug a handkerchief from his pocket and before all of the exalted *ton* gently wipe a tear from the corner of a young lady's eye. "I'm sorry."

"You have a myriad of sins to answer for, Andrews." She gave a charming hiccup. "Can you be more specific as to what you are apologizing for?"

That statement alone signified what fascinated him so. To the point he felt he was teetering on a precipice with unchartered territory at the bottom. "For compromising you. Actually, not that." He took a moment, astounded to realize his hands were not quite steady either. "Let me try again with more sincerity. For everything I contributed to this debacle, for being notorious in the first place, though

I vow I really thought I was the only one affected. I refuse to apologize for the lack of a regular courtship because it wouldn't have happened had our circumstances been different, but for any contribution I've had in hurting you, I am truly sorry."

Now he had her attention, her sticky lashes dark against the whiteness of her skin. "Go on."

Good God, half of London's fashionable circle was pressed up against the windows. He, who had never wanted to make a proposal in the first place, experienced a sort of rueful recognition it might be retribution for his past sins.

Maybe she had no wish to marry him.

Just because he had come to the conclusion he wanted to ask didn't mean a damn thing. She might refuse. After all, two minutes ago she was engaged to someone else.

"I have a title."

It was possibly the least glib sentence of his life, which made him give a choked laugh right away. "May I retract that opening and try again?"

Luminous eyes stared up at him and Elena nodded. "Please do."

He knew then, but he'd possibly known all along, from that first breathless kiss. It was innate self-preservation that made him stumble so badly, but he'd always been wary of innocent debutantes. He was completely bereft of his usual sangfroid.

Luckily, it came to him. Just a few simple words. "You are different."

It was hardly loverlike, said with just a slight edge, but she smiled at him and his heart did an interesting twist.

"I should hope so, my lord."

"You only use formal address to annoy me." He

tugged her closer. Suddenly the crowd in the ballroom didn't matter.

"See? We *do* know each other."

"I think perhaps we do but not as well as I would like. What should we do next? The masses need to be entertained."

"The masses? Oh." She glanced at the terrace doors, where more than a few people were gathered, pretending to sip champagne but instead avidly watching them. Then, as intrepid as he remembered, she set a hand on his shoulder. "Can you believe I'd almost forgotten them? I suppose, since *notoriety* is the word of the day, you could kiss me. I should think they would expect it, and as he just walked away, I somehow doubt Lord Colbert will object. It seems my engagement is officially over, and as I am already quite thoroughly ruined, I can't see how it would make the situation worse."

"Colbert will stay away from you if he values his life." Then he added roughly, "You are mine."

Not quite a poetic declaration of love or a romantic proposal on bended knee, but it served the purpose of at least making his intentions clear.

"Ran." She gazed up at him, the tears gone, and he would do anything—anything—to see that sudden light in her eyes. Her mouth curved invitingly and he knew from personal experience it was soft and warm and inviting. . . .

He leaned forward, his lips brushing hers, and he could swear he heard a collective gasp from inside the house. He murmured against her mouth, "What type of kiss does my lady desire? Soft and sweet, do you think, or suitably passionate?"

Elena slipped her arms around his neck. "You are a terrible rake. Do you know that?"

His tongue traced her lower lip. "I would take offense, but at the moment, with you in my arms, I cannot summon any outrage. Your answer, my sweet? We can't disappoint them."

"Both," she whispered.

Chapter 25

"It appears, at least at a first perusal of the facts, that indeed Lord Colbert was quite correct about Maria Beret."

Alicia, looking deliciously feminine in some sort of muslin gown with ridiculous little puffy sleeves that were actually quite flattering to her slender arms, stopped in the act of taking a sip of coffee. "Darling, it is barely nine in the morning. We did not get home until very late. What facts could you have gathered in that amount of time?"

Quite a lot, Ben wanted to tell her, because after she'd retired he had gone back out and made a few calls. When it was necessary he could do with very little sleep, and he wanted this matter settled quickly so his life could return to a semblance of normalcy.

Though, he had to admit, this had been a much more interesting ten days or so than he'd had in quite a while. Being the earl was definitely not as exciting as his previous employment.

Being a husband, however, was proving to be much more of a challenge than anticipated. Frustrating at times and vastly enjoyable at others. At least he could honestly say he wasn't bored.

"I discovered that the woman in question is financially solvent enough to pay a French chef, sufficient staff, and armed guards. She is also most definitely involved in a romantic sense with Lord Colbert, and, rumor has it, is a bit on the vindictive side when discarded. His upcoming marriage might easily have sparked her somewhat legendary temper."

His wife set down her fork. "All that before breakfast?"

He took her incredulity as a compliment. "Men talk to other men. We just don't talk to women too often when it comes to our private affairs."

"*That's* true."

The swift agreement said on a grumble deflated his brief triumph and he wondered if he should be insulted. "For a reason," he said as he reached for the rack of toast. "All that aside, what I am saying is that it is possible for her to be the culprit. Her lover was marrying someone else and she wished to punish him—and by using Andrews she could punish a former lover who obviously left her some time ago—by destroying the young lady that was taking from her something she wanted."

"Well done." Alicia smiled at him, touching her napkin to her mouth in a dainty movement.

He had to admit a certain fascination with the shape of her lips. They were also a lovely color, a soft pink and tilted up at the corners. . . .

Back to the subject at hand. Good heavens, they were just having breakfast. "Except I am not convinced."

Her smiled faded. "Why ever not? It makes perfect sense."

"It makes no sense at all, my dear."

Dark blue eyes regarded him with all due curiosity

and she pursed her lips in a way that drew his attention back to her mouth. "How so?"

The woman was far too distracting. "Because," he informed her as he took another piece of bacon, "I'm not convinced she would be so clever, and whoever did this is clever indeed."

He wasn't quite sure he was willing to reveal why he thought they were clever quite yet. The bacon was as he liked it, crisp and brown, and he took a bite.

"You just said—"

"I said she has the means, the motive, and, if rumor is correct, the nature to do it, but I am not certain in any way she would know how to actually keep it such a secret."

"I hate it when you get that moody and contemplative tone to your voice."

Ben had to admit the comment took him by surprise. "I wasn't aware I had a tone."

"You know full well you have one. Pfft." His wife sat back and apparently abandoned her breakfast. "Are you telling me this isn't solved after all? I mean, my cousin is so thoroughly compromised by Andrews that she *has* to marry him. Surely he will ask, and I know she will be happy. A bit too happy, considering their behavior last evening, but I assume many a young lady has been kissed on a terrace in the moonlight, however usually not after her former intended has just severed their engagement in front of everyone of consequence."

That was undeniable. Colbert had been in the ballroom when the viscount had kissed Lady Elena in full sight of most of elite society, and the volume of whispers had risen as the embrace went on for a lingering interval.

It hadn't been a perfunctory kiss at all.

Good for Andrews.

"If you are going to scandalize all of society, you might as well enjoy it." He picked up his coffee and went on. "I might be wrong, but my instincts say that Maria Beret *could* be our kidnapper, but I doubt it. Think of it, my dear: besides revenge, what would she gain? Yes, Colbert is humiliated, but she's a wealthy widow with other suitors at hand, and while she might have been piqued at his upcoming wedding, I don't think she has the depth to be this inventive."

"It takes depth to be vindictive?"

"No." He decided to have marmalade on his toast though he didn't usually, because now he had to admit he was self-conscious over hurting the feelings of the cook. "I said *inventive*. It takes someone abnormally clever to arrange to have two people kidnapped in a way that they remember nothing about the event yet are unharmed. My impression of Mrs. Beret is that she would not take such care as to hire a chef and provide them with luxurious accommodations in which to stay during their captivity. She could have spared a lot of expense to achieve the same exact effect. If the purpose was revenge on Elena, Colbert, and Andrews all in one, she was far more subtle than I would expect from what I know of her."

"A valid point." Alicia looked slightly crestfallen. "It seemed so logical. If she'd once had an affair with Lord Andrews and is currently Colbert's paramour, she had the perfect motivation."

"Motivation can be the key to solving a case like this, but all too often the most obvious suspect is not the culprit." Almost as soon as he spoke, he wished he hadn't chosen those particular words, but damned if he wasn't distracted again by the graceful way Alicia stirred more sugar into her coffee.

"I assume that statement means you've solved puzzles like this fairly often, my lord."

"Once or twice." He brushed the curious question aside by deflection. "What are your plans for today?"

"I think perhaps we should go interview Mrs. Beret. Don't you?"

No, he didn't. He did not work that way. The indirect approach was always better. He had every intention of interviewing the woman's banker, the leasing agent that rented the estate where Andrews and Elena had been held and the kindhearted chef who had let them free, but not Mrs. Beret. Right now he had not one shred of evidence except Colbert's—possibly arrogant—assumption she was fond enough of him to commit the crime.

Besides, while he hadn't minded his beautiful wife talking to Lady Elena, he hardly wanted her involved in any other way. It seemed unlikely the situation was dangerous, but Andrews had been convinced at gunpoint that force might be used if he tried to escape, and he'd seen himself that the guard they encountered on the grounds was armed, so it was open to debate.

Absolutely in no way was Alicia going to talk to Mrs. Beret. The trouble was, of course, stopping her from doing as she pleased. He wasn't despotic enough to simply order her—and not convinced she would obey anyway.

"I was wondering if you could possibly visit Lord Andrews's aunt."

His wife blinked. "Why?"

He took a bite of his toast, appreciatively chewed with some surprise because the marmalade was actually superb, and swallowed. "Women notice things men do not and she shares his household and looks after his sister. If there was someone else who might have done this she could offer some insight."

That was safe enough. Randolph Raine's aunt was an upright woman with a reputation for seclusion.

"Good idea." To his relief Alicia agreed with alacrity. "I didn't realize you even considered her as part of this."

"I don't in particular, but she might know some small fact that she doesn't even realize is important. She did point me in the right direction with the mention of the whiskey."

"True. I will find out if possible."

She would, too. He knew it, which somewhat surprised him. Her uncle's words came back. Had he married an intelligent female on purpose? Well, certainly he wasn't attracted to women with no intellect, but he hadn't sat down and thought about it at length either.

It was interesting, he was discovering, to come to terms with how little he might know about himself.

At least the earl agreed to see him, but that did not necessarily mean approval as Ran learned when motioned to a chair with a dismissive wave of Lord Whitbridge's hand.

It grated, he had to admit. Not that he had expected a warm welcome, but surely the man understood he was just as much a victim as Elena, and that aside he was here to petition for marriage, which was not easy for him.

At all.

Yet also it was perhaps the most important moment of his life. That was a paradox. The infamous viscount a beggar at the feet of a self-righteous man whose daughter he hadn't quite ruined but certainly compromised. And Whitbridge not able to refuse his suit, which Ran knew quite well he would have before the abduction.

This should be a most interesting conversation.

"My lord," he said formally.

"Your behavior is quite difficult to accept, Andrews." No preliminary greeting, just that caustic statement.

"How so?" he asked frankly, because that rankled. Though that kiss had been ill-advised, perhaps, at least it had been a public declaration of his intentions.

"A past like yours isn't something any father can ignore."

So the animosity was due to his reputation. Fair enough. In some ways he deserved it.

He said with as much equanimity as possible, "I am not here because of the past, but because I wish to discuss the future."

"Go on." The earl regarded him from under heavy brows. "Explain why you wish to see me."

At least he wasn't unwilling to listen. Ran took in a breath and let it out slowly, tried to pass over how he had not even been offered the courtesy of refreshment, and summoned a conciliatory smile. "I want to marry Elena." He paused and then went on. "This is a formal offer and we can both involve our solicitors in, say," — he extracted his pocket watch — "an hour's time?"

"That soon?"

The sooner they married, the sooner the rumors would die down. Not to mention now that he'd decided he wished to marry her more than he wanted to take his next breath, he couldn't stop thinking about holding her in his arms, preferably in a soft bed. "I want a special license."

"Because you need one?" Lord Whitbridge half rose from his chair, his mouth pinched.

"Because I *want* one. Much different."

The earl sat down again, Ran's scathing tone obviously having an effect. He was younger, taller, and just as socially powerful, but he was not the outraged father of a ruined young woman, and so he gave the elder man due courtesy by saying quietly in the tense aftermath, "Though I hadn't intended on marrying for some time, I do wish to make *her* my wife as soon as possible. May I?"

That was about as humble as he was capable of being. Still, he meant every word.

At least the evident sincerity got through, for Whitbridge finally nodded, looking suddenly quite resigned. "I suppose it is best after all that has happened, so I appreciate the honest offer. Colbert sent a formal letter by special messenger this morning, crying off, which Elena informed me suits her, as apparently she wasn't all that interested in marrying him in the first place."

And since his daughter had been repudiated in such a public manner, this would avert more scandal. But the acquiescence was more gracious than he expected, so Ran simply nodded and stood. "Shall we let our solicitors handle the rest of it, then? I've no need of your money, but if you wish to give her dowry directly to her, please feel free to do so."

"She's a woman," Elena's father objected.

"I have noticed. And gifted with a brain that functions perfectly well. Give her the money or put it in trust for our children."

He spoke before he knew what he was going to say, and the words caught him off guard. The idea of children was startling, and yet . . . most certainly they would have a family, for he was looking forward beyond measure to conceiving them. Lucy would be delighted also in small nieces and nephews. . . .

Life could change quickly in the most interesting ways.

Whitbridge grudgingly said, "Maybe you'll muddle along fairly well together, then, if you feel that way. My daughter is very independent."

"If we can marry quickly, I intend to take her to my country estate and let the gossip die down."

"A reasonable idea. I will see to the formalities. One of my good friends is a bishop and I am sure he can help. The expediency is unseemly, but maybe in this case wise."

"I'd like a short word with Elena alone if possible." Ran knew he still needed to ask her properly. She was being deprived of the fanfare of a grand wedding but she still deserved a true proposal.

"I don't see why not at this point. It is a bit late for propriety." The Earl of Whitbridge's voice was dry. "I advise you keep it very short, because once I inform my wife of this change in plans there will be a great deal of female fussing over gowns and flowers and whatever else would be involved in planning a wedding in such a short time."

When Ran was shown into a small salon a few minutes later, his wife-to-be was already there, her hair simply tied back with a white ribbon. Dark blue eyes regarded him with open question. "I was surprised when I received your card. It is rather early for a formal call, my lord."

"I confess I didn't sleep much last night."

"Neither did I." Her voice was hushed.

She was refreshingly candid, which he'd found enchanting from the beginning. "Were you perhaps thinking of me?"

"You might have entered my mind once or twice." Her smile was teasing but still a little wistful and he couldn't help but admire how composed she was for someone whose life had been recently turned upside down. While he had the benefit of financial autonomy and an indifference to the opinion of society that his rank and title afforded, she had none of that.

"I was thinking of *you*." He moved toward her and took her hand, much as he'd done on the terrace the evening before. "It seems pointless for us both to have sleepless nights, do you not agree? If we shared a bed, I predict we'd sleep quite comfortably. Lady Elena, I wonder if you would do me the honor of becoming my wife."

There was no part of him that thought he deserved the joy in her face, but it did something interesting to his heart, the tightening in his chest maybe a result of holding his breath. Elena laughed. "Trust an infamous rake to couch a proposal with a mention of the bedroom. However, I agree: we did seem to sleep mostly soundly in our tower."

Their tower. He supposed it was, or at least he would always think of it that way.

"Is that a yes?" He tugged her closer.

"I am rather notorious, you know." She reached up and touched his cheek. "Utterly ruined, jilted, and I believe just last night I behaved with shocking impropriety at a fashionable ball, no less."

"I adore reckless ladies with inappropriate tendencies. You will suit me perfectly."

"Are you sure? I am well aware of your attitude

toward marriage. There is no need to be noble on my account."

"No?" He looked into her eyes.

"No." She looked back steadily.

"Perhaps I wish to be noble. Besides, the question of my nobility could be debated, darling. Kiss me to seal the pact because I need to be on my way. I've a rather busy day planned as I am getting married very soon. Tomorrow, if possible."

"Tomorrow?" It was a gasp. "Ran, how could I possibly . . . ? We can't . . ."

His smile was deliberately dangerous. "We can and we will. Might I point out I am very much looking forward to resuming our lessons."

Chapter 26

Janet Raine frowned, walking in long, slow strides, her hands clasped somewhat mannishly behind her back. "Yes, she denies it by all accounts, but my nephew seems to believe that Mrs. Beret is the likely culprit. When I think of it, it is such a perfect opportunity to get revenge on two people at the same time. It is a terrible tragedy your cousin was in the middle of it all, but such things have a way of working out for the best."

Actually, Alicia agreed about the not so nice Maria Beret, but Ben seemed to have finely honed instincts. "Can you think of anyone else? I am certain Lord Andrews does not share many confidences about his private life, but you must hear the rumors, and you and he are fond of each other as far as I can tell."

The other woman sent her a sidelong glance. "Lady Heathton, while I appreciate that your uncle wishes to track down whoever did this to his daughter, I don't think I can help you. Had I a solid suspicion I would have told Randolph. For that matter, he's an intelligent young man and he knows Mrs. Beret. If he thinks the woman would go to such lengths, then so do I."

She supposed that was true but it wasn't very helpful.

There was a bank of scarlet roses and Alicia couldn't help it; she leaned forward to smell one. "Nothing comes to mind?"

"They are getting married, you know. My nephew and your cousin."

That sharpened her attention and she straightened abruptly. "Are they?"

"Indeed. As soon as possible. I feel confident that when you return home there will be an invitation waiting for you."

That *was* hasty, but maybe that was best. She murmured, "Ben and I will be there, of course."

"It is going to be a small affair." Janet smiled, pushing back a wisp of black hair that had escaped her tight chignon. "But I think, given all that has happened, that is wise. Lucy is going to be so delighted at her brother's marriage. Such a satisfactory conclusion to an awkward situation."

"It is indeed."

It was, but didn't change that coercion had been involved. Alicia took her leave, rather chagrined she had nothing to tell Ben except he had better wear his best cravat to the celebration. Her aunt was such a stickler and she could only imagine the dither she was in over both the scandal and her daughter's hasty wedding.

To the rakish Viscount Andrews, who was, Alicia had to admit, very handsome in a devilish way. She could not help but smile as a footman handed her into her carriage. It should be an interesting marriage, because while Elena looked angelic with her fair hair and delicate features, she knew from a lifetime of acquaintance and not a few childhood escapades that there was an adventurous spirit under that demure exterior.

Lord Andrews might have met just the right woman to reform his wicked ways, and the look on her cousin's face when he was mentioned had spoken volumes. Colbert had been a good match in a social sense, and seemed a nice enough man, but it was far from a love match, and every woman deserved that. While her own marriage hadn't begun that way—her naive assumption that Ben would not have proposed if he wasn't in love with her had been erroneous—she still was quite optimistic it would happen eventually.

I love you.

She had told *him*, but in retrospect she'd done it more for herself than for his edification. There was a pleasure in those three simple words, and even more so in loving someone else. She actually wanted him to fall in love with her more for his sake than hers.

What an interesting perspective she had gained on life.

Life was all a matter of one's point of view.

At times he was guilty of forgetting that very basic fact.

Ben was starting to get the irritable feeling that the reason why he hadn't discovered easily who was behind the kidnappings was because females were involved, and it was nigh unto impossible to follow their irrational thought processes. So, therefore, logic didn't work.

So illogic was the order of the day.

"Rather a lovely ceremony, wasn't it? She seems happy." As she stood next to him in the garden, Alicia's observation held a dreamy quality that further convinced him he would never quite understand how women perceived certain situations. If asked, he would have said a hasty marriage in a nearly empty cathedral would not appeal to the average bride, but the new Lady Andrews was glowing, and her husband remarkably relaxed and attentive for a bridegroom whose bride had been engaged to another man just a few days before. He also had to give Lady Whitbridge credit, for the wedding dinner was excellent considering such short notice.

"They both seem to be content with the arrangement." He took another sip of champagne, which was not his favorite beverage, but this was a celebration. "She looks pleased enough."

"She is." His wife surveyed the small gathering. "I haven't said hello to Aunt Beatrice yet and Harriet is beginning to look cornered. Do you mind if I desert you for a moment or two, as I assume you do not want to take part in my sister's rescue?"

Aunt Beatrice, in his experience, was a formidable woman who was not only hard of hearing but also had a habit of not waiting for a person to complete a sentence before interrupting, which made talking to her impossible. "Desert me," he said fervently. "Please. I get the urge to hide behind a hedge if she even looks my way."

His wife's mouth twitched into a mischievous smile. "It would never do for the exalted Earl of Heathton to be found cowering in the garden, so I will go distract her and give my sister some relief."

Then she did something quite remarkable. She gracefully rose on her tiptoes, balancing her glass in one hand, the other braced on his chest, and lightly kissed him. Nothing inappropriate, just a gesture of affection, but it did happen there among the thirty-odd guests, in full view of everyone, and as she walked away he found himself somewhat mystified by the experience. Not that she had *done* it, but his reaction to it.

He was inexplicably touched.

The garden was sunlit—nature had smiled benevolently on the nuptials of the viscount and his new viscountess—and people were wandering about, no doubt also avoiding Beatrice as best as possible. When a voice spoke next to him and he turned, he wasn't all that surprised to see who stood there.

"Miss Raine." He'd wondered if after Alicia's visit Andrews's aunt might not at least comment on his pursuit of the possible culprit in her nephew's adventure.

"My lord." She inclined her head elegantly, though as usual she was dressed fairly plainly. "I did not expect to see you again so soon, much less under such circumstances, but, I suppose, as trite as it sounds, here we are."

"Indeed." He was fairly sure that Whitbridge had decent whiskey or brandy somewhere nearby, but he took a long-suffering sip from his champagne flute instead.

"Just a day ago I was conversing with your wife in the garden about this whole unfortunate affair. How ironic that my nephew has married her cousin the next day in one of the most romantic weddings I have ever seen. Who would think it would turn out this way?"

"Our kidnapper, for one."

"I beg your pardon?" She stopped in the act of taking a drink. "I don't think I understand."

"It was truly a successful and clever seduction."

She looked at him, evidently appalled "You aren't saying my nephew planned any of this."

"No, not at all. He was the one being seduced."

She seemed to consider that. "Are you suggesting Lady Elena is culpable?"

"No."

"Then—"

"Whoever very craftily planned the abduction of Lady Elena and your nephew paid some attention to fine detail that I find hard to believe would be evident in your usual brutish thug. There was no ransom either, which I would think Maria Beret might demand just to recoup the loss of the rental of the manor house and the cost of the staff." He added offhandedly, "If I were to do it, I would have at least asked for a small sum just to avert suspicion."

"Well, I somehow doubt that Mrs. Beret is as clever as you are, Lord Heathton."

"Not to sound too arrogant, but I don't think so either."

There were at least ten footmen with trays—about one to every three guests—but under the ruthless scrutiny of Lady Whitbridge they dared not stand still, so yet another went by, offering more champagne.

They both declined.

He glanced down at the woman beside him. "However you, my lady, are *very* intelligent. Tell me, why didn't you ask for ransom?"

To her credit, she didn't do more in denial except go very still. His point exactly. Intelligent enough to know that he *knew*. When she finally looked up her smile was slightly defiant but still polite enough for the casual observer to not know anything was wrong. "I was a bit dismayed to find out you were involved in this."

"How flattering."

Janet Raine drained her drink and granted an everpassing footman her smile for another, the young man looking absurdly grateful to be doing something. She took a sip and then said quietly, "It *was* a compliment. How did you guess?"

"I didn't."

She regarded him in open speculation and he revised his opinion there and then of Lord Andrews's spinster aunt.

Ben shrugged. "Maria Beret had the means, the motive, and the vindictiveness, but she wouldn't have bothered. I checked with her banker and she has not made any sizable withdrawals lately either, and as her likelihood as a suspect dwindled I thought about the whole abduction from a different angle."

"Such as?" The inquiry was tight-lipped and her hand trembled as she lifted the flute to her mouth again.

"This was matchmaking, my lady, not really an abduction per se. I haven't the slightest idea how you knew they would suit each other so well when they hadn't even met"—his gaze wandered to where one of England's most confirmed bachelors stood next to his beautiful bride, leaning slightly forward to listen to something she said—"but you hit the mark, I'd say."

There was no easy confession but instead silence. That was fine. He had patience. Finally she said, "I was once engaged to the wrong man. Look at her . . . As you said, she's brilliantly happy. And so is Randolph."

"Quite a decision to make on someone else's behalf, isn't it?"

"It is. I agree completely." Miss Raine let her shoulders slump, but almost immediately she straightened in a ladylike way. "It wasn't actually me."

Ben lifted his brows in unspoken inquiry. He'd already come to that conclusion.

"I guess I should say I didn't arrange anything, nor did I hit the mark, as you put it. All I did was answer a discreet ad in the *Times*. It promised romantic intervention if needed. We agreed by post on a sum, and when my nephew suddenly disappeared and Lady Elena as well, I was ... *horrified.* I hadn't intended anything so drastic, and I was certainly concerned about my nephew. When I came to your wife about my uncle's watch being found, I was in a panic."

Luckily, no one seemed interested in approaching where they stood by a small tree of some kind with glossy leaves near an alcove that housed a statue of a Greek god that might have been Zeus. If so, the king of the gods was not very well endowed, but perhaps that was poetic license on the part of the sculptor to protect the delicate sensibilities of any ladies who might stroll by. Ben took a moment to digest this new information. Finally he asked the pressing question, "Why?"

Her pale cheeks took on color and she looked away. "You probably would not understand this, but the small fee seemed worth the gamble. Randolph has always been opposed to permanence, and while I know he does not mean to limit my life, his former stance on keeping his bachelorhood was starting to make me wonder if I would ever be free."

"Of?"

"I've never married. . . . I have my reasons, the old broken engagement one of them. My father's will naturally left everything to be managed by my closest living male relative, which is Randolph ... but with a stipulation than when he married, the portion revert to me, just in case my nephew's wife did not wish another woman in her household." Her smile was brief and brittle. "I am not getting any younger, my lord, and I wish to see the world."

That was a twist he did not see coming. Why were

families so damned complicated anyway? "Pardon me, but from our acquaintance, I do not sense in him venality at all. Could you not skip such inventive measures and just ask him to pass along the inheritance?"

"Lucy needs more than just the staff and his occasional presence. As it stood, he probably would have let me go, as you say, but it wouldn't have been best for her, so I would have had to stay regardless. Young women her age need someone to talk to of their own gender. Lady Elena will be perfect. She is gracious and lovely and of the right age."

It was hard to deny that it seemed all had worked out well enough, but there were quite a few loose threads dangling.

Lady Janet put an imploring hand on his sleeve. "Please do not tell my nephew or Lord Whitbridge."

The quiet request wasn't hard to grant. If she'd known him better, she would never have even felt the need to ask. Actually, he had no problem in telling Whitbridge he'd failed to ever locate the culprit, and he doubted Andrews was still looking forward to revenge in the way he'd tersely stated in the carriage ride to London. Now he seemed quite content with how it had all worked out.

Ben, however, felt a bit different.

His opponent was wily. Worthy. Complicated, because he was sure it had cost far more to rent the castle, pay off the solicitors for their loyal silence, hire the staff, and so forth, than the modest sum Janet Raine had paid. As soon as he'd begun to suspect her, he'd checked with her banker also, so he knew the exact amount.

"I won't tell anyone," he found himself saying even as he pondered his next line of investigation. Then he recalled how he had pledged Alicia could help him, and

God alone knew what she might do if he didn't tell her the case was essentially solved. Reluctantly he amended, "Except I must tell my wife. You can trust her silence. Remember your trip to the man with the watch? I have to keep her from doing anything as reckless as that again."

Janet Raine nodded, her throat working. "I remember it was a rather impulsive decision."

"She is that," he confirmed drily.

"Thank you for granting me this."

"You are most welcome." He stopped in the act of turning away. "Can you possibly gather together any correspondence you had with the person you hired? I'm not certain I will pursue it, but I remain curious. The motivation of the unnamed participant perplexes me. I am sure they didn't give you the truth, but how did they sign their name?"

"I will send it all to you tomorrow." Janet smiled at a passing guest and it was a credible effort. "And whoever it might be didn't sign their name. There is a symbol at the bottom of the page that I don't recognize; that is all."

How interesting.

Epilogue

Three months later

"What on earth are you doing?"

"I am lifting you from your horse."

By now Elena knew that heavy look in her husband's eyes. In her *lover's* eyes. As he deposited her lightly on the ground his arms tightened and he whispered in her ear, "It is bit cool out. Perfect for ravishing a fair maiden."

No. He couldn't be thinking of . . . not *here*.

"Ran." Elena, laughing, pushed at his shoulder, but it was a bit like shoving at a granite wall. "You don't ravish fair maidens, and even if you did, I assume you prefer the comfort of a bed."

Her handsome husband lifted a brow, a dark lock of hair dangling over his forehead. "In case you have not noticed, the bedroom is not all that private at this time of day. If you are in the house Lucy wants to be with you."

"She likes me."

"I do too." He nibbled on her lower lip.

"And she needs a friend. Especially now that Janet has sailed."

"I know." He pulled back, his face taking on a sober cast. "I hope she enjoys her travels, but I must admit I'm surprised my aunt wished to go off on her own. She never told me."

"Men are not the only ones allowed their secrets."

"I suppose not." His grin was boyish. "Just so that I make myself perfectly clear, I am grateful Luce is so enamored of your company, but it is damned inconvenient to my licentious urges. So can I beg a few minutes?"

"For what, my lord?"

His dark eyes held the singular wicked gleam of amusement she loved. He lowered her to the autumn-crisped grass. "Let me demonstrate."

Nimble fingers unfastened her bodice and she gasped at the coolness of the air over her bared breasts, her nipples tightening.

"Don't worry. I'll keep you warm." Ran fairly tore off his expensive jacket, which would make his valet wince, and then divested himself of boots, shirt, and breeches in record time. He was good as his word, covering her with his rangy body, touching, arousing, his mouth traveling in a leisurely trail across her skin until she was panting and gloriously ready when he entered her in one silken thrust.

Perfection.

Her hips lifted to the carnal rhythm, his hand cupped her breast, and before long she didn't care that she was naked in a glen with fall leaves littering the ground, no doubt getting bits of foliage in her hair because he'd recklessly loosened the pins of her neat chignon and sent them every which way.

It was passionate, a little wild, and he was correct, the unorthodox setting just added to the exquisite pleasure.

Being married to a rake, she decided in the breathless aftermath, was even more delightful than being locked in a tower with one.

"I adore you." He finally lifted his head and grinned, but his eyes were serious. "And I never thought I would."

"You never thought you would adore me?" Her tone was teasing. "I think I am insulted."

"Adore anyone."

Her fingertips skimmed his bare shoulder and stilled at the pulse still beating rapidly in his neck. "I know."

"I'm happy."

"I'm so very happy too, my love."

Ran balanced his weight easily on his elbows, his lashes lowering. "I do think ours could be the most unusual courtship known to mankind, however."

"True." His dark hair was disheveled and she brushed a lock from his cheek. "Who else is kidnapped and held against their will?"

"On my brief journey to London last week I saw Heathton at our club."

"Oh? How is Alicia's handsome earl?"

The description brought a faint scowl to her husband's face, but he said, "As enigmatic as ever. When I asked him if your father was still pestering him to find the kidnapper, he merely responded that his desire for revenge seems to have faded with our marriage. Though I swore vengeance for the interference in my life at the time, I find myself in the odd position of actually wanting to thank the perpetrator, so I can't disagree."

"I feel the same way. After all, he gave me you." She kissed his chin, pulling him down closer, and then the corner of his mouth and then his lips.

And he proceeded to show her again the glory of the outdoors on a cool fall afternoon.

A leaf danced across the grass, shining in the brilliant sun, tumbling like a joyous child. Ben watched it absently, walking up the drive with his hands casually in his pockets, the wind ruffling his hair. "It's a Chinese symbol," he said in a contemplative voice. "But even the professor of antiquities I consulted who has visited the Orient many times could not decipher the meaning. He sent it to several colleagues and the answer finally arrived in the post this morning."

Strolling next to him, her cheeks slightly pink from the cool breeze, Alicia sent him a glance. "And?"

"I'm told there are variations in the language and this is from a particularly obscure dialect in the northern part of the country."

"So they couldn't tell you?"

"No, I have my answer."

His wife gave an audible exhale of frustration. "Ben, do not dangle it in front of me this way by talking in circles. Tell me."

"The explanation was rather long-winded and full of dry scholarly rhetoric, but in the end I am told in loose translation it represents divine power."

"Hmm." Her smooth brow wrinkled and she shivered slightly despite the warmth of the sun. "I rather do not like the sound of that, but in an awful way it makes sense, I suppose. Whoever went to such lengths certainly had power over Elena's life, and, for that matter, despite his wealth and position, Lord Andrews as well. Even Lord Colbert and my aunt and uncle were held prisoner by worry and scandal."

All true.

"The brilliance of it all," Ben mused aloud, "is that our devious matchmaker's methods are so extreme that if anyone contacts him and it does not happen to work out happily, like your cousin and Andrews, I doubt the person who paid for the services would dare to complain. It would put the blame on them for starting the process in the first place. Let's not forget, Janet's request put it all into motion, and even though the results are what she wanted she still begged me to never tell her nephew because the way it was handled was hardly what she anticipated."

"So our villain does not run the risk of exposure for his drastic tactics. Clever."

That remained to be seen, though he had to admit the kidnappings were orchestrated perfectly and evidently his opponent was well educated.

Ben said neutrally, "I wonder if this is the first time he has struck. Somehow I doubt it." He added quickly before she could respond, "But though I wanted to tell you what I discovered, that is not why I suggested we take an afternoon walk."

The smile he'd received when he pointed out the beautiful afternoon had been dazzling and he wasn't at all sure he deserved it.

His wife's delicate brows went up in mild inquiry.

He pulled the small box from his pocket. "I never gave you a wedding gift."

"On the contrary," she objected as he handed her the box, "you gave me the Heathton diamonds and so many other pieces of heirloom jewelry, I doubt I will ever be able to wear them all."

"Nothing personal," he corrected quietly. "From me to you, selected with your specific tastes in mind. Open it."

They had stopped walking and stood in front of the house, the façade gilded by sunlight, the air fresh and clean. Alicia hesitated and then took off the ribbon and lifted the lid.

The pearl earrings were not actually the real gift, though she'd told him once that she preferred less heavy pieces of jewelry and they were rare black pearls that had cost him a small fortune. Their iridescent luster reminded him of her hair, and in a sentimental moment he'd purchased them.

Of course, he wasn't even aware he had sentimental moments before he'd married his beguiling wife.

But the card was the actual gift and he knew she realized it when she said haltingly, "It is quite beautiful."

With all my love, Ben

He'd never said it.

Her eyes were luminous when she raised her gaze to meet his, and he slipped his arms around her, accepting the unspoken invitation as he lowered his head and kissed her.

With all his soul. With all his heart. What could a man ask for more than a glorious afternoon, a beautiful woman, and . . .

"My lord?"

A man could *ask for no interruptions,* he thought in irritation and let Alicia go, turning to look at the footman who seemed suitably embarrassed for intruding on such a tender moment. "What is it?" he asked curtly.

"We've been waiting for your return. You have a visitor."

The last time he'd heard that phrase he'd gotten embroiled in the disappearance of Lady Elena, and . . .

He raised his wife's hand to his lips. "Please excuse me. I will return to you as soon as I find out what requires my attention."

And he set off for the house, leaving his wife smiling behind him.

Read on for a preview of the next captivating
Regency romance from Emma Wildes,

A MOST IMPROPER RUMOR

Available in March from Signet Eclipse.

L ondon's most infamous murderess settled into the chair in his study in a swirl of expensive Lyon silk and a hint of floral perfume.

Now, this, Benjamin Wallace, the Earl of Heathton, thought, *is going to prove to be an interesting afternoon.*

"Thank you for receiving me, my lord."

"Not at all, Lady DeBrooke." He sat also, but behind his desk, where a neglected amount of tedious correspondence awaited his attention. "Though I admit I am curious about your call."

An understatement.

"You know all about me. Everyone does."

To her credit, she didn't sound bitter, accusatory, or even defensive. She just sat there, elegant and as exquisitely alluring as rumored, her poise impressive.

To admit or deny? He wasn't sure, and as usual, he took the middle ground. "I certainly know who you are."

"So diplomatic, Lord Heathton." Her smile held a telltale hint of sardonic amusement. "You have a reputation for subtle intrigue, so I am sure you know exactly what I was implying when I said you know about me. Let me be more frank. You know all of the *rumors* about me."

He did, but he was much more concerned about how she'd heard about *him*.

"We've been introduced before. Your husband was a friend."

He actually remembered the meeting quite clearly. She was a raven-haired beauty with crystalline gray eyes, her form graceful yet enticing, with an opulent bosom and narrow waist—she was the picture of feminine allure. Ebony brows were perfect arcs over those silver eyes, and her nose dainty and straight. Her gown was tasteful but seductive, with a fashionable décolletage, and when she reclined and crossed her ankles, the movement was languid and elegant.

The *haut ton* had given her the nickname Dark Angel, and her debut had been the event of the season the year of her coming out, with scores of dazzled gentlemen vying for her attention before it had all gone terribly wrong.

However, Ben was difficult to beguile, or at least he liked to think so.

"My second husband, you mean." Her tone wasn't combative, but instead neutral.

He inclined his head. "Thomas and I knew each other from Cambridge."

"How close of friends?"

"Please tell me how important the answer is to this conversation and I'll give due weight to the answer."

"You have such a way of speaking and not saying anything at all, my lord."

Since he'd been accused of that enough times, instead of replying to the hint of challenge, he asked, "Would you like a sherry before you tell me why you are here?"

After a moment she nodded. "Yes, thank you. Perhaps that will help."

He thought it might. She wasn't nearly as poised as she seemed. The facade was sleek and polished, but the inner trepidation showed to someone who understood how to read the small nuances.

And there was the true question: *Help what?*

He rose to go over to the small drinks table and pour her a glass, taking it back and handing it over with a small bow. "I believe my wife mentioned recently you had returned to London."

As she accepted the drink, her hand trembled slightly. It wasn't much, but it betrayed her, confirming his suspicion that her sophistication was only on the surface. Lady DeBrooke murmured, "Ah, yes, the society pages. They refuse to leave me alone."

"Notoriety can be uncomfortable, I'm sure."

If the frank observation stung, she didn't show it. "Yes."

He could play a game of dancing around the question as well anyone—and better than most, given his past— but at the moment, he just wished to know her purpose. "I assume this isn't a social call."

"I need your help."

The last time he'd heard those words, he'd stepped into a nasty scheme that involved kidnapping and slander. Ben gazed at the woman sitting upright in the chair across from him and almost reflexively refused. His marriage was sailing along smoother waters than a few months ago, his financial holdings were prosperous, and while being the earl wasn't exciting, it was fulfilling in other ways . . .

Perhaps not the ways he craved, though he was happy that he and his wife were more in tune.

"What kind of help?" he asked against his better judgment.

Lady DeBrooke stared at the liquid in her glass for a moment, a fringe of long lashes lending shadows to her perfect cheekbones. "I'm quite desperate and I heard you can clear up small puzzles with amazing skill." She glanced up. "I hope that applies also to large ones."

"Who told you that?"

"I am not supposed to say."

That was fine—he'd find out on his own. Already he had his suspicions on who might have pointed her his direction. "How large?"

"Murder."

He leaned back, taking stock of what that single word implied, particularly in her case, and then he sighed. She was entirely too beautiful to refuse, and besides, he was curious. Intensely so, damn him. He had letters to answer and other dull duties as well and getting caught up in anything else would put him behind. "I cannot promise you anything, but go on. I will listen."

To her credit, there were no theatrics. She simply nodded, the coil of heavy, glossy hair at her nape a contrast to her slender neck. "As perhaps you know, my first husband died almost six years ago of an unknown ailment. He was ten years older than I, and the marriage arranged by my father. I had barely turned eighteen, but William had a barony and he was wealthy. Of the offers for my hand, my father selected to accept his and I had little choice. I will be frank and say it was hardly a love match—he simply wanted a fashionable wife." Her smile was brittle. "He's thought to be my first victim."

"That I have heard." He kept his voice even and unemotional.

"Yes, I imagine you have." Her tone wasn't nearly as dispassionate. "Then I suppose you also know I remarried several years later."

"To Thomas, Lord DeBrooke, who died of the same ailment."

She made a small gesture of humorless affirmation with her glass. "I can see that the gossips have done their work well. Since you knew him, you'll remember Thomas was a nice man, and of my choosing. He was healthy and vibrant, and though once again I only married him because my father insisted I was too young to be a recluse living at our country estate. I was saddened when he died so suddenly."

Was she? He didn't know her well enough to judge— he didn't know her at all—so he didn't comment.

"That was when the rumors truly started. It was insidious at first, and I was in mourning in the country, so I had no idea I was under suspicion until my sister told me. You can imagine how shocking it was to hear."

Shocking because she was innocent, or because she was certain that no one would suspect someone of her grace and beauty capable of maliciously poisoning two husbands?

It was almost four o'clock. He was supposed to have tea with his wife and her elderly aunt, but he was much more interested in having a brandy in his study while listening to his unexpected visitor and her fascinating story. To that end he rose and went over to the table again and uncorked the decanter to pour a small snifter. Alicia would forgive him for skipping tea. When he told her about this visit, she would be fascinated as well. His wife was far more inquisitive than he was.

"My brother-in-law even had me brought up before a

magistrate, but there was no evidence to prove me guilty except his suspicions. The physician that attended Thomas at his death couldn't say for certain it wasn't an ailment of some kind, though the symptoms were very similar to whatever proved to be the end of my first husband."

He recalled the scandal of the trial. She was correct. The society papers had clung to the story and still rehashed it long after her acquittal and Lady DeBrooke had retired once again to the countryside.

"I see." Instead of sitting down he leaned against a bookcase and swirled his brandy while studying her expression. "I take it you are telling me you *do* think they were murdered, just not at your hand."

"Very astute, my lord. This is where I point out I have the advantage of knowing I am innocent." Her fine brows lifted. "A cliché, I know, but quite true. The more and more I have thought about it, the more I think it possible." Her gaze was direct.

It wasn't that he wasn't interested in the challenge but he wanted to be frank. "The *ton* is notorious for its lack of forgiveness. Do you really think if I even could possibly solve two murders that happened years ago it will restore your position in society, Lady DeBrooke? Or is it justice you seek?"

"Neither," she answered quietly. "I wish to remarry."

The Earl of Heathton wasn't quite what she expected. Angelina had met him in passing once or twice, so she recognized him, of course. He was handsome in an understated way with thick, dark blond hair and classic features, tall and wide-shouldered, and to that extent he was like many aristocratic gentlemen she knew, but the difference was in the keen intelligence in his eyes and the way he moved with a subtle athletic grace. She couldn't define it, but there was an air of the hunter about him, and it did not involve horses and hounds.

It had cost her in pride to pay this call. Throughout the horrible series of events after Thomas died she had learned a great deal about scorn and suspicion, including being given the cut direct by former friends, not to mention her husband's vindictive family's strident accusations. There had been no guarantee Lord Heathton would even receive her.

The apprehension proved she wasn't quite thick-skinned enough just yet to weather the scorn of her peers.

"You wish to be able to remarry because the world no longer thinks you poison your husbands, or you wish to marry someone specific?" he asked in the neutral tone he'd used throughout their conversation.

"I am too afraid for him to accept his proposal." After the oblique answer she took a bracing sip of sherry. "It seems possible that the malice is directed at me. I realize that sounds melodramatic and perhaps even self-important, but they were two very different men, with no connection I can find, other than both having the misfortune to be married to me."

"An interesting theory to be sure. If you are correct, do have any idea who might have enough ill will toward you to take the drastic step of actually killing two people?"

"Who has enough ill will toward anyone to do that, my lord?" Her tone was brittle though she tried to control it.

"You might be surprised what drives certain individuals to extreme measures most of us would never consider."

As if she hadn't spent sleepless nights and restless afternoons in her exile contemplating that very question. With conviction, she said, "None."

He didn't seem deterred, but then again, his enigmatic expression seemed to be hard to read in general. "Perhaps a frustrated lover, Lady DeBrooke? You are very lovely."

The compliment was flattering, but she shook her head. "I was faithful entirely to both of them and, when I married William, very young. I'd barely had my coming out when our marriage was arranged. There are no scorned lovers in my past, tarnished as it is reputed to be."

And though he'd treated her more as a possession than a person, William had done her one enormous favor and left her a generous inheritance. After his death she'd discreetly taken the money and invested it under another name with the assistance of a trusted friend, knowing her father was going to insist she remarry. It was prudent that she had, for otherwise Thomas's family would have ended up with not just his money, but hers also. Under English law, a husband controlled anything a wife brought to the marriage. While her brother-in-law hadn't been able to send her to the gibbet, he had seized Thomas's fortune at once and not gifted her with even a stipend.

Had anyone discovered she'd created another identity and quietly accumulated a small fortune, she might have hanged. The thought always made her grow cold. It hadn't been anything more than caution on her part and a bid for some measure of independence, but admittedly, it seemed calculating. As it was, she lived modestly, lest anyone inquire as to where the money came from.

"I will need a list of all servants that were with you in both households, and any friends and even family members that visited you."

That sounded promising.

"Then you will help me?"

"I don't know if I can actually help." His tone was cool and thoughtful. "But I will at least try."

Just the mere possibility of the weight being lifted from her shoulders brought her a poignant joy. She whispered, "That is all I can ask."

"Tell me about your current lover."

"What makes you think I . . ." She stopped, feeling a slight flush in her cheeks, and glanced away. "I suppose I am a mature woman, twice married, and it is logical to assume he shares my bed." Actually, she'd just had her twenty-fourth birthday, but she felt far older.

"That isn't my concern, but understandably, the more I know, the better I can discreetly gather information."

Discreet. That was exactly what she wanted. The assurance Lord Heathton would provide his own brand of secrecy was part of the reason she was sitting in his study.

Angelina nodded once with as much decisiveness as she could summon. "He isn't part of this except to the extent that I now am no longer willing to accept what has happened and do nothing. The awfulness of the trial and the scandal made me wish to hide away from the world. But that, I have found, does not work, and besides, it isn't fair to me or him. Or even to William and Thomas for that matter, to not seek to uncover the truth."

"I understand your motivations and agree, but if you wish me to look into this matter, then let me judge what might be valuable and what isn't."

That was fair enough. Actually, more than fair, for she'd offered him nothing in return. The Earl of Heathton did not need her money. That she knew already. She had little to give him but the challenge.

And she'd been assured that this sticky problem might pique his interest.

"He doesn't care about the cloud over me and thinks he is capable of protecting himself," she said with a careful lack of inflection. "I disagree. How can one protect oneself from some unknown poison? It isn't possible if the murderer is determined, short of having someone else taste your food, and that barbaric custom is long gone, thank goodness."

"At least in England," Heathton agreed. "The rulers in North Africa still employ it from what I understand. It would be a difficult way to live, suspicious of every bite or drink. Do I know him?"

A polite way of asking if her lover was of the beau monde. "Probably," she admitted.

"I thought so."

"Why?" she asked curiously. They had been so circumspect that even her maid did not suspect she was meeting clandestinely with someone. Alternating mornings, evenings, and nights, they used different places, and never acknowledged each other in public. She'd insisted and reluctantly he'd agreed, though he swore it did not matter to him if they were seen together.

However, she was in love for the first time in her life. Deeply, passionately in love, and if something happened to him . . .

No.

She couldn't bear it. She'd survived the rest of it. The accusations, the public degradation, the seclusion with even the servants whispering behind her back, but *harm* to him because of her was inconceivable. She would shatter into a thousand pieces, the damage irreversible.

"We met a half a year ago. I still have a few friends left, and I was invited to a small house party." Remembering that weekend brought a small smile of reminiscence, an indulgence she allowed herself. "I know this might sound like romantic female drivel, but it was one of those moments. He walked into the drawing room and we looked at each other and I *knew*."

God bless Eve for inviting him. As she knew as well.

Angelina added, "Trust me when I say that I was the last person to believe in love at first sight, my lord. I am more grateful than you know to him for adjusting my jaded and weary view of the world. I find love has the ability to heal even the deepest wounds."

Once the words were out, in the resulting silence, she had the impression, just a fleeting one, that she'd just made the erstwhile unflappable Earl of Heathton slightly uncomfortable. Was it the mention of the word *love*?

The earl's expression was too bland to tell. He said, "I take it you are staying in London. Give me the address and I will correspond with you as needed."

She nodded and took the pen and vellum offered and wrote down the address of her rented town house. At least he hadn't demanded to know the name of the man who had given her a glimpse of possible happiness, for she was truly reluctant to give it. He was the catalyst for her to take action, but she wanted to shield him as much as possible.

As she rose to leave, she hesitated and turned back to look at the tall man still standing with one shoulder propped against a bookcase filled with dusty volumes of ancient books with faded gilded letters in Latin on the spines. Lord Heathton looked back with an eyebrow raised in inquiry.

"I do not wish to make you reconsider, for I am more grateful than you know, but why did you agree to aid me?"

"Why?" Hazel eyes looked her with enigmatic detachment. "Because if you are telling me the truth, it appears someone ruined you deliberately, and, I admit, it reminds me of an old friend I'd like to meet again."

Emma Wildes

Spanish Lullaby

AN ORIGINAL NOVELLA
AVAILABLE ONLY AS AN eSPECIAL

Upon his triumphant return from the Battle of Waterloo, the
half-Spanish Marquess de Santorino finds his Juliet is engaged
to another. After four years away, he can hardly blame her, but
that doesn't stop him from getting thoroughly foxed upon
receiving the news. It no longer matters that he still loves her.
She's about to marry someone else.

Lady Juliet Stather is unprepared for Carlos Verde, Marquess
de Santorino, to return to her life. He's still devastatingly
handsome, still the man who broke her heart, but something
has changed. Beneath the surface of his mocking expression,
there's a new seriousness and sincerity. And she realizes she's
changed as well—for she no longer despises him.

Only a well-timed ball thrown by a meddling mother can bring
these two dueling lovers together once more...

**Available wherever books are sold or at
penguin.com/especials**

S0323